I0725121

KEEPING KAT

A SAN SOLOMAN NOVEL

DENISE WELLS

Copyright © 2021 by Denise Wells

All rights reserved.

No part of this book may be reproduced in any form or by any electronic or mechanical means, including information storage and retrieval systems, without written permission from the author, except for the use of brief quotations in a book review.

This book is a work of fiction. Names, characters, places, and incidents are either the product of the author's imagination or are used fictitiously. Any mistakes or misrepresentations are the authors alone.

This book is licensed for your personal enjoyment only. If you would like to share this book with another person, please purchase an additional copy for each person. Thank you for respecting the hard work of this author.

For Courtney Jo McMillon Bonelli

December 7, 1975 - April 13, 2016

You are missed every single day.

Be in love with your life. Every minute of it.

— JACK KEROUAC

ALSO BY DENISE WELLS

STANDALONES

The One I Can't Have, a steamy age-gap novella in **AB Worlds Age-Gap series**

The Three Way, a steamy novella in the **AB Worlds Valentine's Day Series**

Forever Wicked, a steamy novella in the **AB Worlds Halloween Party Series**

Summer Shivers, a romantic thriller in the **Summers in Seaside Collection**

Overdrive, a steamy enemies to lovers romance **in KB WORLDS - DRIVEN COLLECTION**

Pour Decisions, a romantic comedy novella in the **Girl Power Collection**

How to Ruin Your Ex's Wedding, a steamy romantic comedy

I Heart Mason Cartwright, a steamy romantic comedy

Love Off The Rocks, a romantic comedy short

Rebel without a Claus, a steamy, gay romantic short

Breaking Dylan, a coming of age story

AGENTS AND ASSASSINS TRILOGY

Fearless - Book One, a steamy romantic thriller

Careless - Book Two, a steamy romantic thriller

Ruthless - Book Three, a steamy romantic thriller

SAN SOLOMAN

Keeping Kat, a steamy second-chance firefighter romance

Romancing Remi, a steamy enemies to lovers romance

Loving Lexie, a steamy cowboy enemies to lovers romance

Seducing Sadie, a steamy firefighter romance

Trusting Tenley, an emotional second-chance at love romance

ANTHOLOGIES

High EX-Pectations, a romantic comedy short in the **Imperfect Date Anthology**

CAUGHT UNDER THE MISTLETOE - A Holiday Affair to Remember, a romantic comedy holiday short

STORYBOOK PUB CHRISTMAS WISHES - Mistle Oh-No, a romantic comedy holiday short

STORYBOOK PUB - Breezy Like Sunday Morning, a romantic comedy short

LIMITED RELEASES

GIRLS JUST WANNA HAVE FUNDAMENTAL RIGHTS - Charity Anthology

SEEDS OF LOVE A Charity Romance Anthology to benefit Ukraine - Charity Anthology

HOT AS F$#K SUMMER ROMANCE ANTHOLOGY - SULTRY SUMMER NIGHTS

LOCKED AND LOVED: An Isolated Romance Collection

SUMMER WITH YOU: Summer Shorts Collection

JUST A LICK Collection

LOVE LETTERS Collection

STOCKING STUFFERS Anthology

PRAISE FOR KEEPING KAT

My emotions ran the gamut with this well written romantic comedy!!!! Kat and Brad were hilarious!!!!! I loved the push and pull and twist and turns!!!! I can't wait to read more from Denise Wells!!!!

— GOODREADS

I encourage anyone who gets a chance to read this book because once you pick it up, you won't want to put it down.

— GOODREADS

A fantastic read! I couldn't put it down! I laughed, I cried, celebrated, and cried more.

— GOODREADS

INTRODUCTION

I still want my ex. Bad.

Who wouldn't? Brad Matthews is a sexy firefighter with biceps for days and a body that won't quit.

But the two of us together? There's no better way to hit the destruct button on both our lives than that.

So when I get the chance to distract myself helping the (hot) new detective in town on a case - I'm all in.

Except Brad keeps popping up—at crime scenes, around town with his girlfriend, in my fantasies at night.

But I can't take him back, we both know I won't be alive long enough for that. Unless he finds a way to save me first.

KEEPING KAT

PROLOGUE - THE BEGINNING

KAT

Brad and I met in a bar, I know, totally cliché. But once you leave college, how else do you meet someone outside of online dating? I'd already been through my share of right swipes, blind dates, and drunk hookups.

It was happy hour with my best friends—Lexie and Remi—we were at our favorite hangout, *The Recovery Room*, I was up to get our first round. It was 80s night; I was in my groove.

"Hey Kat, what can I get you?" Nate, the bartender, asked. Yes, I was on a first name basis with the main guy at my favorite bar.

"We are all going for the pomegranate mojito tonight, Nate, you've concocted a good one there."

"I aim to please where you ladies are concerned," he said with a wink. I didn't even try to wink back. I can't. It's a long story, just know it's not a good look for me.

"Burning Up" by Madonna, came on the overhead. I bounced to the beat. I fucking loved this song.

"I'm burning up, burning up for your love," I sang to Nate as he handed me all three drinks.

"I'll put my love on your tab," he said. I balanced the three drinks between my two hands and stepped back from the bar.

"Umph!" I heard it before I felt it. My stiletto impaled a toe. I spun to apologize, watching in horror as bright red liquid flew from the glasses blanketing the white expanse in front of me. It was a chest, a wide chest, encased in a white t-shirt that was quickly turning pink. At eye level, with me in my three-inch heels, were finely formed pecs, broad shoulders, and thick biceps. I wanted to run my hands along it, I couldn't help myself.

Sculpted perfection made more visible by the wet material clinging to it. The appeal of wet t-shirt contests becoming clear. My lady parts went all a-twitter. I gave into temptation, running my free pinky finger along the ridges. Belatedly realizing the glasses were still in my hand and all I was doing was rubbing liquid into the shirt. Reality came crashing in like a wrecking ball.

"Ohmigod! I am so sorry!" I said. "Let me get a towel and I'll clean that off for you." I turned to set the remains of our drinks down, asked Nate for club soda and a towel, and began dabbing at the chest. "I think I'm making this worse."

"If you wanted to get my shirt off, all you had to do was ask," the chest said.

I looked up and saw his face.

You know when you see those moments in movies where the girl sees the guy for the first time and the world stops around them? And you think to yourself, ohmigod that is so lame, shit never happens like that in real life? It happened.

I looked up and there he was in all his chiseled, scruffy, and tan glory. With a face that highlighted the most beautiful eyes I had ever seen. Everything around me stopped, I lost myself in his gaze.

"Ohmigod, I'm so sorry. I'm usually not this clumsy. That's not true, I totally am, but it's not intentional, Oh god. Come on." I grabbed his hand and dragged him behind me to the restroom. Pausing for a moment before heading into the men's room. Figuring if one of us was going to be in the wrong place it should be me.

"Hands up," I ordered trying not to look him in the eye again. He was so good looking he made me nervous. Instead, focusing on pulling the hem of his shirt up to try and get it over his head.

I wasn't tall enough. Not even when I plastered my body against his. And especially not with his hands in the air. I got as far as gathering the pink under his chin, leaving my face to get intimately acquainted with his chest in the flesh.

He smelled good. Not like cologne good. More like man, soap, and smoke. I think. My eyes traveled the tanned terrain in front of me examining all the yummy ridges and hard edges.

He was so good looking he made me nervous just being near him.

"My god, are you for real?" I asked without meaning to.

He reached for the hem and pulled his shirt the rest of the way off before looking down and patting his hips and thighs.

"I think so." The corners of his lips turned up and his eyes sparkled. "The better question is, are you?"

I rolled my eyes, pretending that he didn't just flip my insides out, and grabbed his shirt taking care to only get the pink parts wet. He leaned against the wall, arms crossed over his chest, watching me. Looking like a Greek god.

"I really hope I didn't ruin your shirt." I said to his reflection in the mirror. "I promise to pay for it. Oh, and I'll buy you a drink. Shit! This is so embarrassing." I closed my eyes and tried to figure out how to click my heels three times, whisper 'there's no place like home', and get myself out of this situation.

"I'll make you a deal," he said.

"Anything." I placed his shirt over my open hand and held it under the air dryer on the wall. The pink was still there, but it was less obvious than it was before. He took it from me after the dryer timed out.

"You don't even know what I'm going to propose," he said putting his shirt back on.

"Propose?" I said, finally finding my voice. "We haven't even had sex yet."

His smile widened and he put his arm around the small of my back pulling me toward him. I gasped as my hands braced on his chest between us. He looked around, as though to see if anyone else was listening before bending to my ear. "Okay," he whispered, his chin nuzzling my neck making my heart race. "I've got this new move where I get a beautiful woman to spill a drink on me. She feels so bad about it she lets me take her to dinner. How am I doing so far?"

"Really, really well," I breathed.

"Great." He straightened and smiled, holding my gaze while he leaned across me to open the door. "Shall we?"

He and his friend joined me and my girls at our table. He introduced himself as Brad and his friend was Ethan; both firefighters with the San Soloman Fire Department. Brad was an easy conversationalist, funny, quick-witted, and charming. And he sat there all night in a stained and wet (which did eventually dry), t-shirt acting like it didn't bother him at all.

He walked me to my car at the end of the night; we exchanged numbers and kissed goodnight. I was looking forward to the kiss most of the night, but I had not expected how it would affect me. Brad's kiss left me shaking; rocked my world with the barest touch. I'd invited him home with me, and he said no.

"We will have a date first, Kat. At least one, and probably two, before we spend the night together. And when we do, it will be because you find me as irresistible as I find you."

"But—"

"Not just sexually, beautiful girl. We're going to talk and text and get to know one another a bit more. And when we spend the night together, I guarantee it will be nothing short of explosive. And when I get up to make you breakfast the next morning, you won't want me to leave."

"Pfft. Awfully full of—"

He put a finger to my lips to quiet me. Then he kissed me one more time. A soft and lingering kiss that stayed on my lips until long after I'd gotten home.

Sure enough, he'd been right. We had three dates and countless conversations before he came home with me. Our night together was explosive. And the next morning, after he made me breakfast, I never wanted him to leave.

PROLOGUE - THE MIDDLE

BRAD

All I could think about after a grueling forty-eight-hour shift at the fire station was seeing Kat. I'd rushed through my post-shift duties and shower just to get to her a few moments sooner.

"Completely pussy whipped," Ethan, my partner and best friend, joked as he dressed beside me in the locker room. He'd just started, and I was nearly finished.

"Just wait, dude," I told him. "It'll happen to you when you least expect it, and you'll find yourself rushing from work to get to your girl too."

"Never gonna happen, man. There's too much of me for just one love, got to spread all-a-this around." He ran his hands down and back up his bare torso, stopping to fondle his nipples. One of the other guys from our station whipped a towel at him, Ethan shrieked like a little girl when it caught him on the back, causing all of us to laugh at his pain.

I said my goodbyes and jogged through the parking lot toward my truck. Pausing only to laugh at my eagerness. If you'd told me a few months ago that I'd be this gone over a girl I met in a bar I would have laughed my ass off. Yet, there I was, racing through the near empty streets of San Soloman toward her house.

It was quiet for a weekday morning, I remember that. I was one of the few cars on the road. The perfect counterpoint to the loud chaos that was the previous night's shift - apartment fire destroyed most of the building. Twenty families had woken up without a home today, all because the girl in apartment number twelve left a candle burning when she went out for the evening.

I rubbed my hand against my face, the faint smell of smoke still clung to my skin. It was difficult to see the momentary carelessness of one person affect the lives of so many. But were able to take solace in that all twenty families were still around to wake up today - we'd done our job well.

My heart beat faster in anticipation as I made the right turn onto her street. I was certain at that point that I was in love with her. Not that I'd tell her that. She'd get spooked. But it's like my dad always said, 'when you know, you know.' He and my mom married after knowing one another a month. And they were happy right up until the day she died.

While I may not admit to Kat yet how I feel, I had no problems showing her. I know it it's not manly to share feelings. But so much of my life involved turning off my feelings with the amount of death, damage, and destruction that I saw with my job, that sometimes it was nice to focus on them solely.

Part of my excitement stemmed from our not having seen one another in over four days. She'd been pulling a few all-nighters to prepare for closing a big case as one of the most, if not the most, successful criminal defense attorneys in San Soloman. Her all nighters had bumped right into my 48-hour shift, and so there we were. With me pulling into her driveway and sporting a half woodie that hadn't left me the entire trip home.

I tried the knob, surprised to find it unlocked. I'd been anticipating having to wake her up. Now I'd have to chastise her about leaving it open and finagle a key somehow. I made my way through the quiet house, the sun was barely rising, making the ocean still an inky black beyond the large living room windows.

I undressed and slide into the bed next to her. She turned in that half asleep state and curled into my chest. Her hair mussed with makeup smeared under her eyes, and still she'd never looked more beautiful.

It hit me again—with even greater clarity—that I wanted to wake up next to her every day for the rest of my life. Now I just needed her to realize the same. I pulled her toward me to breathe her in, kissing the top of her head. My eyes closed as I relished the moment. Holding her in my arms, the quiet of the morning, the perfection of the moment.

"Hey," she mumbled, looking up through sleep heavy lids.

"Go back to sleep, beautiful. It's still early."

"Missed you." She burrowed further under the covers and into my side. Her arm reached across my stomach, brushing the tip of my hardened dick. I groaned at the soft touch.

"Mmm," she replied waking up a bit, then turned her face up toward me. "Hi there."

I pulled her naked body up my chest and captured her lips with mine. Kissing her deeply, trying to tell her with my touch everything I couldn't yet voice. One hand holding her head in place, while the other slid down her back to slip between her legs; she was already wet for me. Like always, it was such a goddamn turn on. She moved her hips until the head of my cock was at here entrance, teasing us both with the promise of more.

I flipped us so she was on her back and kissed her some more, moving my lips down her face and throat to pull one nipple in my mouth. She bucked her hips in invitation.

"In!"

I reared back, reaching between us to take my cock in my hand and used the tip to spread her arousal around.

"Please, Brad," she groaned. "I need you. I missed you."

"I missed you too, baby." I told her, sliding my length along her opening, prolonging the pleasure for both of us. She grabbed my face and brought it back to hers, bit my bottom lip sharply, then soothed it with her tongue. I slid inside of her inch by aching inch, loving the way her pussy walls pulled me in. Filling her like my cock was created for that sole purpose. It made me want to weep with pleasure.

I didn't stop the moans that rose from my chest as I sank all the way down into her and stayed there. Luxuriating in the feel of her around me. "Fuck, Kat, you feel so good."

She pushed at my shoulders and I let her roll me to my back to straddle me. Let her take total control of her pleasure. I hoped to never forget that moment, how she looked riding me. She was mesmerizing like that with her hair cascading down her shoulders, and her head thrown back. Lips parted as she gasped, her hips rocking back and forth, hands gripping at my thighs behind her keeping her stable.

Her nails dug into my skin and the scent of her shower gel blended with the muskiness of sex in the air around us. Muscles tightened around me as she ground down, teasing her clit with the smattering of hair on my pelvis. I bit my cheek to keep me from coming too soon, wanting her to get off before I did.

I ran my hands up her thighs to her hips and held her in place while I pistoned my hips at an angle that made her lose her mind. She was close, I could feel it in how she tightened around me. How her eyes dropped to half-mast and the crooked smile took over her face.

Her hands rose to her breasts, fingertips pulling at her nipples. My hands followed, wanting to experience the same. I pinched the tips then ran my palms across their fullness to soothe the sting. Kat had—has—the most beautiful tits, their globes filled my hands, round and pert with a tear drop shape. I could have squeezed them all day long and never tired.

Her body stiffened as she came, muscles tightening all around me, her mouth falling open emitting the most beautiful sounds. She kept going, leaning away from me slightly, bracing her hands behind her on my thighs, as she rode out her orgasm. With her head thrown back, the ends of her hair tickled my thighs.

The soft of the tickle in direct contrast with the fierceness of the fucking. I kept thrusting, needing her to come once more, but this time with me. Her tits jutted out, begging for more attention, and I complied. My fingers graced the sides as my palms caressed her nipples.

And then . . . a lump?

I moved my fingertips back to where they'd just been feeling around, trying to catch what I'd just touched before.

And there it was.

Small. Palpable. Potentially deadly.

Holy fuck.

I slowed my hips, my heart pounding for a different reason now.

"Baby," I said, alarmed.

"No! Don't stop! I'm so close," Kat groaned.

But I did.

I stopped.

And our lives were never the same after.

PROLOGUE - THE END

BRAD

I'd come home from an off-site training followed by happy hour with the station guys to find her sitting on the deck with bloodshot eyes and a half-empty bottle of tequila next to her. When I asked her what was wrong and how the doctor's appointment had gone, she turned and handed me her engagement ring, and said, "I need you to pack your stuff and leave."

"What do you mean?" I asked her.

"Just what I said. I need you to pack your stuff and leave. We are over."

"What the fuck, Kat!? Did something happen today? What did the doctor say? Are you all right? What's going on?" I couldn't get my questions out fast enough. But she wasn't supplying any answers. She sat there staring out at the dark sea, fiddling with her shot glass.

"Just go, please," she said.

"I'm not going anywhere. What the hell's going on? We're getting married in two weeks. Tell me what's going on. Is it the cancer? Is it back?" She'd been diagnosed shortly after we got together with breast cancer. But with treatment and a double mastectomy we thought we'd caught it in time.

She choked out a bitter laugh.

"It's back all right and it's spread to my lymph nodes." Tears streamed down her face. "I don't want you here, so get the fuck out."

I kneeled in front of her and grabbed her hands. "Babe, please. We're getting married and I'm not going anywhere. This doesn't change anything."

"Doesn't change anything?" she yelled. "Are you fucking kidding me, Brad? This changes everything. Nothing is the same and it never will be. We're over. This is it, Brad. Don't you get it? This is *it*!"

She stood and paced around the deck. I stood and waited to see if she would calm down. Instead of the pacing calming her, it made her more upset.

"You need to go. You need to go. You can't stay here. You can't be here anymore. I don't want you here." Her voice was shaky and her hands trembled. All I wanted to do is comfort her. Take her in my arms, remind her how much I love her, and soothe the pain she was feeling.

"Kat . . ." Tears pooled in my eyes.

"Brad - you need to go. Can't you see? We're through. I can't make it any plainer for you. We're not married. I'm not beholden to you. You don't owe me anything. So, pack your things and get the fuck out."

"I'm not leaving you. We aren't married yet, but I've made a commitment to you Kat. To love you no matter what. To stay by your side during good times and bad. I plan to stand by that commitment."

"You plan to stand by that commitment?" she asked. "Stand by it? That's exactly what I'm talking about. I'm not going to be that person, the one that makes you stand by them and watch them die. If the cancer has come back once, it's going to come back again." She was crying harder now.

I knew she was thinking about my mom and how she died. And worse, how my brother and my father and I all watched her die.

Slowly. For months.

And there was nothing we could do about it.

Little streams of snot were sliding down her upper lip and into her mouth. She kept trying to wipe it away on her arm, but it wasn't doing much good.

I had this extreme urge to laugh. To take her in my arms and let her blow her nose in my shirt and have us both laugh about the snot and the absurdity of this conversation.

"I don't need you standing by anything. I need you gone. Get your things and leave. You don't need to take everything; I'll stay away tomorrow and you can come back then to get the rest. I'll get the key from you another time."

"Kat, you aren't thinking straight, baby, there is no reason for me to leave. I'm here. We don't know it will come back again. I love you. I want to be with you. I want to help you."

"I don't need your help!"

"Okay, clearly I'm not saying all the right things here, but Kat, you know how much I love you and how badly I want to spend the rest of my life with you. The rest of *your* life with you. We are better together than we are apart. A bad day together is always better than a good day apart, right?" I felt my chest constricting and I couldn't breathe.

Was she serious about this?

She couldn't be.

There's no way she wanted me to leave. Right? Inklings of panic settled in my chest.

It doesn't matter. I'll never leave her when she's upset. I looked at her puffy face, red eyes, and runny nose. She needs me. I'm not going anywhere.

"If you don't get your things and go in the next five minutes, I'm calling the cops."

"Oh, come on! For fuck's sake. You're being ridiculous. Let's sit down and talk about this. Or better yet, how about you lie down, I'll make you some tea, you can get some rest, sleep off the tequila, and we will talk about it in the morning when we've both had time to calm down."

She looked at me—"Five minutes."—then turned and walked into her home office, locking the door behind her. I sat down outside the door to her office and tried to reason with her. Tried to get her to open the door. She wouldn't answer me. I was getting worried about whether she was even conscious after half a bottle of tequila.

The front doorbell rang, and I stood to go answer it. Before I could even get to the door, I saw the blue and red flashing lights through the window.

"Aw, come on, Kat! Are you fucking kidding me with this?" I yelled.

I opened the door to two officers.

"Can I help you, officers?"

"We received a domestic disturbance complaint, sir. Was that you we heard yelling?"

"Yeah," I started, rubbing the back of my neck to loosen the tension that had gathered there. "But it was just because it was ridiculous and unnecessary for her to call you."

"I think we'll be the judge of whether or not the call was necessary. Can you tell us where the lady of the house is now?"

"Kat is her name. She's my fiancée, and she is in her home office down the hall there," I turned to point toward Kat's office.

"Do you mind if we come in?"

"For what purpose?" I ask dumbly since I already know the answer.

"We'd like to talk to her, make sure everything is okay."

"Everything is okay. I would never hurt Kat. We're getting married in two weeks. She's trying to break it off. But she doesn't realize what she's doing. That's all."

"Sir?" He motions toward the inside the house.

"Yeah, sorry, come in." I wave them through the door. They come in cautiously, looking around.

"Which way to the home office?"

"That door there." I point out Kat's office door.

One officer stands by me, and puts his arm out in front of me, as though to stop me. The other officer approaches the office door and knocks.

"Ma'am? This is Officer Neal with the SSPD. Are you okay? Can I talk to you for a minute?"

The door opens and Kat peeks her head out. "Can you make him go away, please?" she asked, pointing at me.

"Kat, what the hell?" I yelled.

"Sir, please stay quiet," the officer next to me said, as he'd moved from blocking any forward momentum to grabbing my upper arm.

"I haven't hurt her," I said. I tried to shake off his arm, but he wouldn't let go. "I could never hurt her. I love her. She's drunk, and she's just found out her cancer is back. She's trying to break up with me, and I don't want to go. I'm not going anywhere. Do you hear me, Kat? I'm not going anywhere!"

"Why don't we step outside?" The officer holding my arm turned us around and tried to pull me outside.

"No. I don't want to go outside. You aren't listening I'm not leaving her!" I wrenched my arm from his and turned to face him at the same time as he stepped toward me. My hands went up in front of me, an automatic reflex, and I pushed him backward.

I barely got the words 'man, I didn't mean' out before he's got me twisted back around, both hands behind my back, and handcuffs locked tight over my wrists.

I heard him say something about assaulting a police officer as he pushed me outside, shutting the front door after him. His words whooshed around me without taking hold, my brain in a fog that I wasn't able to clear.

"You don't understand," I said.

"I understand, sir."

"I'm a firefighter with the SSFD, I would never hurt a woman. Especially not Kat," I said.

"That may be true, sir, but assaulting an officer of the law is a serious offense."

"I didn't assault you; it was a reflex."

He opened the door to the back of the squad car and said, "Watch your head," as he pushed the top of mine down and in, directing my body to the inside the car.

"This isn't even a real disturbance call, I promise you. This is just Kat being irrational," I said as he shut the door.

The other officer came outside a brief time later and shut the door behind him. The two talked in low voices, looking from me to the front door of the house, and back again.

By this time, some neighbors had come outside, watching to see what was going on. The blue and red swirling lights acting as a beacon in the foggy night for nosey gossip mongers.

The other officer opened the front passenger door and leaned in to talk. "Sir, the lady said you've both been drinking tonight, and I understand that you're both upset. I need you to calm down, then I will give you a couple options for tonight."

"For fuck's sake. This is ridiculous! I didn't fucking do anything!" I struggled against the handcuffs, trying to pull my hands free.

The officer looked at me.

"Sir, how much have you had to drink tonight?"

"I went to happy hour after a Haz-Mat training. I had two beers over two hours, I wouldn't exactly call that drinking. So, in answer to your question, not much. Unlike Kat who's had a half bottle of tequila and clearly isn't thinking straight. Can you give me a minute to talk to her?"

"No, sir, I cannot. The lady has asserted that she is frightened and does not feel safe with you. In addition, my partner says you got physical with him."

"Well, then you're going to have to fucking take me in, 'cause I'm not leaving her willingly."

"Planning on it."

I spent the night in a holding cell, and Ethan bailed me out the next day. I've checked myself every so often, trying to see if I can muster anger toward her, but I can't. At least not for the break-up part. Intellectually, I know that she acted out of fear and love.

Fear for herself and her life and love for me in not wanting me to watch her fight the cancer again. I needed my head to remind my heart every so often.

But as far as the decimation of my career? That I'm still angry about. And, if I'm honest, I'm still pissed off that she beat the cancer again. Because this time apart—eighteen fucking months—has been a total fucking waste.

1

KAT

I wake up slowly, every inch of my body aching. The memory of the night before dim and convoluted. My brain stuck in a fog of too much alcohol, not enough food or sleep. Or water if the feel of my bloated tongue in my mouth is any sign.

My eyes stick together from a combination of last night's makeup and tears. I don't remember how much I cried, but the puffiness I feel around my eyes says it was a noticeable amount. I rub at my lashes to loosen them enough to lift the lids and see.

I lie still, taking in the sounds and feel of the room around me. An oscillating fan hits me with a light breeze every twenty-seconds or so, the head clicking with itself trying to complete its turn, but something blocks it from the full rotation.

Sweat soaked sheets stick to my skin as I try to turn from my back to my side. Nausea roils through me, my stomach turns, the bitter taste of vomit creeping up my throat. I barely make it to the side of the bed before I throw up in the wastebasket beside the bed. If the contents are any indication, it's not the first time I've done it.

I flop to my back, forearm thrown over my eyes, and wait for the feeling to pass. Easing myself out of the bed and heading toward what I think is the bathroom once it does.

The sink is one of those pedestal kind with a medicine cabinet above it. The mirrored door hangs crooked with a crack through the middle, making the face that reflects at me look disfigured. I splash tepid water on my face and use the dried cake soap on the sink rim to rub away as much makeup as I can.

Then, seeing no toothpaste or mouthwash anywhere, try to do the same with my mouth, using my fingers to brush away the taste of vomit. The efforts of both stealing most of my limited energy.

A basket of partially opened newspapers sits by the side of the toilet, I use the rubber band from one to collect my hair on the top of my head, knowing it's going to pull my hair out later when I remove it, yet not caring enough to look for anything else.

The toilet bowl has a ring of black at the edge of the water, with stains of brown muddying the sides. Not trusting it's sanitariness, I squat over it to pee. Ignoring the irony of letting the owner of said bathroom put his penis inside of me, but not wanting to touch my bare ass to his toilet.

The sting as I relieve myself is palpable. But I'm not sure if it's the beginnings of a UTI or that I was dry when he entered me last night and that didn't change. Getting fucked while dry isn't my idea of a good time. But it definitely lets you know you're still alive.

Ignoring the tinge of blood on the toilet paper, I flush and wash my hands. Then ease the bathroom door open and push my toes along the floor to feel for my clothes.

I get dressed slowly. Not finding my underwear, but not really caring to take too much time looking for it. Instead pulling tight jeans against my chafed vagina, wincing as I go.

I don't put on my shoes for fear of the sounds they'll make will wake the stranger. So I just grab my jacket and purse and slip out of the guy's house as quietly as possible, not stopping to put on my shoes until I reach the front sidewalk.

I pull up the LYFT app so I can get home, then try to mentally review the day ahead of me. If memory serves, I have about an hour before I need to be at the police station. I'm helping Detective Sherman solve another case. Not that I don't enjoy it, I do. It keeps me from the monotony of life as a semi-retired, ex criminal defense attorney with nothing more to do than count down the hours of her life until it's finally over.

2

BRAD

I leave the gym and sprint to my car. I'm running late and now only have ten minutes to make a twenty-minute trip to the San Soloman fire station for an all-company meeting and workout. I'm A-shift so my team and I aren't on today, but that doesn't mean we don't get together for workouts and the meeting is required.

I text Kat while stopped at a red light. Just a short text to say good morning. I want her to know I am thinking about her even though that doesn't seem to make much of a difference most days. Then, to be fair, I send Stacy one too.

Stacy is the woman I'm fucking, but Kat is the one I love. Stacy knows I'm not in love with her and that I'm still in love with Kat. She also knows we aren't serious, and that this won't lead anywhere. But that doesn't deter her from continuing to sleep with me. And I fear that the longer I continue to sleep with her, the more hope she'll have that it will turn into a relationship.

And it won't.

Ever.

Continuing to see Stacy, knowing she wants more from this, is a total dick move but I can't help how I feel. I wasn't planning to date again at all after Kat. I knew she was the one for me the first time I met her. But life doesn't always go as planned. The more time that goes by, the less patient I am waiting for Kat to come back to me.

My throat clenches, a direct correlation to thinking about life without Kat. I take a deep breath and let it out slowly, wincing as my ribs expand. They're sore, and I realize I will have to wrap them for the next few days. I must have a death wish having just sparred for over an hour with a guy from the semi-pro MMA circuit, especially since my primary purpose in the ring is to let this guy beat the crap out of me. I defend myself, but I also intentionally take a beating.

The pain keeps me real and gives me something to focus on.

I needed to feel alive again to make sure I was still here. When she left me, I died inside. Became an empty shell of the man I had been when I was with her. And it wasn't possible to return to the man I was with her. It wasn't even possible to return to the man I was *before* her.

Life with Kat is hi-definition full technicolor, everything before and after her is just gray-scale.

My life as I knew it ended when Kat left me. It's been eighteen months and I'm still not over it yet.

This morning's all-company work-out was a five-mile run. Which sucked considering what I've been doing at the boxing gym. Every few times we do an all-company run, we use a route that takes us along the beach in front of Kat's house. The point of the runs is to be doing an exercise together as a team.

So, we encourage one another if one guy falls back; we move as one unit and there is no competition to see who can finish first. It's like when we are fighting a fire, we are moving as one cohesive whole, and not individual pieces. It's hard to explain if you haven't experienced it before. But it is why the chief called me into his office when we got back to the station.

Today, I left the group to check Kat's house. I thought I saw someone on her balcony as we were passing by. The balcony was empty by the time I got up the steps to the cliff top. But I know they saw me coming. My guess is I scared them off. The exterior of the house was undisturbed, and I saw no one inside or an extra car in the drive or garage.

I checked the mobile app for her alarm as soon as we got back to the station; it showed no alarm activity. Which means no one tripped the alarm or activated it. So, I tried calling Kat, but she didn't answer. I sent her a text asking her to call me as soon as she can. And then I waited for what I knew was coming, right about now.

"Matthews, get your fucking ass in here now!" the Chief yells, his voice bellowing through the halls.

No one wants to be called into the Battalion Chief's office, especially not when he's yelling your name loud enough for it to echo off the walls. But when you have me leaving a group activity, combined with reckless behavior at a site early this week, and then the fresh cuts and bruises on my face of late from the boxing gym, you get a guy who's about to get his ass reamed.

I head down the hall, passing through the bunk area. Ethan is there gathering sheets for laundry.

"Dude - I warned you. Get it together, man. I know you're a fucking train wreck, but you can't handle it like this. We've got to find another way."

I give him a fist bump as I pass. "Thanks, man."

I appreciate what he's saying, plus he said, 'we've got to find another way' instead of 'you have to find another way.' I know he has my back. But this is something I need to handle on my own.

He keeps talking as I walk past, "I got you, bro, you just gotta let me."

I nod to Ethan in response and continue to the Chief's office. I stand in the doorway and wait for him to look up and acknowledge my presence. It doesn't take long.

"Sit your ass down, Matthews. You want to tell me what the fuck is going on with you and why you have such a death wish lately?"

I play stupid just to see how long I can drag it out before he really lays into me. Not my smartest move.

"I'm not sure what you mean, Chief."

"Don't fuck with me, Matthews. You know exactly what I mean. What was that the other day - running into the house with no fucking helmet? Not even a fucking Nomex hood? And without waiting until I gave an all clear? And then today with leaving the group run? And while I'm at it, what the fuck is going on with your face? You look like hell." He pauses as though waiting for me to say something, but then continues anyway.

"It's not just you. When you do something stupid, you are putting every single member of the team in danger. I will not tolerate that. If you want to put yourself in danger on your own time, fine, go jump off a cliff or a bridge, or out of a plane for all I care. But when you bring that shit into my house, on my time, we've got problems."

He runs his hand through his hair. "You are a great firefighter, man, a fucking lieutenant, you're smarter than this and we both know it. You could have been a captain by now without all these fuck ups and the shit with your girl. Don't forget you set an example for the others, you have responsibilities to the family and the community. Don't fuck this up."

I nod at him in agreement.

"What's the sign say, Matthews?" he asks, pointing to a large sign on the wall.

"Two go in, two go out," I tell him in response.

"That's right. That's not just literal either. It's the motto for how we live our life. With everything we do. Now quit being such an asshole and live by it instead of just reciting it back."

I hang my head in shame.

"You're right, Chief. I'm sorry. I fucked up, it won't happen again."

"Make sure it doesn't."

I turn to leave, but stop when he calls my name again, "Matthews?"

I turn around. "Yeah?"

His voice is softer when he speaks this time. "I know a lot of this has to do with Kat and I'm sorry for that. Whatever's going on with her, work it out. Talk to someone, get shit-faced, run twenty miles, I don't care, but work it out. And not by doing whatever bullshit it is that gives you all these bruises on your pretty boy face. I won't give you another chance. You've already taken more than your fair share of chances, and you know it."

"Got it, Chief. Thank you."

He nods in response, my cue to leave. "Shut the door behind you," he says.

I pause outside the closed door. I had fucked up earlier this week. I didn't wait for the Chief to size-up a fire or to give the all-clear. I didn't wait for status on electric or gas utilities; I didn't even wait to put most of my gear on. I charged into the home after the neighbor told me there was a little girl and a babysitter trapped upstairs.

I don't know how, but he must have known a thing or two about both the house and about fires because he also told me the stairs were on the immediate left when you enter the home, and the young girl's bedroom on the immediate left at the top of the stairs.

If I'm honest with myself, that's the only thing that saved me. There was zero visibility in the home because of poor ventilation and heavy smoke. And I never would have been able to make my way into the house and upstairs before succumbing to smoke inhalation without my equipment. Let alone saving the two people inside and getting them out safely.

3

KAT

I'm uneasy walking into the police precinct. Still sick to my stomach from last night, on top of feeling nervous over being here. Which is silly since I've been here plenty of times before to do the same thing I'm here to do today; help solve a crime. I just don't know yet what type of crime, and Detective Sherman was not forthcoming with any other information when he asked me to meet him here.

Apparently, being a (former) criminal defense attorney with a high acquittal rate in San Soloman qualifies me to help the local police with solving some small crimes. Which is how I first met Sherman, he's the lead investigator for the San Soloman Investigative Homicide Team (SSIHT). An acronym that my brain reads as 'SSHIT' every time. He didn't look happy when he asked me to meet him this morning. Then again, every time I've seen him, he's been unpleasant and looked unhappy.

I tell the woman at the front desk that I am there to meet with Detective Sherman. She raises her head to me.

"Oh, you must be Kat?" She seems surprised.

"I am."

"They are in conference room three, up the stairs and to the left. You can't miss it."

"They?" I ask.

"The task force."

Shit.

This isn't just a little low-key gab session with Detective Sherman about something he's stuck on. This is another case they need my help on.

A case with a task force.

Which means a big case. Excitement and dread fill me in equal measures as I make my way to conference room three. Stopping to grab a cup of coffee on my way. They are out of paper cups, so I have a choice between two ceramic mugs. I go with the least grungy of the two.

Sherman is off to the side talking to a big beefy guy I don't recall seeing before. He has his back to me, hands resting on his hips with his legs spread, easily taking up the space of two men.

The base of his neck is clean shaven, but his profile is rugged. Dressed in a tight black t-shirt, well-worn faded jeans, and scuffed motorcycle boots, he's about as opposite from most of the police officers in San Soloman as a guy can get. I can tell just by looking at it that his hair is soft to the touch and a tad too long for regulation. His t-shirt highlights broad shoulders and a strong back leading down to a great ass and thighs showcased in those jeans.

And just like that, I'm thinking about fucking a stranger again. As though last night didn't happen. And I haven't promised my therapist that I'll put a stop to my downward spiral. Like my friends aren't counting on me to take care of myself even though I'm still hell bent on total self-destruction. As though it doesn't gut me—feeling like I'm cheating on Brad every fucking time.

I shake my head to clear it, belatedly noticing three other men sitting around the conference table with an assortment of coffee cups, notepads, muffin wrappers, and donut boxes in front of them. I know there is a joke in there somewhere, I just can't think of it.

Detective Sherman turns. "Kat. Good, you're here," he says and pivots toward me, motioning for the guy to do the same.

There must be a hot-cop prerequisite where this guy comes from. I look around for the boom-box convinced he's really a stripper and any second those jeans will come flying off and he'll start to gyrate like crazy—

"Chance, I'd like you to meet Katarina Walker." Sherman gestures toward me. "And, Kat, this is Chance Bauer."

I feel my stomach tighten.

He's a dead ringer for Bradley Cooper, circa 2010. When he was in the *A-Team* movie? With hair that's just a little too big on top and a little too long at the neck, begging to have a woman run her hands through it.

Maybe even begging to get wet in my hot tub and help me create sexy new memories that don't involve Brad, my ex.

And now I'm thinking about Brad.

Again.

Fuck.

I know what you're thinking.

It's been how long, Kat? And you're still hung up on your ex?

You'd be right. And with the more time that passes, the harder it gets to stay away from him. I need a Brad distraction, just not necessarily in the form of Chance Bauer or anyone I work with.

The two men stare at me, Sherman as though waiting for me to start performing party tricks or something equally entertaining. And Bauer with his steely gaze and chiseled jaw.

Focus, Kat. You've got a job to do.

Ah yes, the case that Sherman has yet to present. Set aside the sexual thoughts and make room for the professional ones. I made that mistake before, sleeping with an investigator on a case, which ended up being nothing but trouble.

Big, embarrassing trouble.

Note to self: ignore the distraction that is the dream-boat detective and every other doable male on the planet (read: Brad) and focus instead on the task at hand.

Which means no flirting

"Ok, now that we're all here," Sherman says. "Let me tell you why." He clears his throat for emphasis. "We've got a stalker in our midst. He's hit four families so far." He glances down at his notes. "The Taylor, Jones, Martin, and Shaw families. Let's make sure we don't get a fifth, yeah?"

I force myself to pay attention as Sherman lays out the case for us.

Someone has been breaking into people homes and replacing their normal framed family photos with candid shots that the perp has either taken themselves or acquired in some other way. He hangs or places the framed shots among other pictures in the home, so the families don't always notice them right away. No evidence of forced entry or signs of anything disturbed or missing.

He looks at each of us pointedly, pausing as he gets to me. "Kat, besides reviewing the pictures, you'll be working with Bauer, visiting the houses of these four families."

He gives tasks to the rest of the guys before turning back.

"I think between the two of you, you and Bauer should be able to produce something to go on. Soon. Plus, if we don't, the mayor will have my ass on a platter."

An image of Sherman's ass on a platter pops into my head.

And it's a huge platter.

"I'm on it," I tell Sherman, holding back my snicker.

We all stand to leave the room. I look to Bauer; he looks back at me, his eyes twinkling again. And for just a second, I let myself wonder what his eyes look like when he's turned on.

When he's fucking.

Would they still twinkle, or would they grow darker and more intense?

Does he fuck hard or soft?

"Ready to get started?" he asks.

I nod dumbly.

He makes a hand motion as if to say *after you*. The twinkle is still there. So is the cocky half smile. How does someone even smile cockily?

Chance grabs my elbow and leads me out the door. Mid-hallway, he switches from holding my elbow, to steering me with a firm hand on my lower back. Confidently guiding me down the hall to where he wants me to go. His alpha-ness rearing its head, never doubting that I will follow.

Crazy thing is, I do.

We end up in a smaller room with a table and two chairs. He motions to a chair while shutting the door, then turns and says, "We've got a fuck ton of work to do. Are you ready to get started?"

He gives me a very direct stare, no more twinkle, his eyes all steely blue with an edge.

Shit. Fuck. Piss.

Chance Bauer is *so* the kind of guy that fucks hard.

4

____

KAT

Bauer and I work through the morning, stopping only to grab a quick bite to eat before we set out to visit the houses of San Soloman Stalker's victims. We hit the farthest first and then work our way back toward the precinct. A woman with short blonde hair in her early thirties answers the door: medium height, yoga pants and a tank top, an infant in one hand and burp cloth in the other.

She looks back and forth between the two of us; her gaze lingering on Bauer.

"Can I help you?" she asks.

"Are you Amber Jones?" Bauer asks.

"Yes, what is this regarding?"

Bauer pulls out his badge and shows it to her.

"I'm Detective Chance Bauer, and this is Investigative Consultant, Kat Walker. We'd like to ask you a few questions about the day the stalker broke into your home and left the photographs of you and your family."

"Is this because you haven't caught him yet?" she asks. "Do you have any leads? I'm sure any clues you might have found are long gone. Plus, I've cleaned the house since then. What do you hope to find?" She lets us in and leads us to the living room.

Bauer counters her questions with a few of his own and soon she is telling us her entire life story. She grew up in Virginia, married her high school sweetheart, military widow as of four years ago, and on her second marriage. Two kids from the first husband, a girl twelve, Makayla, and a boy ten, Michael. One child from her current husband, five-month-old infant, Marcus. A stay-at-home Mom who needs to leave in an hour to get the older kids from school.

While Bauer talks to her, I roam the room to see if I can note anything that may have been missed, unlikely as that may be. Not that I'm some kind of super-sleuth or anything. I'm not. But years of defending criminals gives you a glimpse into their minds and thinking like a thief becomes a little bit easier. It goes a long way in trying to catch them, to be sure.

A high-pitched female laugh breaks my concentration.

"You are too much!" I hear Amber Jones nearly scream. Judging from the giggles in the living room, Bauer is clearly scoring.

I turn back in time to see her squeezing Bauer's bicep, asking him how often he works out.

WTF?

My eyes narrow as I look at her, surprised I'm jealous. He looks up and I turn away quickly. Then head outside. He joins me a few minutes later.

"You know she's married, right?" I ask as we get in the car.

"Who?"

"*Mrs. Jones.*"

"Yeah. Why?" he asks.

"Uh, you were hitting on her… duh… totally not professional, Bauer."

"I was not hitting on her. We were just discussing… you know what, it doesn't matter. Let's go."

We've been driving a while when he turns to me and asks. "You ever been married?"

"Close, but no," I say, at once feeling guilty. "You?"

Instead of answering, he asks, "What happened?"

"Uh, I called it off. It's complicated. He's still . . . around. He's a firefighter here San Soloman. He didn't want to break up. But I had cancer, so." I shrug as if that explains everything.

"Fuck. I'm sorry, Sherman told me about your cancer, I wasn't thinking." He reaches over to pat my knee. I feel a zing straight down my center at his touch.

"It's cool," I mumble distractedly.

And it is cool, I think.

"You're in remission or whatever it's called now, right? Like, you're okay?"

"Mostly good."

"Glad to hear it, Cookie.

The rest of our drive is quiet and subdued. Me thinking about how his hand felt on my knee and him thinking about

I don't know what. But for my own good, I don't try to figure it out.

Unfortunately, we don't get much from the other two houses, but that doesn't surprise me. Returning to a scene long after they committed a 'crime' to try to solve it is not an effective means of catching a criminal.

Bauer agrees.

"I knew this would be a waste of time, but I told the mayor I would follow Sherman's lead until that lead became ineffectual. I think we can both agree that with today, it became ineffectual."

"Yup!"

It's late by the time he pulls into the precinct parking lot and stops behind my car, and I can't wait to go home and go to bed. I'm exhausted.

"So, let's reconvene sometime tomorrow to devise a new strategy," he says.

"Sounds good," I say with a smile.

I get out of his car but then turn back.

"Quick question?"

"Shoot," he says.

"Bang." My inner thirteen-year-old girl strikes again.

He smiles.

I continue, "Why are you calling me Cookie?"

"Well, you didn't like babe or Kit-Kat and calling you chocolate bar is ridiculous, so I settled on Cookie."

"Why would you call me chocolate bar? Or anything but my name?"

He doesn't respond.

"Did it occur to you I may not like nick-names?"

"Not really," he says.

"I don't like nick-names," I lie.

"Well, I like nicknames. And I like you. And when I like people, I give them nicknames. But more than that, I like that you *don't* like it." He winks at me and drives away.

5

THE STALKER

I spend my afternoon trying not to watch the schoolgirls while I rake. Even though I watch them daily, I'm unsure if my favorites are friends with one another. But I do know they are all the same age, in the same grade, and at the same school.

My school.

My girls.

I watch them here. I watch them at home.

Their home. My home. Doesn't matter now. I watch when I want.

My job as the school groundskeeper allows me to roam freely about the grounds. I'm supposed to only work on the playground while the kids are in class. But all too often, the pull of the girls is magnetic, and I am the metal within their reach.

They spend their free time to run around in their little skirts, swinging, jumping rope, dancing, twirling in circles. It's impossible to look away. I continue raking the same spot repeatedly. The ground now bare of leaves and scored repeatedly by the blades of my rake. My gloves cut into the sores on my hands; my fingers burn with the same repetition of my movements.

Glance down, pull the rake, look up, watch the girls, glance down, pull the rake, look up, watch the girls.

The twirling girls are mesmerizing. Skirts flaring up, to the point of being revealing. Shiny hair sparkling in the sun, arms flung out to their sides, faces raised towards the sun. Taking turns twirling until they fall, laughing all the while.

An inkling of a happy memory nudges my brain. I'm twirling in the sun, happy and carefree. Mother brought me to an orchard. We were going to pick apples and bake pies, I was so excited.

We got to the orchard and claimed our collection baskets. Neither of us able to reach even the low hanging fruit. I dragged a step stool under one of the trees and began plucking my apples and tossing them in my basket. Mother stood on the step just below mine doing the same. A good strategy. Soon we had collected more apples than we could ever possibly use. We took a break, mother wandered off, I sat below a tree to eat some of my apples.

It was short time later that I roamed into the sun and began to twirl. My face tilted up towards the sun, my arms thrust out for balance, my head dizzying after only a few seconds. For a moment I was happy and at peace. I could not imagine that anything bad would ever happen again. After I tired, I laid down on the grass, content and full, falling asleep quickly in the warm and welcoming arms of the sun.

I don't remember how long I slept, but when I woke it was cold and there was no one else was in the orchard with me. I wandered through the rows looking for mother, calling her name, but no one answered. Row after row of trees with empty baskets beneath them. My happy feelings quickly coming to an end, I curled up under a tree and cried softly. Mother's didn't just leave their sons in apple orchards. Did they?

I remembered the barn where the man had shown us the tractor, the tools, and the apple picking sticks. That was where I found mother with the man. She was leaning over a table with her skirt raised above her waist. His pants were down around his ankles and he was pushing at her from behind. Mother had her head bent at the neck and the man had his head flung back, both had their eyes closed.

I watched until they stopped. The man cried out, like he was in pain, his whole body tensed and arched. Mother turned at the waist smiling at him. That was when she saw me and yelled for me to leave. She stayed mad at me as she drove us home. I know she wanted to yell more, but instead she just kept looking at me and sighing.

The apple man came to our house that night, which made mother happy. I loved it when mother was happy. Her smile would change her entire face. Creases sunk so far into her face, you want to trace the lines with your finger. Her mouth, ordinarily shaped into a constant frown, suddenly bending in the opposite direction as sadness transforms into gladness.

I lived for the moments I could make her face do that, but mine were rare. The man's moments more frequent.

It was the apple man's idea to take pictures while mother and I played the game. And we always did whatever the apple man said.

6

KAT

I use the Bluetooth connection in my car to check new messages on my way home. I have a message from Brad.

"Hey, it's me. We did a run by your house earlier today and I thought I saw someone on the balcony. I checked out the house but saw nothing. And the app shows no alarm activity. Can you call me as soon as you get this and let me know if you had someone at the house doing work or something? I'll send you a text too."

I hesitate to call him because suddenly the thought of talking to him makes me nervous. But so does the thought of someone having been on my balcony.

Shit. Fuck. Piss.

I can't handle this right now. The situation is either freak the fuck out over someone on my balcony and not talk to Brad about it. Or call Brad and feel better. Because Brad always makes me feel better. *But* then I'd have to talk to Brad and I'm trying to not lean on him. It gives him the wrong idea about us. *But* if I don't call him, he'll worry. I hate to be the reason for his worry. *And,* if he left a group run, he got in trouble for it. I hate to be the reason he gets in trouble.

I dial, half hoping that he's asleep or something and I get his voicemail.

No such luck, he answers after the second ring.

"Hey, hang on," he says softly. The sound of his voice gives me goosebumps. Will there ever be a time he doesn't affect me all the way to my core?

"I'm so sorry," I whisper. "I didn't mean to wake you up; I didn't want you to worry if I didn't call as soon as I got your message."

"Why are you whispering?" he asks, now at a normal volume.

"I don't know," I say, still whispering. "Why were you whispering?"

"Because I'm at the station, and some guys are sleeping, I didn't want to wake them up," he says.

"Why are you at the station? Shouldn't you be off tonight?" I cringe as soon as I say it, not wanting him to know I still remember his schedule.

"Ethan and I are covering for the Nelson brothers - they went to a family reunion or something."

"Oh, that's nice of you."

"Why are you still whispering?" he asks.

"Sorry. I didn't realize I was still doing it. I guess because it's so late at night and the streets are empty. It feels weird to speak in a normal voice," I say at a normal volume.

He laughs, so I do too.

I forgot how much I love the sound of his laugh.

"So, did you have someone doing work on your balcony today?" he asks, getting right to the point.

"No. Are you sure you saw someone?"

"I'm sure." The finality in his voice leaves no room for uncertainty, making my heart race and my breathing shallow.

Ok, so I guess I'm going to freak the fuck out over talking to Brad AND the fact that someone was on my balcony!

"What about an overnight guest overstaying his welcome?" he asks tentatively.

"No," I say sighing. "No overnight guests."

He lets out a breath I doubt he realized he was holding. He seems happy with that answer. I knew he would be.

"Are you home now, does everything seem okay? Did you have your alarm set?"

"Um, no I'm not home yet, but yes, I had my alarm set. Should I be worried?"

"I don't know. I'll stay on the phone with you until you get there to make sure everything is okay," he says.

"You don't have to do that, Brad."

"I know I don't," he says.

The conversation seems to stall, so I ask him, "How was the run on the beach?"

"It was spectacular, as always."

"Mmm, I'm jealous."

"You'll get back there, baby. Just be patient," he tells me.

My lady parts go all atwitter, they love it when he calls me baby.

"I know." I hate the melancholy tone that gets in my voice and the longing I feel. For running on the beach. For Brad. And for running on the beach with Brad. For life with Brad.

Needing to abort those thoughts, I ask a little too loudly, "How's Stacy?"

Bringing up his girlfriend effectively sucks all the warmth from our conversation.

"Fine," he says.

"Great," I say with absolutely no sincerity at all whatsoever, hating that I even brought it up. Then, because I now feel like a total bitch, I also ask, "How is your shift going?"

"It's been slow today. Two car accidents and one residential pipe burst pipe. No major injuries, luckily. Hoping the second twenty-four hours will go as smoothly. "

"I still find it to be so ridiculous that you guys get called out for pipe leaks in someone's house."

"It's because of the water intrusion meeting electricity."

"I know, I remember. I still think it's dumb."

He laughs.

I sink into that laugh and let it envelop me.

"I'm pulling into my garage now," I tell him.

"Okay, I will stay on the phone with you to make sure everything is okay. I'm sorry I can't be there to check it out personally."

Instead of telling him it's no longer his job to do that, I let it be.

He continues, "Do you still carry your Glock? Do you have it on you?"

"Yes, but what exactly do you think I'm walking into here? Aren't you overreacting just a bit?" I ask.

"You can't be too careful, Kat. Just, please pull it out."

"Fine." I get it from my purse wanting to giggle when Brad says, 'pull it out.'

Focus, Kat!

I am at the ready as I open the door leading from my garage into my house. The alarm is still armed, so I disarm it, and turn on the kitchen light; nothing seems amiss.

I report all this back to Brad, then check the rest of my house while he's on the phone with me. Everything looks to be as it should be, which is what I tell Brad.

"Will you just look on the deck too?" he asks.

"Sure thing, boss-man."

But everything on the balcony looks normal, except for a plant that's fallen off the railing. It happens often.

"Everything is good; one of my plants blew over again, but that's it."

"Don't touch it!"

"I know! I'm not! Wait, why?"

He sighs. "Kat, someone was on your deck today, I'm certain of it. I didn't call the guys at the police department because I wasn't sure if it was a guest. But they could still be out there.

I'm contacting the PD and sending someone over to check it out."

"If someone was on my deck, I would see them. I'm out here now. No one is in the house or on the deck," I say with a confidence that I don't feel. I can't be vulnerable with Brad, not now, and especially not tonight.

"Kat, I wouldn't have called you if I didn't think it was important."

"And here I just thought it was a ploy because you missed the sound of my voice."

Face palm!

I know better than to flirt with Brad. Still, I do it anyway.

I clear my throat and continue before he responds. "Don't call the precinct. I've got Detective Sherman's cell number, I'll call him and let him know. Does that work?"

"Yes," Brad says. "Call him now please and then call me back to let me know what happens."

7

KAT

I waste some time not wanting to wake Detective Sherman with my call just in case he's asleep. This doesn't feel like that big a deal, despite what Brad says. I walk quickly through my house checking all my pictures to make sure the stalker hasn't been in my house. Once I'm satisfied there are no new candid shots of me anywhere that I didn't hang myself, I pick up the phone to call Sherman.

"Sherman," he croaks.

He seems to do about as well when first waking up as I do, which isn't saying much.

"Detective Sherman, it's Kat Walker. I'm sorry to call so late, but I may have had an intruder on my deck earlier today and I'd like to have someone come check it out."

"Mmm. Now?" He still sounds asleep. I thought detectives were supposed to wake right up when the phone rang. Like they trained for it or something.

My foot starts to tap of its own volition. A spazzy tap with no rhythm or beat.

"Yes," I say, suddenly realizing I won't be able to sleep unless someone aside from me checks everything out.

"Address?"

I give him my address trying to still my tapping limbs. The fingers on my free hand have joined my foot. Maybe I'm more nervous about this that I realize.

I check the house one more time just to make sure nothing is amiss and before I know it, I've got three police cars in my driveway, with lights flashing and sirens silent. They ask me to stand outside with one officer while the others enter the house, knocking first on the door and then loudly announcing their presence.

"There's no one—" I tell the officer as my phone rings.

It's Bauer. "Cookie, I'm—" he says.

My call waiting beeps, I pull the phone away from my ear to look at the screen. Brad is calling.

"Bauer, can I call you back?" I interrupt.

Before I even hear his answer, Brad and Ethan screech into my driveway in the rescue truck. I hang up the phone.

Brad is out of the truck before it's even stopped. "Kat? Baby? My god, are you okay?"

He pats me down and checks me out before pulling me into his arms and holding me tight. A shiver runs through me. He feels so good.

"I am so glad you are okay. If something happened to you, I would never forgive myself. I should have been here. I'm so sorry." His voice is low, his words for my ears only. They make me feel good.

Too good.

I need to distance myself.

"I'm right here, I told you on the phone that everything was okay," I say.

"Right, but then we got a call saying there was an intruder outside your house."

"You know there's no intruder, I already told you that."

"Ma'am, did you say there's no intruder? Did you call in a false report?" the officer asks. He pulls out his walkie-talkie to tell the others in the house that there's no intruder, it was a false report.

"I didn't call in a false report. I asked Detective Sherman to send someone out to check for fingerprints or something. Brad, I mean Lieutenant Matthews, thought he saw someone outside my house earlier."

"Were you here earlier?" The officer turns to Brad as he asks this.

"No, I saw someone from the beach. My unit runs together in the afternoons. I ran up when I saw him, but he was gone by the time I got here."

"You're sure it was a man?" the officer asks.

"I'm sure."

The other officers walk out of the house. "You called in a false report?" one of them asks me.

"No! This is all just a misunderstanding. I'm sorry! I wanted someone to check for prints or something. Someone was here earlier, Brad saw them," I tell him and the other officers at the same time. Brad looks like he wants to hug me, but holds back, then turns to inspect the house.

Ethan steps closer. "Stirring up trouble again, Kat?" he asks with a slight smile.

I sigh. "This must have gotten mixed up somehow between me telling Sherman and him telling dispatch. You guys didn't have to come all the way over here. Brad knew no one was here."

"We were dispatched, Kat, doesn't matter what Brad knew or whether or not your report got mixed up, when we're dispatched, we have to respond. No way was Brad not going to respond when he heard your address. Especially after he saw someone on your balcony today," Ethan says.

"Did you see them too?" I ask Ethan.

"No, but I'm not exactly interested in looking at your balcony when I'm running on the beach and it's still bikini weather. Ya know what I mean?" he asks with a wink.

I try to wink back. "Got it." My winks are not very appealing. Luckily, Ethan knows me and knows better than to ask if I have something in my eye or if I'm about to cry. My winks are more like Quasimodo with a face spasm than anything flirty or charming.

Brad comes back outside. "When did you get security cameras on the balcony?" he asks.

"I don't have security cameras on the balcony," I say.

"Well, there's a small camera up in the eaves over the balcony."

"What do you mean there's a camera in the eaves? Like a *camera* camera?" My voice grows shrill. "Like one that takes pictures and records me when I'm out there?"

"Yes, a *camera* camera. A small video camera."

"Let me see."

He leads me through the house out to the balcony and shows me where the camera is; I'm amazed he saw it. And tell him so.

"I only noticed it because I was looking to see if the doves had returned this year and put a nest up there," he says. "Otherwise, it's not even visible. Fuck." He groans, seeing the look on my face. "You didn't know it was there. I need to tell the guys outside."

I smile at the thought of Brad remembering the bird's nest. For such an alpha-male-hard-ass firefighter, he's a total softie. What I'm assuming are the same pair of doves, have returned for the past three years and built nests in the same spot under my roof.

He puts his hand on the small of my back and we walk back into the house; Ethan is heading for us with two police officers and Bauer bringing up the rear.

"Cookie, you good?" Bauer comes over and grabs my upper arms, looking me up and down.

I look at Brad; he raises his eyebrow at me. I'm sure over Bauer's touch and use of "Cookie" when addressing me.

"Yeah, yeah, I'm fine. There's a camera on my balcony though, and I didn't put it there."

Bauer heads out toward the balcony.

"Who's that guy?" Brad asks.

"That's Chance Bauer, he's a detective. I'm working with him on The San Soloman Stalker case."

"Yeah, I get that. Who is he to you?"

"No one, we work together, that's it."

Brad scoffs. "He calls you 'Cookie'?"

"I've asked him not to."

"How's that working, Kat?"

Bauer comes back in the room, and I feel Brad tense beside me.

I turn to introduce them, but Bauer beats me to it.

"Chance Bauer, Detective, SSPD, Downtown Precinct," he says, holding out his hand.

Brad takes Bauer's hand and shakes it.

"Brad Matthews, Lieutenant, SSFD, Station 76."

Even from where I'm standing, I can tell both men are taking their shaking duties very seriously.

Ethan laughs behind a cough, muttering something close to "down boy," then steps forward and offers a hand to Bauer.

"Ethan Stewart, SSFD, Station 76."

Bauer drops Brad's hand, reluctantly, and moves in to shake Ethan's.

Their shake is brief and not as intense. I look back and forth between Brad and Bauer, who are just glaring at each other, engaging in some non-verbal testosterone driven communication.

"So, hey," I say, hoping to break the tension, "did y'all see the camera? Should I freak out now? Good thing I haven't done naked hot tub in a while, huh?"

All five men turn to look at me. Well, I guess that got their attention.

One of the uniformed officers clears his throat. "Ma'am, since it was a false report, we will excuse ourselves. Have a nice night and stay safe." He tips his hat to us and leaves.

"It wasn't a false . . . oh never mind. Thank you, officers," I say.

That leaves the four of us.

Oh goodie.

"So, now what?" I ask as I swing my arms back and forth making my hands clap in front of me and behind me. It's not as easy as it sounds, believe me, but it is a great stress reliever, loosens up the shoulder blades and releases tension.

From the looks of it, Brad and Bauer should do it too.

"I'm going to dust for prints," Bauer says. "But I'm guessing there won't be any. That camera was well hidden. It wasn't a sloppy installation. How did you know to look there?" He turns to Brad with his last question.

"There is usually a bird's nest in that spot, I was looking for that."

Bauer just stares at him.

"He used to live here," I say.

"Oh, you lived here before Cookie?" Bauer asks.

"I lived here *with Kat*," Brad says.

"Brad and I were, um, engaged," I say, sounding as awkward as humanly possible.

"Ah, this is the one you gave the old heave-ho to, huh?" Bauer asks, making the situation even more uncomfortable, which I hadn't thought was possible.

I nod dumbly.

Bauer makes a pseudo-sympathetic clicking noise with his mouth that I can't think of the name of. He pats Brad on the shoulder as he walks by, even from where I'm standing it looks condescending. "Doesn't look like you live here anymore, bud."

Shit. Fuck. Piss.

Brad lunges for Bauer, but Ethan grabs him by the arm before he reaches him.

"Dude," he warns Brad in a faint voice. "Not worth it, three strikes you're out, man."

Brad rubs his hand over his face, turns to give me a hard stare, then walks out of the room. I turn to look at Ethan; he gives me a none too friendly look.

"Glottal!" I say, hitting my forehead with the palm of my hand.

Ethan looks at me, one eyebrow raised.

"Uh, that's the noise that Bauer made just now. It's called glottal, it was a GRE word. I took the GRE before I took the LSAT. I like standardized testing... "

My voice trails off when I see the slightly disgusted look on Ethan's face. I don't think he cares about my tangential recall skills. But the English teacher for that thirteen-year-old girl inside me is beaming with pride.

Brad comes back in the room. "We gotta go," he tells Ethan. "Chief wants us back. There's no medical or rescue reason to be here."

He turns. "Keep me posted on the camera. You okay with him still being here?" He motions toward the balcony where Bauer is still dusting for prints and examining the camera.

"With Bauer?" I laugh. "Totally, he's harmless."

Brad nods in response and leaves without saying goodbye.

I turn to Ethan as he follows. "He okay?" I ask.

He pauses at the door. "Really, Kat?" He looks at me with a furrowed brow, shakes his head, and then follows Brad out the front door.

Bauer comes back in. "They wiped it clean, no prints, nothing on it. As far as I can tell, it's activated remotely or by motion sensor, battery operated, and totally wireless. There are no audio capabilities, so they can't hear you. I don't think it's transmitting but that would make sense given the time of night."

"Who would put a camera on my balcony?"

"Pissed off client? Stalker? *Ex-boyfriend?*"

"No. No. *No.*"

"Well, they've got it positioned to span across the entire deck, across the entire back of the house, living room, office, and bedroom since you've got more windows than the fucking Chrysler Building."

"I like natural light."

"Given that the ex *claims* to have seen someone on your balcony today, I'm going to guess that either they installed it today, or they adjusted it somehow today."

"I'm kind of creeped out by this."

"You should be."

"Well, did you disconnect it?"

"No. If we disconnect it, we won't be able to catch who it is. We need to leave it running, be careful with what you do on your balcony and anywhere within view of your windows. We stand a better chance of intercepting the signal and catching this guy if he doesn't know we're on to him."

"So, I'm a stool pigeon? Stalker bait? Creeper Catcher?" I say, oddly titillated by this.

Bauer laughs. "Exactly. But I'm serious about you needing to be careful. I'm sure Sherman can schedule drive-bys throughout the day, which would be the front of the house, so it won't be on camera. Wait, did anyone check the front of the house? Or inside?"

"I have a security system for the inside, and it showed no activity, so I think we are good there. I believe Brad checked the front; he knows this house better than anyone."

"Well, can you check with him?"

"On it."

I grab my phone and step into the other room to call Brad. I'm not too excited about calling him when I know he's mad at me, but even I realize it's important to know if he checked the front.

He answers after the second ring. "Matthews." His tone is short and clipped.

"Hey, it's me. Kat. Do you have a second for a quick question?"

"I knew it was you . . . what's up?" he asks.

"Did you happen to check the front of the house to see if there were any other cameras there by chance?" I hate that I sound so unsure of myself and so meek.

"I checked the entire exterior of the house, there weren't any other cameras or anything else that was out of place or unusual."

"Thank you," I lower my voice. "I really appreciate it."

His voice softens. "Anytime," he says and hangs up. I hold on to the phone for a minute trying to recapture that softness from before he disconnected.

"Well?" Bauer stands in the doorway looking at me expectantly.

"The rest of the outside has the all-clear."

"And he's sure?"

"He's sure."

"Okay, if you're good then I'm going to go try to get some rest. Unless you want me to stay." He waggles his eyebrows at me.

"Nope. I'm good. I've got my security alarm and you on speed dial." I push him out the door, arm the security system, and close every blind in every window.

Feeling exhausted, I sit on my bed and debate whether I want to take a shower before bed. Cringing at the thought of having to get in the shower, wash my body, wash my hair, dry my body, and then dry my hair, I decide against it.

It sounds like so much effort.

I don't have enough energy to freak out *and* be clean. It's one or the other. So, I set my alarm clock, strip down, and crawl between the covers.

Sleep totally escapes me as I try to figure about who has put me under secret surveillance and why. I go back through all my past clients from when I was working, all my exes from when I was dating, as many of my drunk fucks as I can remember, and anyone else I've met in the last five years. But come up empty.

Except for my drunk fucks, I'm boring post cancer-resurgence. The most exciting thing to happen to me in a long time is when Netflix dropped ten seasons of "Criminal Minds" all at once.

I can think of plenty of people who don't like me, but I don't know if watching someone via remote camera is an indication they don't like you. I can't really think of anyone who would have a desire to watch me via remote camera whether or not they liked me.

At least, I don't think I can.

8

KAT

After a sleepless night trying to figure out who the hell is recording my every move, I wake up late and almost don't have time for my morning constitutional, my favorite part of the day.

I do some light yoga and water meditations in my hot tub, typically first thing in the morning just after the sun has come up. When everything is quiet, and the only sounds I hear are the hot tub on my deck and the waves of the ocean below. I like to think it counteracts the rest of the shit I do to my body to help destroy it—whether in the name of medical science or social activity.

Bauer is already at the precinct when I get there. He's got coffee and a bagel waiting for me. I moan appreciably.

"I think I love you for this," I tell him.

"Pfft, you love me anyway." He smiles his sexy smile back at me. My stomach flutters appreciatively.

Down, girl. We already have one big bundle of testosterone we can't handle. We don't need another.

We are working on developing a strategy for catching The San Soloman Stalker, the problem with that being neither of us really knows what his motivation is. No rantings of a crazy man, no manifesto, no inkling of motive. Just breaking in and leaving the picture(s), with nothing else missing or disturbed. It's like he just wants to take a shower and waste the water with no real reasoning or rationale behind it. And the worst kind of criminal to try to catch is the one with no rationale behind their crime. Just a new family each week.

"Let's go back through the files," he says. "And see if anything jumps out at us."

I groan. I'm really starting to hate these files.

"You know I'm not really a detective, right? I'm a consultant. A part-time consultant. Not some kind of lackey you can force to sit here all day and play with files. This is your job."

He rolls his eyes in response.

I stick my tongue out when I think he's not looking.

"I saw that," he says.

At some point I will have to rid myself of these juvenile responses when he pays attention to me. Where's the grown woman who is cool, calm, and collected? The one that could freeze out an entire courtroom and focus only on getting her way and winning her case? She's not the one in the room with this guy, I can tell you that.

My phone beeps with a text from Brad in response to my lame one from earlier thanking him for yesterday. Technically he was just doing his job last night, so thanking him for that was the lame part. The things I didn't thank him for: Watching my house. Finding the camera. Looking out for me. None of that is his responsibility. And I didn't draw attention to it. Yet, he still comes through me for every time I need him, whether I realize I need him or not.

BRAD: You know I will always help you. Anytime. You doing okay today? Need anything?

ME: I need a break in this stupid case we are working on.

BRAD: Which case?

ME: The one I mentioned last night, The San Soloman Stalker?

BRAD: Been to every scene as soon as they called it in.

ME: You're kidding?!?

ME: Oh, duh, of course you have. Well, that's what we are working on.

BRAD: You and Bates?

ME: Bauer.

ME: Yes.

BRAD: I'll come help.

ME: You can't come help.

BRAD: Why?

"You going to sit there playing around on your phone all day, Cookie, or are you going to help me out here?" Bauer asks.

BRAD: Hello?

BRAD: You still there?

"God, just give me a second to think," I say. I'm just not sure if it's in response to Bauer's question or to Brad's text.

Bauer mumbles something under his breath in response I don't quite catch. Though I'm sure it was about me. And it wasn't flattering.

ME: I'm here. Don't you have to work?

BRAD: I would be working.

BRAD: You at the precinct? I'll be there soon.

Shit. Fuck. Piss.

Now what have I gotten myself into? I ponder what to say and how to say it.

"Hey, guess what?" I say to Bauer. "Brad is going to come help us with the case." I take a drink of my coffee, and peek at him from over the rim of the cup. Not really wanting to see his reaction.

"Who's Brad?" he asks, without looking up from the file.

"You met him last night. Brad Matthews. He's with the fire department. He's my, ah, ex."

"What do you mean *help us with the case?*" He looks up at me and he doesn't look happy.

"Well, he's been to every scene, you know, because the fire department always responds to everything that's called in. So, he's seen it all."

"And how is that going to help, exactly?"

I take another sip of coffee to avoid answering. Because I really don't know how that will help. Brad is smart, but he's not a detective. He's a firefighter.

Bauer gives me a stern look.

"This had better be because he will actually help, Cookie. I don't have time to entertain some little firefighter who wants to play cop, 'cause he's got his panties in a bunch over his ex."

"He doesn't want to *play cop*. And he doesn't wear panties." I hear a deep voice from the doorway.

Brad.

He's in his uniform still, dark blue slacks, short-sleeved SSFD button-down shirt, and SSFD ball cap. He looks nothing short of amazing. His shirt pulls tight in all the right places, across his chest and arms. My heart does a little pitter pat, and my vagina butterflies force themselves from temporary hibernation and charge forward, full speed ahead.

How did he even get here so quickly? And then I see his pager and realize he must be on call and was close by when he texted me. The fire station is only a couple blocks from the precinct as it is.

Bauer sighs heavily and gives Brad a head nod.

Brad nods his head in return.

I look around for something to cut the tension with. A chain-saw, maybe?

"Hey, thanks for coming. I think we can use all the help we can get," I say to Brad.

"Speak for yourself," Bauer says.

Brad sits at the table next to me and I show him the file I'm working with and the pictures.

"We are missing something big," I say to Brad. "I mean, this is just evidence, and evidence always leads to a crime. I should be able to figure this out more quickly given all the criminals I've defended in the past. It's just deductive reasoning and I am a master at that. Or at least I was before . . ."

"You'll get back there, it takes time," Brad says. He moves his arm as if he's going to touch me.

I want him to touch me.

Even though the idea of it makes me tense up. Which he sees before dropping his arm.

But I'm still disappointed when he does it.

Bauer seems to accept that Brad is helping and lists out everything about each victim. Four in all so far. I stare at the board, willing my brain to produce something, anything really that will move this case forward.

"Don't forget about the kids," Brad says.

"What kids?" Bauer asks.

"Well, if you are listing out the commonalities with each of the four families affected, they all have a twelve-year-old girl."

"That's got to be it," I say, snapping my fingers.

"What?" Bauer asks.

"What Brad said, it's about the twelve-year-old girls."

"How?" Bauer asks.

I shrug in response.

"Isn't that what you're supposed to be figuring out?" Brad asks Bauer with a smirk.

"That is what the entire task force is trying to figure out, yes," Bauer says, his mouth tight.

"Task force? That sounds like a lot of people working on one thing," Brad says.

"Because one guy can put out a fire?" Bauer asks.

Brad looks at Bauer.

Bauer looks at Brad.

I look between them both.

"Hey, so," I say. "An amnesiac walks into a bar and asks, 'Do I come here often?'."

I'm the only one who laughs.

Brad's phone rings. He pulls it from his pocket; I see on the screen it's Stacy.

His girlfriend.

Fire erupts in my soul. No pun intended. "You should get that," I sneer, turning my back toward him.

Brad sighs as he stands and walks to the other side of the room, answering his phone along the way. I can't hear much of what he's saying, just little snippets. But I lean toward that side of the room anyway, to try to hear more.

"Glad you're home. . . working. . . happy to. . . of course."

Bauer looks at me, one eyebrow raised.

I straighten in my chair trying to pass off the lean as a stretch.

"It's his girlfriend," I say loudly. Brad turns back toward us as he's finishing his conversation. "Yep. . . see you soon," he says and hangs up the phone. He heard me tell Bauer who was on the phone.

"You have to go, I take it?" I ask when he hangs up, hating that my voice sounds so bitchy, but still unable to control it.

"Don't stay on our account," Bauer adds. "If your *girlfriend* needs you."

"Stacy is an elementary school teacher," Brad says. This, I already knew so he must be saying it for Bauer's benefit. "She was out of town and just returned to work today. A little girl was kidnapped the other day, turns out it was one of her students," he says. "She wants me to talk to the other kids in the class and reassure them. They are all a bit freaked out, understandably."

"How nice," I say. Still in bitch mode.

"What's a fireman going to say about kidnapping?" Bauer asks snidely.

If we're ganging up on Brad, I like that Bauer is on my side.

"Probably the same thing a detective would say," Brad says with a sigh. Only he sounds tired now, and not as combative as earlier. "I'm going to go talk to the class before we get called out again." He motions to the pager on his belt.

"Thanks for the help," I say lamely.

"Yeah, thanks," Bauer says.

Brad looks at me, then turns and walks out the door with a wave of his hand. I feel a little empty now that he's gone.

"I need sugar," I say, standing suddenly. "Want something from the vending machine?" I ask Bauer.

"Skittles."

"Skittles? You don't seem like a Skittles kind of guy."

"Hey, don't knock the rainbow of fruit flavor until you've tried it," he says.

"Oh, I've tried it. But after they swapped out lime flavor for green apple, skittles lost it for me," I tell him.

"Funny, that's when they became perfect for me."

I laugh at him and head to the vending machines. I stop to read to the BOLOs board on my way. A leftover habit from my criminal defense days when I wanted to see if a past client was at it again.

One posting stands out at me.

Missing! 12-Year-Old Girl

Sofia Carter - last seen leaving Sail Point Middle School wearing blue jeans, a white shirt with ruffled sleeves, and red tennis shoes. Answers to Sofia. Caucasian, shoulder length straight Blonde hair, blue eyes, 4'9", 92lbs, age 12.

Age Twelve.

Holy shit.

I rip the flyer from the board and race back to our office.

"Look! Look! Look!" I thrust the flyer in Bauer's face. He scans it quickly.

"And?"

"It's a twelve-year-old girl!"

"Think this is the one from your ex's girlfriend's class? She hasn't been missing long," he says, frowning.

"This has got to be the girl from Stacy's class. How many twelve-year-old's go missing around here?"

"I'm not seeing the connection. You think there's something here?" Bauer asks.

"Fuck yes, I think there's a connection here."

"But this girl isn't from one of the families with a ransacked house."

"Maybe all the families haven't reported it happening to them yet."

"You think there's a chance someone broke into their house and left framed photos on their walls and they *still* haven't noticed?"

"Yes. I don't know. Maybe. It doesn't matter. I've got a good feeling about this."

"What do you mean by a good feeling? Is this some kind of woman's intuition? Or are you actually basing it on something?"

"What difference does it make—we've got nothing else. Stop bullshitting and start policing, Bauer!"

9

———

BRAD

I leave the precinct to head toward the elementary school. Once I'm in the truck, I radio the station to let them know where I'll be. The station has a large SUV we use about town, or when the Chief has to be somewhere and it's not an emergency.

Or, like today, when I want to check on Kat.

Or visit Stacy Hunter's class.

A feeling of dread comes over me as I pull up to the school. The kids are still at recess and Stacy is in the yard with them. She must have been looking for my station truck because she waves as soon as I pull up. The kids all run to the fence to say hi. I steel my shoulders and make my way on to school grounds.

"Hey hon," she says. "We are so happy you are here, aren't we kids?"

The kids chime in with cries of 'yes' and scramble over one another to reach the gate I'll be entering the playground from.

Stacy comes over and gives me a quick peck on the lips.

"Not appropriate, Stacy," I say wiping at my lips. She giggles.

One girl taps me on the elbow. "Are you Miss Hunter's boyfriend?"

"No," I say at the same time Stacy says, "yes."

I need to break it off with Stacy. There just never seems to be a good time to do it. Now it's gone on too long and she's getting too involved.

We both agreed in the beginning it was casual, just sex, and that it wouldn't lead to anything more because I'm in love with someone else. I was brutally honest with her about it. She said she wanted to fuck a firefighter. That it was a fantasy of hers. That she's not a commitment type of girl.

I should have known better. Every girl I've met who says she's not a commitment type of girl is the exact opposite.

The bell rings, signaling the end of recess. Stacy's class aide herds the kids into the classroom. Stacy grabs my forearm and hooks her arm through mine to walk into the class. I carefully disengage myself from her.

"Stacy, I'm on duty."

"I know, but I've missed you," she says, with a pout. "Can I make you dinner tonight?"

"I can't tonight. But we need to get together, to talk," I saw as we walk through the classroom door. She claps her hands at the same time to get the attention of the kids, so I'm not sure she heard me or not.

"Class," she says. "We have a special treat today. A real-life hero is going to talk to us about safety with strangers. He's an extremely brave firefighter, and someone who is very special to me. Let's give him an extra warm welcome, Lieutenant Brad Matthews with the San Soloman Fire Department."

I'm not happy that she introduces me as someone who is special to her. I can't be any clearer about our situation, and my lack of feelings for her. It's like she doesn't process what I'm saying, and just believes what she wants to about us. I know this game she's playing, and it doesn't end well for her.

I finish with my part of the talk in about fifteen minutes, then spend another ten answering questions about being Miss Hunter's boyfriend. She walks me out to my truck after, leaving the class in the hands of her aide.

"Shouldn't you be in there with them?" I ask.

"No, they're fine with Anna. I often have other things to do that take me out of the class. Besides, if I stayed there, I wouldn't be able to do this." She reaches down to cup me.

"Stacy, what the fuck!" I pull her hand away from me and thrust it back at her.

"Baby," she whines.

We reach the truck and I open the door to get in.

"Stacy, look—"

"I know what you're going to say."

"You do?"

"Yes. And I just, I'm feeling scared right now. My students are being kidnapped. I don't know how to handle that. I'm just so grateful you are here. I don't know what I would do right now. I mean, they are so innocent."

She has crocodile tears in her eyes.

Which makes me feel like an asshole.

It's crazy to still fall for fake tears when you know you are being manipulated, right?. Yet, here I am, taking the bait hook, line, and sinker.

I give her a hug and tell her to be strong and I will check in with her later.

Then I head back to the station.

I took Stacy out to dinner for her birthday last month.

That was a big mistake.

Now, she wants to eat together all the time, mostly she wants to cook for me. I don't want to eat with her. I just want to fuck her and go home.

When I'm at Stacy's, I'm in and out. No pun intended. I don't spend the night; I don't leave clothes there; I don't bring a toothbrush. We don't cuddle; we don't have dates. Which is why the birthday dinner was a problem.

I have no issues talking to a classroom of kids about safety issues. Our station does it all the time. It's that Stacy wanted something from me, and I delivered. It feels like a promise of something more.

And if I give the impression, we are something more than we are, it's not fair to her.

I mean, I'm not a total asshole. Just a partial one.

10

————————

KAT

We begin by tracking down the detective on the Sofia Carter case - Detective Benson. He's a smallish man, with bright strawberry blond hair and bow-shaped lips. He fills us in on what's happened so far, his voice too unsure and effeminate to carry much authority.

"The, uh, abduction happened when she was on her way home from school. At. . . uh . . ." Benson consults his notes. "Sail Point Middle School. Uh. Less than three blocks from her house."

"Was she alone?" Bauer asks at the same time I ask, "How'd he do it?"

He looks back and forth between the two of us, unsure who to answer first.

So, I ask, "Was she alone?"

Just as Bauer asks, "How'd he do it?"

I backhand him in the stomach. "Knock it off!"

His stomach feels hard and firm. I stop myself from reaching out to touch it again. You know, just to be sure.

Sigh.

"Tell us what happened," I say to Benson.

"Well," Benson begins, "she and two of her friends all walk home together. They, uh, live on the same street. So, every day they walk home together, Sofia and one of the other girls both stay at the third girl's house. And that's because, uh, her mom works from home. So, they, uh, do homework or whatever until their own parents get home."

"Is this your first case or something? How did you get assigned?" Bauer asks, annoyed.

I smile at Benson and nod, encouraging him to continue.

"He makes me nervous," Benson says, motioning to Bauer. "Can't I just talk to you?"

"How did you even get through the fucking academy?" Bauer practically yells at him.

I turn to Bauer. "Go away." I point down the hallway toward a few benches that line the walls. He glares at me. For a minute, I think he won't do what I ask. But then he turns and stomps down the hall.

I smile at Benson again, reaching out to touch his arm as I ask him to continue.

His voice much firmer now. "Per Sofia's two friends, a man in a police uniform, driving a plain white car, pulled up beside them, got out of the car and walked up to the girls." He pantomimes the moves as he speaks. "He pointed to Sofia and said, 'Sofia Carter, you are under arrest, I need to take you in to the police station.'"

"Sofia started crying and said she didn't do anything. Then asked why he was arresting her, but the man just said, 'you know why'."

Benson tries to deepen his voice for the male part of the conversation and raise his voice when he speaks as Sofia. I stifle a laugh, inappropriateness rearing its ugly head once again.

"He handcuffed her, put her in the back of the car, and drove off. The other two girls ran to tell the mom at home what happened. She called Mrs. Carter first, who knew nothing about it, then the precinct to find out what was going on.

"Meanwhile, Mrs. Carter, went directly to the precinct, the desk officer told her we would never arrest a minor without a parent present. And that there was nothing in the system about Sofia Carter. So, Mrs. Carter reported Sofia missing.

"An Amber Alert was issued at once. We found Sofia's phone a few blocks from her house, the screen cracked. I'm guessing it was tossed from the car so we couldn't use GPS to track her."

"What about the other girls?" I ask. "Were they able to give us any useful information?"

Benson shakes his head. "The other two girls couldn't definitively tell anyone what the man looked like. One said he had brown hair, and the other said he had blonde hair. Both were certain he was wearing a police uniform, a police hat, and sunglasses. And both were certain it was a white car that looked like a police car without blue and red lights on the top.

"This is the card for the first responders," he says, handing me a business card. "In case you have questions. I know he filed a report too. I doubt there will be any more information than what I've given you, but there might be."

I thank Benson and look down at the card he gave me.

Ha!

Brad Matthews
Lieutenant, San Soloman Fire Department

I'm tempted to call him.

Because I need the file.

And not for any other reason.

But instead, I head down the hall to Bauer and relay the information to him, as he continues to complain about Benson and his competency as a detective.

"I got the info for the first responders too," I add. "In case we need to talk to them. But all that info would already be in Detective Benson's report, right?" I'm hoping I'm wrong, and we need to call Brad, just as strongly as I'm hoping I'm right so I can avoid him. My emotional inconsistencies know no bounds, it seems.

Bauer extends his hand for the business card in mine. I hand it to him.

"Is this your jealous little ex-Romeo, Cookie?"

"He's not jealous," I mumble, but still nod my head.

"Our next step is to talk to Sofia Carter's parents, Cookie. Not your boy-toy," Bauer says as he crumbles up Brad's card and tosses it to the ground.

Well, so much for that.

11

THE STALKER

I follow my Kitty-Kat to the girl's house. I watch her walk around looking behind bushes, peeking into trees, studying the ground. As if she would actually find something. In her ridiculously tight jeans and her tall boots. Out playing detective with the Pretty Boy.

Through my binoculars, I can see when she bends over, her giant tits swinging down in her loose sweater. The sweater is way too big for her. I would prefer it be smaller and tighter, I would prefer she be smaller and tighter.

If Ronald were here, he would say the sweater leaves just enough hidden for the imagination to run wild. He would say her tits are the perfect size for fucking. I shudder at the thought. I know some of the things that Ronald does and he makes me sick. His predilections are disgusting and vulgar. Though, I'm sure if he knew about mine, he would say the same.

I wonder if I should bring my Kitty Kat to Ronald as a surprise. I can watch as he fucks her tits. Maybe he'll even fuck her ass. I wonder if she will like it. Most of the time they like it. Of course, most of the time they are whores. Whores like everything. Unless he hurts them; even the whores don't like it when he hurts them. Ronald is a good guy; he just gets a little out of hand with the whores sometimes.

My Kitty Kat is not a whore though; she's different. Even with her huge tits and her tight pants, I know she's good. She could have been one of My Girls. But she's grown already and once they grow, they are of no use to me any longer. Growing taints them in a way that I no longer find appealing. Their innocence leaves them so quickly as they grow. And it is their unsullied embodiment that I need to survive; to thrive. Their chastity of thought, virtuous touch and sincere intent. It's a beautiful thing to experience.

I didn't have my purity for long.

I blame Mother for that. She took it before I had a chance to tuck it away and keep it safe.

Ronald never had any to begin with. But with him it was just because he wasn't made that way.

Mother would blame me when he didn't obey, which was hardly fair. Especially since he never obeyed. Oh, how she hated when Ronald didn't obey. She would hurt me, and I would cry; begging for her to stop. She would laugh and tell me not to be a pussy. The apple man would always be there, taking his pictures, no matter what she did. Ronald told me not to show weakness, that the man could inflict more pain than Mother did. But I didn't listen. I think weakness was all I knew. And for that I paid the price; again and again.

12

KAT

The Carter Family lives in a two-story Tudor style home on an ordinarily quiet street at the end of a cul-de-sac. Today, the street is unusually busy because of the search command center they set up in their home shortly after Sofia went missing.

Volunteers have been taking phone calls with tips, scouting the wooded areas behind the house, and searching the surrounding streets in the neighborhood. But there has been no sign of her or the white car. She's been missing now for forty-eight hours.

The parents—as expected—are extremely upset and not able to give us much information. No one contacted them for a ransom, and they have no clue who might have taken their daughter.

An inspection of her room doesn't yield much either it's clean, organized, and tidy.

A twin bed with a white ruffled comforter in the corner, bookshelves with a built-in desk on the same wall as the door, windows on the opposite wall from the doorway, and a closet taking up most of the fourth wall. One bookshelf has books, stuffed animals, a few knick-knacks, and a Bose speaker system for her iPod. A MacBook Air sits on the desk along with a calculator, pad of paper, and a pencil cup filled with brightly colored pens, markers, and pencils with fuzzy animal heads stuck over the erasers.

"She's got a better stereo system than I do," I joke with Bauer. He doesn't respond.

"Totally kidding," I say. "I have a killer system. Rock on!" I flash him the rocker sign and stick my tongue out Gene Simmons style. He doesn't even look at me.

"Uh, trying to work here," he says irritated.

"Sorry," I mumble.

What is it about this guy that makes me act like such a juvenile idiot? I graduated from a top ten law school, fifth in my class. To see me with Bauer you'd think it was a top ten rodeo school and I was head clown.

I keep looking around. There is nothing shoved under her bed; her clothes are all neatly hung in the closet and nicely folded in the drawers. Her shoes were in a rack on the closet floor arranged by style. Her nightstand held an iPad, a charger for an iPhone or iPad, alarm clock, and a bedside glass/carafe combo she must use for middle of the night water breaks.

I am amazed at the order and cleanliness of it all. There is nothing unusual about Sofia Carter's room. In fact, it is the perfect room for a twelve-year-old girl who's cared for and loved. Still, I know we are missing something; I just can't get a beat on it.

Bauer finds me after speaking with Mr. Carter, I'm still standing in Sofia's room trying to figure out what I'm missing.

"Well, there goes that theory," he says. "They say no one ever left unfamiliar framed photos in their house. So much for tying the two together. I guess we are back to the proverbial drawing board now."

"Sorry, Bauer. I really thought we had a connection here."

"No worries, Cookie, I did too. We'll figure it out."

"I just want something to click in this whole situation, so I don't feel like we just wasted our time."

"Welcome to police work," he says. "Where things rarely click, and you always feel like you're wasting time."

13

BRAD

I get back to the station and join Ethan and the guys on the clean-up and restocking of the rig.

"How'd it go, bro?" Ethan asks.

"Which part?

"I thought you went to help Kat with the case?"

"I did," I say. "But then Stacy called and said her class was scared and so I went to talk to them."

"Oh," Ethan says flatly.

"Exactly. Dude, she introduced me to the kids as her boyfriend. And she kissed me in front of them. Then she followed me out to the truck and grabbed my dick. She's a fucking nut job."

"Crazier in the head makes 'em better in the bed!" Ethan says.

I laugh at him.

"Seriously though, bro, I've got three words for you. Break. It. Off," he says.

"I know, E. I've tried. She gets all upset and starts crying then next thing I know we're fucking."

"I get it. You're like a victim in all this. You have no control over the situation," Ethan says.

"Fuck off, dude," I say with a scowl. Even though I hate when he calls me on my shit, I need it. It's why he's my best friend.

My phone buzzes with a call, I grab it from my belt clip and see it's Kat calling.

"Be right back, E."

"Hi," I say into the phone.

"Hi," she says, sounding a little tentative.

"Everything okay?" I ask.

"Oh, yeah, totally. I just. . . I talked to Detective Benson, the lead on the Sofia Carter case, and he said you were the first responder when she went missing, and then he gave me your card in case I had questions. Which I found funny since you're like the only person whose phone number I know by heart." She laughs, so I do too.

After a slight pause, she continues, "But I wasn't sure if you maybe had anything you could add to what you helped us with this morning. That thing about all the houses having twelve-year-old girls was brilliant. And despite what Bauer says, I think we need all the help we can get with this case."

"I'm always happy to help you in any way I can. But I'm not sure I have anything more than what I saw you guys had in the file. I can bring you my report if you want to verify. Do you have any gaps in the information you're trying to fill? I can help with that," I tell her, hoping that she'll say we should go over the report together.

"Well, we thought we had something a bit ago, but it turned out to be nothing."

"What was that?"

"We were trying to make the connection between the kidnapping and The Stalker, but Sofia Carter's house wasn't visited by him. Or her."

"You'd think they could have come up with a better name than The San Soloman Stalker, right?" I ask her.

"Ohmigod! Yes! Like they couldn't produce anything better than the literal description of the crime? And then, is it really a crime? I mean, I know it's breaking and entering, but it's not like he removed anything from the home. It's more like he's leaving them a gift. So, they'd be hard-pressed to prove criminal activity since he wasn't caught in the act."

"You would know better than anyone," I tell her.

"You're right, I would," she says, laughing. "Ah, that's funny."

I smile when she says that even though I know she can't hear it through the phone. There's just something about her voice. Her laugh. Her thoughts. It makes me feel all put back together again.

"I guess it's better than pretend prowler," I say.

"Counterfeit crook," she says.

"Proclaimed pick-pocket."

"Bogus burglar," she says as her voice dissolves into hysterics, she's laughing so hard.

I love that sound. The sound of her laughter. If I could pick one sound to hear for the rest of my life that would be it.

"Okay, okay, stop, you're killing me, smalls," she says. "I forget how much fun you are sometimes," she says, her voice much softer this time.

"Kat–" The need to tell her we should try again too overwhelming to not bring up. But she interrupts me before I can.

"Um, okay, well, I gotta go. But I'll call you if we need the file. Thanks, I appreciate it! Bye."

She disconnects before I say anything else. I'm not sure what I would have said had she not interrupted, but I would have rather had that chance and still be on the line with her, than standing here on the side of the fire station holding a silent phone.

14

KAT

If you had asked me five years ago if I would ever be comfortable going to the doctor, for anything, I would have said no. It was all I could do to force myself to get my annual check-up and gynecological exam. When I was young, I was that child who would throw such a tantrum when getting a shot, they would have to restrain me in a straight-jacket type device so I wouldn't be able to hit the nurses or the doctor when they administered it. More than once, I'd contaminated the needle because my flailing caused it to fall to the floor or stick in the wall.

Now, sticking me with shit is like second nature. And being locked in confining little scanning machines that make lots of noise is a normal happenstance.

Thus my afternoon appointment with my oncologist to check-in and get a full body scan. The building I'm going to is a smaller one in a much larger complex. They've tried hard to make the *Curtis Cancer Center* look more like a resort than a medical complex. Trees and grass line the paths to the buildings, and a large waterfall hides the entrance. There's even a Koi pond in the lobby.

The atmosphere is always quiet. As though all the cancer-free inhabitants are continually paying homage to those who are dying. I hate the way my stiletto boots sound on the slate floor, trying to push through the silence and create a constant agitation. Not that I'll stop wearing them. Once I left the courtroom—where it was all suits all the time—I decided that revealing shirts and skirts, tight jeans and slutty shoes were the way to go.

I get through my appointment, blood draws, and scans quickly and change to leave. The nurse stops me and says my oncologist wants to see me for a moment in her office. I walk back toward the office and knock lightly on her closed door.

"Come in," I hear through the door.

I go in and she motions for me to take a seat. "How are you doing lately, Kat?" she asks.

"Good. I feel good. A little tired, some muscle soreness, and a little emotional, but that's to be expected, right?"

"Any tenderness in your breasts?"

"Nope, these bad boys are still good to go," I say of my reconstructed twins. Which even I have to say are fantastic. Kudos to the boob doc.

"And you aren't working still, correct?" she asks.

"No, I took a leave of absence and my partner is slowly buying my share of the law practice from me. I am doing some consulting for the police department; I've helped with a few cases."

"How many hours a month are you doing that?"

"A month? It's kind of more like how many hours a day right now. I had a busy day today, and I don't see that letting up. I think that's why I'm feeling off."

"Don't overdo it, Katarina," she says.

"I'm not. I won't."

"Okay, well, your estrogen levels are not where we would like them to be. I'm having them run a full panel from today's draw and we should have the results from the scans in a few days. I'll have them update you on both at the same time."

"Who's them?" I ask.

"I'll be out of town for the next couple weeks," she says. "I have another doctor covering for me. He will be the one to contact you with the scan results and the blood test results. How are you on your meds?"

"All good, no worries there," I tell her with a smile, thinking of my little stockpile of Valium and OxyContin. Not that I plan to use them for anything. I don't think. But I find it comforting to know that if I had to Kevorkian myself, I could.

"Great. Are you seeing your therapist regularly?" she asks.

"I have an appointment tomorrow morning."

"Perfect," she says. "Make an appointment to come in and see me in three weeks, and you and I can go over your scans and results together then."

I thank her and am out the door. My phone pings with a text as I'm getting into my car.

BRAD: How'd the appointment go? All okay?

I can't believe he still keeps track of my appointments. I mean, I know he's still listed as my cancer caregiver in my medical file, so he gets the auto-notifications by email. But that he pays attention, and then follows up with me, blows my mind.

I text him back a thumbs up emoji and turn my phone off. Not wanting to get too involved in texting him back or too preoccupied in thinking about how his texts makes me feel.

How his texts always make me feel.

Like I matter, more than anything else. When all I usually feel is alone and unseen.

Which makes me think about him. And miss him. And no matter how many times and how many ways I try to get him out of my head and out of my heart, he stays.

No matter how much I drink, or how many nameless drunk fucks I bring home, and how many times I let them fuck me in the dirtiest, most debasing way possible, it isn't enough.

I still wish it was Brad every time.

15

BRAD

I spend most of the night tossing and turning and wake up with zero motivation to do much of anything except make sure Kat is safe. Hard to do when she doesn't respond to my fucking texts. I take a cup of coffee to my living room and try to decompress. She pisses me off when she gets like this, uncommunicative and uncooperative. Regardless of our relationship status, it's my job to protect her as the man who loves her.

I flop on the couch and turn on *SportsCenter* to catch up on what's happening with my teams. One cup of coffee turns into a breakfast beer and I find a *Die Hard* marathon while channel surfing.

"Now we're talking."

I have a man-crush on John McClane, the main character in the *Die Hard* movies, and I'm not afraid to admit it. I have a well-worn t-shirt that says, 'Yippee-ki-yay, motherf**ker!' on the front. I have all five movies on Blu-Ray. And I have a framed print of a pencil drawing of McClane crawling through the air ducts with the lighter during the "come out to the coast" scene.

I pull into the fire station, with no time to spare, race up the stairs to join the pre-shift meeting already in progress. The Chief is reviewing the schedules for the next three weeks, all of which still revolves around whether we are called out.

"Nice of you to join us, Matthews," Chief says wryly.

"Sorry, Chief, lost track of time."

I halfway listen and halfway think about how I plan to end things with Stacy and convince Kat that she needs me back in her life. The latter being the main thing to occupy my mind of late. Stacy has been hinting that she wants to meet my dad and brother, which would take us to that next level. One I have no intention of going to with her.

My phone buzzes with a new text. I pull it out of my pocket to peek, hoping it's from Kat.

STACY: Since it's your day off tomorrow, can I make you breakfast?

She has a string of heart emojis at the end of the text. At times like this, I hate predictability of my schedule. I hit the shortcut button for an auto-response:

ME: Can't respond right now - can I contact you later?

STACY: Of course! Whenever you're available is fine.

Which is a lie. If I hadn't responded she would have continued to text until I did. I've *got* to find time to end this with her. We haven't had sex in a few weeks, so the timing is good. Even if the expectation—on her part—is still there.

The meeting concludes and I limp slightly out of the room, my body even more sore today. Ethan comes up behind me. "Were you the volunteer punching bag again?"

"It's not like that," I say.

"Yes, it is," he replies, laughing.

"I worked out at the boxing gym, yes."

"You're moving a little gingerly, man. Want me to set you up with my massage therapist?" Ethan has a massage therapist he sees, both professionally and personally.

Before I respond, we hear the familiar chimes and buzzer ring through the firehouse, spurring us all into action.

Alpha situation involving an elderly woman who can't breathe. We classify traumas or emergency medical situations as either alpha, bravo, or charlie. With alpha being the most critical and charlie being the least critical.

Ethan and I are out the door less than thirty-seconds later and in the rescue truck on the way to the residence. He gets an update from dispatch on the way. They believe the woman called 911 herself, so at least we know that she isn't unconscious, which is good.

I always worry when we have the senior citizen calls because it could be anything with them. They have a tendency toward strokes, falling, debilitating illnesses, and too many are living alone with no one to check in on them or help them throughout the day.

We pull up in front of the home, a smaller ranch style house at the waterfront end of what seems to be a quiet block running perpendicular to the ocean. There is a large tree in the front yard that desperately needs trimming. The branches are far too overgrown and heavy to be that close to her roof.

I make a mental note to see if she has someone to trim the tree. If not, I'm coming back to do it myself. One bad wind and those branches are breaking through the roof. Not to mention the fire hazard they present.

I grab the medical kit and we continue to the front door. It opens before we knock; there stands a small, silver-haired lady with chin length hair, super short bangs, and big red glasses. She's wearing flannel pajamas, a loosely tied cotton robe, and large slippers with elephant heads on the ends. Two small dogs are barking and yipping, winding themselves in and out of around her feet. She's holding a box of tissue in one hand and the door open in the other.

"*Oy vey!*" she says, sounding congested and stuffed up. "I could have died in the time you took to get here. Clearly you don't understand emergency."

"We got here as soon as we could, ma'am. Can you tell us where the emergency is?" Ethan asks her.

Yip! Yip! Yip! Yip!

"Don't be a *putz*, I'm the emergency, *boychik*! I can't breathe! Nothing is helping. I've tried everything," she tells him.

"You're the woman who isn't breathing?" I ask.

She looks at me now like I'm the *putz* and turns to walk back in the house.

Ethan leans toward me. "Did she just call me a boy chick?" he asks in a muffled voice.

"My nose is completely stuffed up and I can't breathe! Are you going to help or not?" she asks over her shoulder.

We follow her in, and I take her pulse once she's sitting down.

"Would you feel more comfortable if we took you to the hospital?" Ethan asks as he sets our kit up on the coffee table.

One dog is pulling at Ethan's pant leg and growling. I can't tell if it's playing or if it seriously thinks it can take Ethan down. I see him gently shake his leg to try to get the dog off.

Yip! Yip! Yip! Yip!

"No!" she says. "No doctors and no hospitals. My late husband, *alev ha-sholem*, died in a hospital. I am not ready to die, and especially not over something as ridiculous as not breathing. And they don't know what they are doing at that hospital. So, no. You be a good *boychik* and fix me. You do it here at my house."

I laugh under my breath at her calling Ethan a boy chick again.

"Ma'am," I say securing an oxygen mask around her head.

"Mavis," she says, smiling at me, her voice muffled.

"Mavis," I say. "We are licensed EMT's, emergency medical technicians, and can assist when there is a medical emergency, but we are not licensed physicians, we did not go to medical school, and we are not equipped to help you with something that is much better suited for a doctor's visit." I listen to her heart as well as her lungs from the front and the back.

"*Feh!*" She moves the mask away from her face. "I told you, no doctors. No exceptions. Don't you know who I am?"

"You're Mavis," Ethan says, gently moving the mask back in place.

The dogs have stopped pulling on Ethan's pant leg, but still seem disturbed by his presence and continue to *yip* at will. Mavis flicks her hand at him. "*Oy khokhem attick*. I am Mavis Strassburg, perhaps you've heard of my late husband, Stone Strassburg?"

We had heard of Stone Strassburg; he was a pillar of the community before he passed, very philanthropic with both his time and money. He was widely loved and admired. His son had passed away years before him and the entire town showed up to his memorial. They called the SSFD in to aid with traffic control; it was that busy. She's close with Kat and her best friends, Lexie and Remi. I'm surprised that neither Ethan nor I recognized her.

She quiets the dogs, finally. "Stella! Clyde! *Shtum*! *Shtum*!"

Then sits back to let us continue our examination. We take her blood pressure, measure oxygen levels, gauge pupil reactions, take her temperature, test her reflexes, listen to her heart and chest again, check her breathing, and look in her ears and throat. Nothing is out of normal range enough to be alarming. It looks like she has a common cold, so we tell her so.

"*Feh*! What am I supposed to do now?" She frowns and the dogs growl at Ethan and me again.

"I suggest rest, warm liquids, vitamin C, and maybe some chicken soup," I tell her.

"I don't want to make soup. I'm too weak." Her voice quivers. The dogs jump up beside her and paw at her lap, whimpering. She continues, "*Oy vey iz mir*. I'm tired, I can't breathe, I can't sleep, I want it to go away. My son is dead. My husband is dead. My *bubula* is too busy with her grapes to care for me.

I have no one!" She throws her arm over her eyes, the move is dramatic, but also effective.

I look to Ethan; he raises his eyebrows back at me.

Before we realize what we're doing Ethan and I make promises to visit, make soup, mow her lawn, and trim the big tree. She looks up at us with big, watery blue eyes.

"You *boychiks* would really do that?" She blows her nose with a soft honking noise. Ethan and I are both nodding our heads enthusiastically, not caring that now we are both boy chicks.

I kneel next to her and place one hand on her knee. Clyde, or maybe it was Stella, licks my hand.

"Mavis," I say. "When we get back to the station, I will make you some chicken soup. Then I will bring it back here for you. One of us will check on your periodically to make sure you are okay."

"Oh *danke, danke.*" She blows her nose again. "But I'll need it to be matzo ball soup you know. That is the cure for everything. People think the cure is chicken soup, but a good Jewish woman knows the difference." Her voice is suddenly much clearer than it was a minute ago.

I smile at the request. "Matzo ball soup it is," I tell her. We move to leave, Ethan steps outside to call in our status to dispatch.

Mavis surprises me with a quick hug. "You're a real *mensch.* You're too thin, but you've got a nice *tuchus.* Are you married?"

"No, ma'am."

"Mavis."

"Right, Mavis. No, Mavis, I am not married."

"Well, you should be," she says. "If I was still a *maydl*, I'd give you a run for your money."

One dog yips in agreement. She pinches me on the butt when I turn to walk out the door. The move surprises me and I jump with a little yelp, Ethan looks over at me with a questioning look on his face. I motion him toward the truck and follow quickly behind him.

"*Danke*, boys, *danke*!" Mavis yells after us.

Yip! Yip! Yip! Yip!

Her voice is back to throaty and congested.

Ethan and I get back in the truck at the same time.

I turn to him. "Dude, she pinched my ass!"

"She called me a boy chick," he says. "Multiple times."

"She said that to me too," I say.

"Once. She said it to you once."

"And then she pinched my ass!"

Ethan just laughs. "

As we head back to the station, I realize I need to figure out what the hell a matzo ball is.

16

KAT

The day goes by excruciatingly slow; Bauer and I sit and review pictures and reports for hours, taking notes, making comparisons, sharing speculations, drinking copious amounts of coffee; all with no results. I'm staring at the same things repeatedly; seeing nothing new, connecting zero dots.

It makes for an unproductive day, giving me plenty of time to let my mind wander. And it seems to wander the most to thoughts of Brad.

"Earth to Cookie, you in there, girl?"

My eyes come in to focus and I see Bauer waving his hand in front of me. I feel a ping of sadness for just a moment it's not Brad.

"There you are," he says. "I don't know about you, but I'm about fried with all this." He motions to everything strewn across the table between us. "You wanna wrap this up and grab something to eat?" He looks at me questioningly.

"I'm meeting my girlfriends for dinner in about a half hour, so I'll just eat then," I say. My besties, Remi and Lexie, and I have a standing dinner date once a week, and tonight is it.

He looks disappointed. And I remember that he's new to the area and doesn't really know anyone and that the highlight of his evening will be going back to some drab apartment with fast food and watching pay-per-view. So, to be a charitable colleague, with no ulterior motive at all, I ask, "Would you like to join us?"

He smiles. "Are you asking me if I want to join three hot babes for happy hour?"

"I guess I am." I attempt an exaggerated wink, but based on the way Bauer looks at me, I'm sure I look like I'm trying to pop my ear on one side. I may be a sucker for a wink, but if I haven't mentioned it before, I am not a good winker.

He gathers his stuff together. "Show me the way." He grins, stands, and motions me out the door.

I try not to have crazy sex on a motorcycle fantasies each time I glimpse him in my rearview mirror and see Bauer following me. There's just something about a guy on a motorcycle.

Sigh.

The restaurant is in downtown San Soloman—it's my favorite place to unwind with salty chips, spicy salsa, and the best margaritas in town.

We arrive before the girls. The hostess is different from one I've seen before. She ignores me and smiles big at Bauer, asking him how many; he tells her four. She puts her hand on his arm and leads us to a table directly adjacent from the hostess station.

Bauer goes to sit, but I stand and look toward our usual booth, which is empty, and ask if we can sit there instead. She huffs, but when Bauer smiles at her, she leads us over there. Which I then realize is out of her line of sight. She wanted to seat us where could make eyes at Bauer all night. The little tart.

We settle into the booth.

"You know you drive like shit, right?" he asks.

"*Excuse* me?"

"That car of yours, she deserves to be driven. Hard. Fast. By a man who will treat her right." My body starts to heat at the tone in his voice. I have to wonder if we're really talking about cars.

I glance at him only to find he's staring me down. Like a cobra, his eyes capture mine and refuse to let go. I allow myself a brief moment to indulge in the image of those same eyes looking up at me from between my legs before I shake it off.

"Oh yeah?" I ask, clearing my throat and finally coming to my senses. "You mean like you?"

He shrugs. "Just sayin' it's a sweet ride, Cookie, and I know how to treat sweet rides right." He crosses his arms over his chest, the movement tilts the detective badge that hangs from a chain around his neck, causing it to glisten in the light.

I don't tell him it was because I was trying to multi-task between watching him and texting the girls on my Bluetooth connection, to let them know he was coming. But my phone kept searching the web for Bradley Cooper in *The A-Team* lookalikes, instead of texting them I was bringing my own lookalike.

So, finally I had to dig through my purse to find my phone and text them the old-fashioned way, with my fingers. All of which combined distracted me and caused me to—as he said—drive like shit.

Our regular server comes to take our order. "Well, well, who's the hottie and where are the rest of my girls?"

I laugh and tell her, "The hottie is my colleague, Chance. Chance, this is the best server in the entire world, Maureen."

"Nice to meet ya, handsome. What can I getcha?" she asks him with a big smile.

"I'll take whatever you want to bring me that is icy cold and from a tap, gorgeous," he returns, with a wink.

She turns to look at me. "Usual, baby girl?"

"Yes, please. Make it three since Remi and Lexie will be here any second."

I turn to Bauer. "So, my girlfriend Lexie owns a winery here in town called *Lovestone*. She makes killer wines and names them all after iconic old Hollywood characters and lines from romance movies. My girlfriend Remi is a chemical engineer who is going to change the world. And they are both gorgeous."

"Remi, huh?" He asks. "I knew a Remi in college."

"Did you date her?" I ask, only half teasing.

"No, well, almost. It's complicated. Killer looks, but a stone-cold bitch."

"Well, my Remi is not a bitch. She definitely has killer looks though."

"Well, then I think I'm gonna enjoy this evening just fine, Cookie." He looks at me with a wicked grin on his face.

Lexie appears at the edge of the table, blue eyes dancing, pink ponytail askew atop her head, stained white tee, dirty jeans and purple Doc Martens. "Guess what? Guess what? Guess what?" She bounces in front of the booth not waiting for us to answer. "I got a call from The Wine Educator and they are reviewing *We'll Always Have Paris* and *As You Wish* in the next issue! Aaahh! I can't stand it!"

I jump up and hug her. "Lexie, that's amazing! I'm so proud of you!"

While Lexie has received a lot of recognition for her wines locally and throughout the state, she's yet to receive much recognition nationally, and this could take her business to a whole other level.

Lexie sits down and drinks half her margarita in one straw pull.

I count to five in my head, waiting. . .

"Ack! Brain freeze!" She grabs her head with both hands and shakes it slightly. Bauer and I both laugh. He breaks the moment by reaching a hand out to her across the table. "Chance Bauer," he says, as an introduction.

"Oh my god, I'm so sorry! Chance Bauer, this is Lexie Harrison. Lexie, this is Chance."

Lexie giggles and bats her eyelashes at him. "Well, hello there. You might have to be my next dashing leading-man blend."

He grins widely at her. "I have no idea what that means, but I think I like it."

I can't decide if I'm jealous or intrigued.

Remi approaches from behind Bauer. Today she dressed "casually" in high-waisted, slim-fitting black cigarette pants with two rows of buttons decorating the front, paired with a bright red scoop neck tee, bolero cute black blazer with white trim, and black platform peep-toe Mary Janes. Her hair is twisted in victory rolls and her make-up is flawless. She looks amazing as usual.

Remi slides into the booth. "Sorry I'm late," she says before looking around the table. She narrows her eyes. "Wait a minute . . ."

And I swear the temperature in the booth goes up at least ten degrees.

"Chance?" she says at the same time Bauer says, "Remi?" and I realize that my Remi must be the Remi he knew in college.

"You guys know each other?" I ask, an expert at saying the obvious.

"Unfortunately." Remi has a dour look on her face.

"Hey." Bauer puts a hand over his heart. "That hurts. Not that I would expect anything less coming from you, Ice Queen."

"That's so original, Neanderthal."

"And cue the frostbite," he says, leaning back in his chair. Remi just glares at him.

Lexie and I look back and forth between them.

"Uh, so hey, Rem, I ordered you a margarita already," I say, gesturing to the table.

She turns and smiles, her expression at once warming. "Thanks, sweetie."

"And I'm guessing there is no real need to introduce the two of you."

"No," Bauer says. "We know each other *quite* well already."

"I know everything I need to know about this guy," Remi says. Bauer just looks at her with one eyebrow raised. I'm sensing there is a story here that Remi will tell Lexie and I about later.

"I will tell you guys all about it later," Remi says, smiling at Lexie and me.

Told you I was the master of the obvious.

"What's your wait, Ice Queen?" he all but sneers at her. "You may as well tell them now. I mean, I for one am dying to hear this." He settles back in his chair, stretching his legs out and crossing his arms over his chest. The move makes all his muscles bulge in all the right places. And judging from the expression on Lexie's face, I'm not the only one who notices.

Remi ignores his retort, choosing instead to study her menu even though she knows everything on it.

I catch Bauer staring at Remi whenever he thinks none of us are looking at him. Chance Bauer still wants to thaw the Ice Queen. Remi, on the other hand, looks like she's tuned everyone out, staring down at her hands fidgeting with her napkin.

"Hey, so, have you heard from sexy ex lately?" Lexie asks. "Or can we not talk about him in front of Officer Hottie over here." She motions to Bauer.

"I won't take offense at the Officer Hottie comment," he says. "But I do not want to engage in your little chick chat. Especially not if we are talking about Mr. Pansy-ass."

"He's not a pansy ass!" Lexie and I both say at the same time.

My phone rings. And as though summoned, I see that it's Brad calling.

As does Lexie. "Speak of the devil," she says.

I move from the table and answer.

"Hey," I say.

"Hey," he says. "I know this is your girls' night, am I interrupting?"

"No," I say. "We just finished eating and are just doing the usual gab session. What's up?"

"They called us out to Mavis Strassburg's house this evening—"

"Ohmigod, is she okay?"

"Yeah, just a head cold. Maybe you want to stop in and see her or tell Lexie to. She made a comment about Lexie caring more about her grapes than Mavis herself."

"Oh, poor thing. And that's not true. It's just a busy time for the winery. I'll make sure we all get over to see her."

"Good. I also want to see if you know if she has anyone to do any maintenance around the house for her. You know, like trimming trees, cleaning rain gutters, and such?"

My heart skips a beat. It's so like Brad to notice something like that and then to want to do something about it for Mavis.

"She used to have a guy, but I'm not sure if he's still around. I can check with Lex and see."

"Okay, if not, I will go take care of some of it for her."

"That's nice of you, Brad."

"Well, some of it is a fire hazard, so really it's like my job," he says.

I hear the sirens go off in the background.

"I gotta go, be safe," he says and hangs up before I can respond. I make my way back to the table in time to hear Lexie talking about her upcoming movie night at the winery.

"What movie are you starting with?" I ask her as I sit down.

"Goonies!" she responds, bouncing in her chair excitedly.

"Awesome!" Remi and I both say.

Lexie turns to Bauer. "And you can totally come. I show movies in the tasting room at my winery, and we have popcorn."

"I've never seen it," Bauer says.

We all look at him in disbelief.

Remi is the first to speak. "You really are a Neanderthal, aren't you?"

Bauer just shrugs his shoulders.

"Of course it's good. Otherwise, no one would come," Lexie says as though that's the logical answer to Bauer's question. "Bring snacks and a blanket. I'll comp your first bottle of wine, and we can introduce you to cinematic genius!"

I catch Remi glaring at Lexie. Bauer does too.

"Hey, your iciness, there is no reason to be upset . . ." he trails off as his phone rings. "I've got to take this, excuse me." Bauer leaves the table and steps into the corridor leading to the bathrooms. Remi motions to the server to bring another round of drinks.

Lexie turns to Remi. "So, is Officer Hottie tickling your fancy, missy?"

Remi blushes in response. "God no!" she says. "Been there, done that, bought the commemorative coffee mug and broke it. Maybe one of you should go for it." She turns and looks at me.

"Don't look at me," I say. "I've got enough trouble keeping my body cancer free, slowing down my slutty ways, and re-breaking up with my ex without bringing another guy into the equation."

Bauer comes back to the table looking upset. "Cookie, we've gotta go. Someone returned Sofia Carter and she is in the hospital."

"She was *returned?*" I ask. "Wasn't she just taken?"

"Yep. And yep. Dumped back at the same place they took her from," Bauer replies.

I pick up my margarita and down the rest in one gulp. The three of them all look at me with wide eyes.

"Don't judge," I say. "It's going to be a hard night."

Bauer digs out his wallet and hands Remi a hundred-dollar bill. "Here," he says. "This should cover what we've had and anything else you two ladies want to order."

"This is way too much," Remi says.

Bauer winks, his voice husky, "I'll collect from you later, Your Iciness."

Remi blushes. Again. "I just mean this is what? At least your weekly salary. Can you afford it?"

Bauer glares at her before turning to me. "Let's go."

Oh yeah, this would definitely be interesting.

17

———

KAT

We get to the hospital in a short amount of time, thanks to Bauer's driving skills, and find out from Detective Benson that Sofia has yet to wake up. As he talks to us, it's clear Bauer still intimidates Benson.

Regardless, he tells us the doctors are hesitant to give her anything other than hydration for fear of any interactions with whatever the kidnapper has given her. Lab results to show what is in her system won't be back for a little while. Though they are certain it was Flunitrazepam (Rohypnol). But that he has no other information outside of that.

I turn to head to the waiting room when I see Brad and Ethan walking toward me.

I smile before I can stop myself.

"Kat, what are you doing here? Are you okay?" Brad asks, worry on his face.

"I'm fine, I'm here on another case. Kidnapping. They returned the girl if you can believe it," I tell them.

"Yeah, Sofia Carter," Brad says.

"Word travels fast," I say.

"We brought her in, Kat," Ethan says.

Duh.

"Sofia is the one that is Stacy's student?" I ask.

Brad nods.

"How's she holding up? Stacy, I mean?" I ask. Brad looks at me like he's questioning my sincerity. I don't blame him, I am too.

"She's shaken up. I talked to her class, they're tough kids. I think the kids handle it better than the adults."

"I'll bet," I say.

Brad cups my shoulder with one hand. "Hey, how was dinner with the girls?"

"Awesome, as always. We actually just left them at *Crazy B,*" I say.

"We?" he asks.

"Bauer and me."

"You brought Bauer to your girls' dinner?" he asks.

"Well, there's a funny story there—" I say.

Both Brad and Ethan's pagers go off. Brad curses under his breath. He looks at me, his face unreadable. "We have to get back to the station. You be careful out there tonight, okay?" He squeezes my shoulder and turns to walk away.

"Aye, aye, Captain," I say.

"That's Lieutenant to you," Ethan says from down the hall, bringing back an old inside joke from when Brad and I were still together. My heart pangs with a longing so strong it takes my breath away.

I take a moment to regroup before heading toward the waiting room to find where the Carter family is sitting; the doctor let them in to see Sofia, but only for a brief period. So now they are back in the waiting area with the rest of us. I see Martina, the Carters' nanny/housekeeper looking at us.

I give her a small smile and am surprised when she walks toward us. She approaches cautiously, looking warily at the officers.

"Excuse me, officer?"

"Oh, I'm not an officer," I tell her. "I'm an investigative consultant. My name is Kat."

I reach my hand out to shake hers. I didn't formally introduce myself when I visited the Carter household previously.

"Kat," she begins shakily. "I heard you just now talking about the thief who steals nothing. And, well, I thought nothing of it at the time, but there was a day a few weeks ago when I got to the house later than normal because I had a flat tire and had to wait for road services to repair it. Someone had stuck a screwdriver in it. I didn't see how it was connected, but I wonder now if I was wrong. I'm so sorry."

She starts crying.

I can't handle when people cry.

I pat her shoulder awkwardly and tell her it's okay. Not knowing exactly what I'm excusing.

"There was a picture, out of place, just sitting on the coffee table. I didn't think anything of it, I just put it away in Mr. Carter's study on one of the shelves. Now I'm wondering if that was the wrong thing to do."

"Did you ever ask anyone in the Carter Family if they had left a new framed picture in the living room?"

She shakes her head, no.

I push her gently toward Mrs. Carter and thank her for talking.

I turn and walk back to Bauer. "Do you have the pictures of the Carter's home from when we were there? Specifically, the study?"

"Their house wasn't hit. Mr. Carter already told us that in the beginning," he says.

"Right, but let's say the nanny found a random framed photo in the living room one day and didn't say anything because she didn't think it was important?"

"Seriously?" he asks looking through the photos on his phone.

"Seriously," I say.

"Shit." He hands me his phone, the pictures of the Carter house already pulled up.

"Ok, I will go ask Mrs. Carter if she recognizes any of the photos on the shelves as not theirs." I look across the room at Mrs. Carter; she is sitting in a chair with her hands together and pressed between her thighs, rocking back and forth slowly.

She looks up when I approach. "Mrs. Carter, I'm so sorry to bother you, but I wonder if I could ask you a quick question."

I kneel in front of her, my knees cracking as I go down. I cringe, hoping she didn't hear them. "I'm wondering if you remember the day a couple weeks ago that Martina had a flat tire and didn't show up to the house until early afternoon?"

"Of course. It was a terrible thing to have happen. That someone would deliberately flatten her tire is horrid."

"The police have been trying to catch a criminal, perhaps you've heard of him? The San Soloman Stalker? I know this is an odd question, but if I show you some pictures do you think you might be able to help me with identifying something in them?"

She stiffens, then speaks coldly, "Are you really sitting here asking me questions about a different crime and expecting me to help you solve it while my daughter lies in a hospital bed after being abducted?"

Her voice gets increasingly loud and shrill as she speaks. "During a time when we don't even know what happened to her while she was gone or what kind of condition she will wake up in?"

"No!" I cry. "I mean absolutely no disrespect. We believe there might be a connection between whoever abducted Sofia and The Stalker."

She looks at me like I'm crazy. Then seeming to decide about that says, "How so?"

"Well, Martina mentioned that there was a framed photo on the living room table when she arrived that day but thought nothing of it. She put it on the shelves in Mr. Carter's study while she was cleaning up."

Mrs. Carter's face pales. "I didn't know that. Well, what does this have to do with… oh god… you don't… do you think this Stalker person is the one who abducted Sofia? Why would he do that?"

"We aren't sure yet. But there could be a connection."

She sighs. "I'm sorry I yelled at you, officer, I am so upset over all of this. Whatever I can do to help, I will."

I want to tell her I'm not an officer, just a consultant, but decide it probably doesn't matter right now. Instead, handing her the phone so she can flip through the pictures. "This one, here,"—she zooms in on the photo, pointing to something on one of the shelves—"I'm fairly sure it's new. And not one we took. Oh God! What does this mean?" She calls out to her husband and he comes rushing over.

Not wanting to intrude on what I'm guessing is about to be an emotional time, I thank her for speaking with me, and turn away. I head to the water fountain to get a drink. The water shoots out wonky and straight up my nose, making me cough in response. I grab a tissue from my purse and blow my nose to try to get the water out, still coughing.

Bauer comes over and pats me on the back. "You okay?"

I try to wave him off. "I think there's a connection," I croak.

"No shit, sherlock."

"You don't have to be a dick about it," I tell him

"You don't have to state the obvious."

"If it's so obvious, how come you have pointed it out yet?"

"Okay, fine, what *is* the connection, Cookie?"

"I don't know. Hell, you're the big, fancy detective, you figure it out."

"Ok, Cookie. You're right. I am the big, fancy detective. And I will figure it out. And I sure as shit won't need you pointing out the most obvious of observations to do it."

I look at him, feeling tears sting my eyes. I can't tell if I'm feeling more pissed off or hurt. He rubs his hand over his face and lets out a big sigh.

"Fuck. I'm sorry, Cookie. It's the first real thing we've got to go on until Sofia wakes up. I feel like I'm failing right now and I'm having a hard time with that."

My pissy mood immediately dissipates. I want to give him a hug.

"And," he continues. "Fuck if I don't actually need you to help me figure all this out. Not my finest hour, you know. And don't take that personally, it has nothing to do with you. That's my observation on me. Got it?"

I nod at him in response.

"Maybe we should get some sleep so we can attack this fresh in the morning. What do you say? I'll connect with you in a few hours."

Realizing I'm exhausted, I tell him, "It better not be just a few, I've got beauty sleep to catch up on."

"You don't need any beauty sleep, trust me." He winks and motions me out the door with his hand on the small of my back. The heat from his hand feels nice.

I'm not attracted to him.

Girl code dictates I no longer find him attractive. Especially not when he's got the hots for Remi and I'm waiting to get back together with Brad.

Wait? What did I just think?

I halt in the doorway.

Did I just think I'm getting back with Brad?

I can't be back with Brad.

I mean I know I still think about him all the time, but Brad and I are over. Brad has Stacy now. I can't be with him. Where did *that* come from? That is some crazy, ridiculous—

Bauer bumps into me from behind. "Whoa, everything ok?"

I shake my head to clear it.

"Yep!" I say a little too brightly. "Just confusing myself in my head."

"You definitely need sleep," he teases. "Let's get you home so you can rest that poor taxed brain."

Unfortunately, I couldn't agree more.

18

THE STALKER

I watch as the action unfolds in front of the missing girl's house.

It makes me itch with anticipation.

The sounds of women crying blends with the ever-increasing volume of men shouting orders, dogs barking, and the general chaos of a crowd. All ringing through the cul-de-sac at the same time, as though each one is trying to drown out the other. Uniformed officers push past me to cordon off the area and immediately begin to stake their claim. They think just because they are here, that their very presence will somehow aid in the girl's return.

It's only been a couple hours since she disappeared and already a search party is gathering to comb through area surrounding her home. With all the orders being barked from such a variety of sources, it's surprising that anyone can make sense of the melee that is transpiring.

Movement in my periphery pulls my attention and I see Goofy Gumshoe and Slapstick Sidekick heading in my general direction with Chubby Cohort bringing up the rear. The small one, the tall one, and the fat one. My three favorite members of the malicious crimes task-force in San Solomon. We've seen one another before at other such sites as this, not that they will remember.

I was different then.

Sadly, they haven't brought in my Kitty-Kat to aid in the search; which makes them behind schedule. And if she isn't ready for this part of the investigation, then she's definitely not ready for me.

The excitement of watching the reactions to the missing girl begin to wear off. I wait a few more minutes before heading to my car. An older blue Toyota Corolla that looks like every other older blue Corolla, which helps me blend in seamlessly. I take one last look at the large gathering of people and grin; pleased with the knowledge that I am the only one who knows that there is nothing to discover here. So while they all go home hoping they helped, but still filled with despair.

I will go home safe with the knowledge that the girl will only be found when I want her to be. And there is nothing they can do about it.

I drive away from the impromptu search command center without anyone even noticing. Which is how it is most of the time; I'm that guy you never notice. The one you might even bump into because he is so unremarkable he doesn't even register in your field of vision. The guy who is content to remain in the background, staying unseen and unheard.

At least for now.

19

KAT

Even though I often get up early, I'm not a good early morning person. Which is why when the buzzing of my phone wakes me up mere hours after I get to sleep, I'm not amused. I grab it without even looking at who is calling.

"This had better be good, you're interrupting my beauty sleep," I croak.

"He's got another girl, he took her from her house while the family was sleeping, and patrol on the house didn't see a fucking thing." Bauer sounds despondent. "I'll be there in ten to pick you up."

I wake at once, throw on a baseball cap threading my hair through the hole in the back, grab jeans, a t-shirt and flip-flops. At the last minute adding one of Brad's old SSFD sweatshirts for comfort. Bauer rings the front bell just as I finish brushing my teeth. He fills me in on what he knows while we drive to the scene.

"Dad wakes up around three a.m., goes to get a glass of water in the kitchen. Notices the front door is open, checks the rest of the house, notices that the daughter is gone, and her bedroom window and screen are missing from the frame. He wakes everyone in the house; no one has seen or heard anything. He calls the cops."

We pull onto Hudson Street a few minutes later; it's easy to tell which house the Taylor Family lives in with all the cars and flashing lights in front is. Engine 82, Brad's rig, is parking in the middle of the street.

I don't want to see him when I'm with Bauer again. Or else I don't want him to see me with Bauer again. It's hard to know the difference.

We pull up to the house and park. I look around to make sure I don't see Brad anywhere. Even though the coast seems clear, I crouch as I get out of the car and run to the cover of a shrub, look around again and bolt straight for the house.

It isn't until we get inside that I realize this is the multi-generational family whose file I've studied so many times. I smack Bauer on the arm. "Holy shit! Do you realize who this family is?" I hiss.

"The Taylor's," he replies.

"The Taylor's who *were* The Stalker's first victims, except that now we know he really targeted the Carters first thanks to Martina the merry maid."

"Fuck!" he roars. I shush him and pull him back outside, forgetting all about Brad and Engine 82.

"Okay, okay," I say excitedly. "So, we now know the Carters were the first of the Stalker's targets, and Sofia Carter was the first kidnapping victim, before he returned her. The Taylor's were the second Stalker target and Madison Taylor has just gone missing."

"I think it's safe to say we already know all the targets and who will be next. And that The Stalker is our perp!" Bauer says, before he turns to rush back into the house leaving me to either stand there or follow.

20

BRAD

Ethan and I finish a medical call and join the rest of the station at a small kitchen fire. We get back to the station and finish reloading the truck and changing out the equipment just in time to hear the speakers roar to life again.

Engine 82, Truck 37, Rescue 13. Amber Alert – Child Abduction – 7032 Hudson Street. Residential

The same street that Mavis Strassburg lives on.

We pull onto the street in a matter of minutes, lights on, no sirens, luckily there is no traffic at three-thirty a.m. which makes for a quick trip. Even though there isn't always much we can do with an Amber Alert, they still require us to answer the call. We show up to everything.

This time arriving simultaneously with the first responding police, so the captain goes inside with the officers to see if they need us. The guys and I get out of the rig and roam around. I see a light on at the end of the street where Mavis lives and make a note to go back and check on her soon.

Another car pulls up a short while later. Bauer gets out before the car is completely stopped and heads into the house. I recognize Kat as the passenger and lean back against the truck, slightly out of view, to watch her.

She pulls her baseball cap low on her brow before she gets out of the car. She looks around and ducks down near the side of the car.

Ethan comes up beside me. "Isn't that Kat?" he asks.

We watch as she runs stooped over from the car to the side of a shrub and from there straight into the house.

"She's with that fucking guy again," I say.

"Yeah. I'm sure he just picked her up."

"I don't like him. At all."

"Hey, you ever notice he kind of looks like Bradley Cooper?" Ethan asks.

"What?" I scoff. "No way. That guy looks nothing like Bradley Cooper. He looks like a douchebag."

"You sure you're not jealous, bro?"

"Pfft. Of him . . . no . . . yes. I mean, fuck, look at that guy," I admit.

"He's got nothing over you, man."

I smile, grateful for the support.

"Hey, you jump, I jump, right?" he says with a smile and a wink.

My eyes widen. "You promised never to tease me about that move! I told you that in confidence."

Ethan cackles like a hideous horror movie clown.

"In my defense, it's a great movie, the special effects with the ship sinking are amazing and Kate Winslet is hot." I cross my arms over my chest, feeling defensive. It's hard enough to keep some sense of masculinity around the station with the guys knowing I'm an animal lover who likes to cook and garden. If they knew one of my all-time favorite movies was *Titanic,* I'd lose my man card forever.

"Sorry bro, my bad," he says, chuckling. "Be right back."

21

KAT

"Nice sweatshirt," a deep voice says in my ear.

Not Brad's.

I turn and see Ethan grinning at me.

"Hey E," I say.

"Kat, fancy meeting you here."

"Yeah, well, I'm on the case." I try to peek around him to see if Brad is nearby. If Brad sees me wearing his sweatshirt, I will die.

"Right, the case," he says rocking back on his heels, arms crossed over his chest. "It looked more like you were trying to hide from the rig."

"Pfft! Why would I hide from the rig?"

Oh, I don't know, Kat. Maybe because you've finally admitted to yourself that you're still in love with Brad and want to be with him again?

"I'm guessing so you don't see Brad again tonight."

"Give me a little credit for being a grown-up, Ethan. I wouldn't hide from Brad. I'm working a case and I was looking for clues," I tell him.

"Looking for clues," he says.

"Quit repeating what I say. I am working a case. And I'm terribly busy."

"I can tell," he says as he looks me up and down. I cross my arms over my chest.

"You're wearing my boy's sweatshirt."

"Possession is 9/10ths of the law, which makes this my sweatshirt." I'm not at all proud with that retort, but it's the best I can come up with given the situation.

"Hmm."

"Well, great seeing you... again... tonight... gotta go, I'm needed inside," I say.

I turn to go back in the house and run smack into a brick wall. A familiar brick wall, outfitted in a tight blue t-shirt and turn-out gear, who smells a little like smoke, and a lot like coming home. I put my hands on his chest and look up.

Brad looks down at me, a smile in his eyes, his hands on my hips to steady me.

"Twice in one night," he says, with warmth in his voice. "How did I get so lucky?"

"I was just thinking the same thing," I say. A little breathless from the proximity to Brad. "I'm working on another case," I say, lamely. "Were you the first responders?"

He nods in response. Then says, "It's scary, he took her right from her house. That's either stupid or really ballsy." He tucks a stray piece of hair that slipped from my cap behind my ear. I shiver in response.

"Are you warm enough?" he asks with a slightly teasing tone. "This sweatshirt doesn't look thick enough for the chill tonight. Do you want my coat? I have an extra at the station."

So, he's seen I'm wearing his sweatshirt.

Great.

Embarrassed, I start to say no, then figure fuck it. I might as well get as many pieces of the man's clothing as I can. Because even though I want to be back with him, I won't ever do that to him. And I need more of him to keep with me.

He unties his jacket from his waist and wraps it around me, running his hands up and down my arms once it's on.

The Chief comes out of the house. "Let's rally, boys. Back to the house," he says, spinning his hand in the air, with one finger pointing up in a rallying motion.

Brad bops me on the nose with his finger and leaves before I thank him for the jacket.

I head back into the house. Bauer has moved down the hall to speak with one of the detectives. I take a moment to look around at these people I feel like I know so well. At least I know their *file* so well.

The grandmother and the mother, still in their nightclothes, have their arms around each other and are crying, rocking back and forth. Officers mill around looking for clues and intermittently asking questions. The father is pacing in the living room, the older sister is making coffee in the kitchen, and the younger brother is sitting on an opposite couch looking very frightened and alone. Not wanting to intrude on any of them, I smile softly in their general direction and go track down Bauer.

I find him in Madison's room.

I don't step into the room as the detectives and crime scene crew have marked clues and are in the middle of taking pictures. Bauer is off to one side speaking to one of the C-SECT guys, he doesn't look thrilled. He sees me at the door and gives me the one moment gesture.

Madison's room is much like Sofia Carter's in the décor and furnishings, but unlike Sofia's room, it's clear that a young girl lives here.

Dirty clothes on the floor at the foot of her bed, shoes and toys scattered about, posters and pictures on the walls, shelves filled with books, stuffed animals, puzzles, and games. Papers, pens, an iPod, older laptop, brushes, hair ties, and ohmigod—

"Is that Lip Smacker lip gloss?"

Bauer, the C-SECT guy, and the photographer all turn to look at me, mouths agape. I hadn't realized I'd said that aloud.

"Uh, I'll just step out to the living room and wait there," I say as I back down the hall. The gentlemen turn back to what they were doing before I interrupted.

I make a mental note to check the drugstore for grape Lip Smacker next time I'm there. I haven't seen that shit in twenty years. I know, completely inappropriate reaction given the circumstances.

Don't judge.

I have cancer.

When I get back into the living room, I notice the father is now speaking in low voices with one officer, his hands gesturing animatedly. The older sister is trying to console the mother and grandmother who are still crying, though silent now, but I don't see the little brother anywhere.

Bauer comes into the room and grabs my arm to lead me back outside.

"Where'd you get the jacket?" he asks. "Never mind. I don't care. We don't have a lot to go on," he speaks in a faint voice even though there really isn't anyone else around. "He came in through her bedroom window, no prints so he was probably wearing gloves, we're assuming he drugged her here, then just walked her out the front door. There's a concrete walkway around the perimeter of the house, so no footprints either. No alarm system, no one heard anything." His face is all stress and worry.

He looks down at his phone and his frown deepens, something I didn't think was possible. "Hang on, I gotta take this."

He walks out of earshot, but turns at once, grabs my hand, and pulls me with him, his phone already back at his side. "Let's go, Sofia Carter is awake."

22

KAT

The hospital is abuzz with activity even though it's still before dawn. We head toward Sofia Carter's room. Detective Sherman catches up with us before we get there.

"Good, you're both here. I can catch you up on what we know so far so we can make any necessary connections."

He fills us in on what little Sofia could tell them, which jives with what her friends also reported. She was walking home from school with her two friends and she thinks she remembers a police officer. Everything after that is hazy.

She thinks she slept a lot and drank a lot of either juice or something like a smoothie and that she wet the bed a few times. Sherman confirms that she was already showing signs of Flunitrazepam withdrawal – restlessness, muscle pain, confusion, and some delirium.

I look to Sherman; I have to know. "Did she say if he did anything to her?"

Sherman sighs heavily. "There is no physical evidence of rape or any kind of penetration, thank god. We will have psych talk to her when she's more coherent, but if she doesn't remember anything it won't do any good. It sounds like he took her, drugged the shit out of her, and brought her back. Now we've got to figure out why."

Bauer looks at me once Sherman has moved on. He looks worried and I don't blame him.

"It sounds like we got lucky, for lack of a better word, with Sofia Carter, but who is to say we'll have that same luck again with Madison Taylor? And why did he bring her back? Not that I'm complaining, but you must admit it's odd behavior, right?"

He's asking me questions that there are no answers to, at least no answers I can produce. He sighs heavily, running his hand up and down his face. "Fuck, Cookie. This case defies everything we know about kidnappings, There's got to be a reason. What is the purpose? Personal enjoyment? Kiddie porn black market? Let's be realistic, he could have gotten her to do whatever he wanted, regardless of the drugs, when he had her in captivity. This doesn't play out like a typical pedophile or child molester scenario."

I stay silent and let Bauer continue to work out his thoughts aloud. "We're missing something. Something obvious. This just doesn't jive otherwise. Why take her? Why bring her back? No ransom. No signs of rape or beating. Fuck, this guy is driving me crazy."

He's pacing around the waiting room, intermittently talking with his hands, and then running them through his hair, creating an even more tousled look with each pass.

"I'll be back. Let me know if anything happens."

And with that, he walks down the hall that Detective Sherman had met us in a few minutes earlier. I'm not sure what he expects to happen during the time he's gone, but I nod affirmatively at his retreating back, nonetheless.

23

KAT

By the time we leave the hospital, the day has begun. Bauer decides he wants to stop by Madison Taylor's house one more time before taking me home. He's convinced we missed something the first time around.

The house is still an active crime scene. Bauer flashes his badge at the guy guarding the perimeter and we drive up to the property. In the daylight, I realize the Taylor Family lives a few houses from Mavis Strassburg, and I'd told Brad I would check in on her. I tell Bauer I'm going to visit with her while he checks for whatever it is he thinks he missed. The sun coming out has warmed the day, so I leave Brad's jacket in the car. I'm hoping Mavis has coffee already brewing.

Mavis and her late husband, Stone, mentored my bestie Lexie when she was in college and graduate school. Then offered her a job after she graduated. When Stone retired, he sold the tasting room, the vineyards, land, and equipment to Lexie at a reasonable price. It's why she named the winery *Lovestone,* as a tribute to Stone and his generosity. Sadly, he passed a year after retiring. And Mavis has been alone ever since. I'm sure she is probably eager for company.

I hear her dogs, Stella and Clyde, barking before I even make it to the front door to knock. I can hear Mavis saying something to them

She answers the door; her nose is as red as her glasses.

"Oh Katarina, my other *bubula*," she says. "How lovely of you to visit. Come in, come in." She sounds congested.

"Oh no, Mavis, are you sick?" I ask.

"*Oy vey*. Yes, so sick. I feel death coming, Katarina. Knocking on my door. Waiting to take me to my *gelibteh*." She coughs delicately. "*Alev ha-sholem.*"

"May he rest in peace," I repeat.

"Now come," she says gesturing to her kitchen. "You can get us some coffee and *nosh* and we will talk, yes?"

We sit down in her kitchen, which always feels so inviting with its light-yellow walls, white cabinetry, and stainless-steel appliances. I get us coffee and strudel while she makes herself comfortable in her built-in breakfast nook.

"Tell me, Katarina, how are my *bubalas*? You all are good, yes? Happy?"

She's asking about Remi, Lexie, and me. Even though Lexie is technically the one that Stone and Mavis took under their wing, Remi and I definitely came along for the ride. We are all without family in one way or another.

I know that even though Mavis doesn't get to see Lexie often; they speak on the phone daily, so there isn't much to update her with. But I still update her on the basics with all of us.

"And your health, Katarina? Is good, no?"

"I still have no evidence of disease, so it's fantastic."

"*Mazel tov.*" She takes small sips of her coffee and even smaller bites of her strudel. And I pretend not to notice that she slips more strudel to the dogs than she eats herself.

I lean over the table toward her. "Are you ready for a juicy story?"

Her blue eyes twinkle behind her big red glasses and I swear I can see her rubbing her hands together in glee even though she isn't moving. She loves a good gossip story.

"So, believe it or not, the detective I am working with at the police department, used to date Remi in college. I think they still like each other." I don't tell her the real story of Remi and Bauer, instead I make it juicy and romantic. Embellishing for the sake of the story when needed. When I'm finished, Mavis has tears in her eyes.

"Oh, that makes my heart happy, Katarina. Everyone deserves a second chance at love. I do hope you are happy with this *boychik*," she says, blowing her nose loudly.

"Not me, Mavis, this is about Remi," I remind her. She nods and waves her hand at me.

Yip! Yip! Yip! Yip!

The doorbell rings and the dogs go crazy running in circles around one another, like little tornadoes making a path for the door. I look at the time and realize it must be Bauer coming to get me.

I open the door to a frustrated looking Bauer.

"Nothing new?" I ask.

"Not a thing," he says, running his hand through his hair. The dogs jump in the air and fling themselves at the screen door trying to get at Bauer.

Yip! Yip! Yip! Yip!

Mavis makes it to the door and quiets the dogs. "Stella! Clyde! *Shtum*! *Shtum*!"

The dogs sit at her feet, tails spinning in little circles as they wait to envelop this newcomer in their swirling vortex of fur-filled love.

"*Oy vey* my little *kinderlachs*," she says to them. "So feisty today." She looks up at Bauer. "They rarely like gentlemen callers," she says, as she opens the screen door to let him in.

Stella and Clyde both jump as high as his thighs, trying to get his attention. They look like little ping pong balls bouncing back and forth off the floor and his leg.

"Mavis, this is Chance Bauer, the gentleman I was telling you about," I say.

"Pleasure to meet you, ma'am," Bauer says, reaching out his hand to shake hers.

Mavis takes his hand, then turns and says, "Katarina, if I was still a *maydl*, you'd have to beat me off this one with a stick, no?"

Bauer tries to cover a laugh with a cough, clearly surprised by her comments.

"You'll get used to her," I tell him. "She's got *chutzpah*, isn't that right, Mavis?"

She reaches up and cradles my cheek in her hand, then pats it twice. "Oh, my Katarina, such a dear."

I can't tell if it's a loving gesture or a patronizing one.

"I don't mean to cut this visit short ma'am," Bauer says to Mavis. "But we need to get going."

I lean down to give Mavis a hug. When I straighten, Bauer puts his hand on the small of my back and turns me toward the front door.

"Ah, the *libe* of the young," she says.

I say goodbye one more time and head out the door with Bauer right behind me. We get a few houses away when he stops me and says, "You know she totally grabbed my ass, right?"

I look up at him, a huge smile on my face. Because that sounds like Mavis.

"Twice," he says. "And I think I liked it."

"Of course, you did," I say laughing at him.

I want to be Mavis when I grow up.

24

BRAD

I always considered myself to be a good chef until I tried to make matzo ball soup for Mavis after my shift. I used the kitchen at the station since I have yet to remodel the kitchen in my house.

The recipes seem simple, and the videos online make it look foolproof. But a matzo ball staying together once it's in the soup, is a freak of nature. It's taken me countless broken balls, and four different batches of soup, to get one small bowl of clear broth and one ball. And it's not even a big ball.

If Kat were here, she would giggle at my continued use of the word ball.

If Kat were here, her balls would be flawless.

Now *I'm* laughing at the word balls.

I grab the bowl of soup for Mavis and am out the door to bring it to her. I let one of the guys at the station borrow my truck today so he could help someone move and am driving his sports car. I take a minute to get my bearings in a vehicle that is the opposite of my own: low to the ground with scant leg and headroom.

I pull on to Mavis' street a short time later with a sigh of relief. I didn't spill the soup. A feat considering my knee would get stuck at the steering wheel every time I had to push any of the pedals when trying to shift, accelerate, or stop.

I see that the Taylor house is still an active crime scene as I pass it by. I also see Kat and that guy, Bauer, walking away from Mavis' house and toward his car. I move to honk the horn and get her attention when I see the two of them stop and she looks up at him like he's the center of her universe.

How she used to look at me.

Instead of honking, I drive past, circling in the cul-de-sac, and parking on the other side of the street. I wait in the car until Kat and Bauer drive away, my emotions rapidly switching between jealousy and anger. I take a deep breath to calm myself before grabbing the bowl and heading up the walk to Mavis' door. She answers before I knock. The dogs having already alerted her to my visit.

Yip! Yip! Yip! Yip!

"Oh, I can't believe you would do such a thing. Such a good boy. A true *mensch*," she says when she sees the container of soup in my hands. She opens the screen door, then reaches up and squeezes my cheek. "Come in, come in."

She steps back to make room for me. The dogs are running in circles behind her.

"I can't stay long I'm sorry to say," I tell her. "I have a shift that starts soon."

"One cup of coffee," she says.

I notice there are already two cups on the table of her break-fast nook. I offer to clear them for her, then grab two new cups, fill them, and bring them back to the table. She's seated on the bench with a dog on each side of her. It's amazing how quiet it is when they aren't barking.

"Did I just see someone leave?" I ask her.

"Oh, yes. That was my *bubula*, Katarina, and her new beau," she says.

"Her beau?"

"Oh, yes. In fact, I would introduce you if she wasn't in love. Such a good *boychik*, you are."

My heart stops beating.

"In love?" I ask, my voice not much clearer than a croak. I try to clear it and ask again.

"Such a wonderful story. I tell you. *L'chaim.*" She claps her hands together, then clasps them over her heart. "Young *libe*. Such treasure, no?"

I nod my head, not entirely sure what she's saying.

"Not her new beau," she says. "Oy, such *meshugaas* coming from my mouth. Is not Katarina's new beau."

My breath catches as I wait for her to right my entire world.

"Is old beau returned. And now a second chance at love."

The floor falls out from under me.

I'm left alone.

Adrift. Anchorless with no foundation and no destination.

All I can do is nod at her dumbly, not believing what I'm hearing. My head bobbing up and down like it's attached to a spring.

Kat told me nothing was going on between them. Said he was harmless. And she definitely didn't say anything about knowing him before.

"They lost each other once," Mavis says. "But now have found each other once again. So good to see my *bubulas* so happy. You will find a young *maydl* soon, no?"

I smile, politely, and continue to nod my head. Not trusting that my voice will even work right now. Mavis doesn't seem to notice; she just keeps prattling on about love.

I feel numb all over.

I stand and stumble toward the front door, mumbling a poor excuse for goodbye to Mavis.

"*Danke*, my young *mensch*. *Danke!*" she yells after me.

By the time I reach my car, I can't breathe. The pain threatens to swallow me whole. Tears that have pricked my eyes since I left Mavis' drive begin to fall over.

Fuck this shit. If Kat is moving on, then I am too.

I reach for my phone to call Stacy.

25

KAT

Sherman makes us all go home after a couple of hours to get some sleep. I am exhausted but can't imagine sleeping right now. I make myself a cup of Sleepy Time tea and head out to the balcony to drink it before I take a nap.

I send Remi a quick text to ask about her date. She quickly responds with lots of capital letters and exclamation points. Adding that she plans to bring him to movie night at Lexie's winery. I say 'yay' in my text, but really, I'm dying just a bit inside.

I mean, I'm happy for her, I really am.

Actually, no I'm not.

I am a shitty friend.

Like the shittiest.

Because at the same time I'm happy, I'm jealous. So jealous and so fucking sad. And if I'm honest with myself, it has more to do with opportunity and what this new beginning for her represents. And no one deserves a new beginning more than Remi does.

I will never have another new beginning with a man. That time in the beginning of a relationship where everything is all about hope and optimism and the future. When the bad has tainted nothing yet and all you know is what you can dream. And everything is as sweet and wonderful as candy, rainbows, puppies, and kitties.

I go inside the house, rinse my teacup in the kitchen sink, then text Brad to see if he can go to lunch tomorrow before collapsing on my bed. If you had doubts about what an asshole I am with just my Remi issues as an example. Well, I know that A-Shift works tomorrow, and Brad will not be available for lunch.

So now I can tell myself that I've tried to set him straight, but just haven't been able to yet. My phone beeps back at once.

BRAD: Where? I have the day off.

That surprises me. Before I can stop myself, I text,

ME: You have the day off?

That was stupid. Now he will know I remember his schedule. And then he will wonder why I asked if I thought he was working.

We make plans to meet, and I turn off my phone and head to my bed for a quick nap before movie night.

Except that I can't fall asleep.

Even though I'm exhausted.

All I want to do is sleep. Bury myself as far under the covers as my bed will allow, and sleep. All that usually helps when

I'm at this point is tequila or my vibrator, or both. I'm too tired to get out of bed, and it's the middle of the day and I'm a new responsible Kat who follows her therapist's recommendations.

So, vibrator it is.

Against my better judgment, I think about when Brad proposed.

~

He was still inside me when he said he wanted to ask me a question, I looked at him, waiting, and he said, "Marry me?"

"For real?"

"Fuck yes for real!"

Of course I said yes. A great big, breathy yes with tears in my eyes and a sob in my throat. Whatever I'd done to deserve Brad Matthew's love and devotion, I was thankful for every day. I hugged him and kissed him all over his face and felt him get hard inside me again. I moaned and that's all it took for him to start fucking me again.

Until he wasn't.

He stopped fucking me so he could start making love to me.

With every swipe of his tongue, every brush of his lips, every caress from his hands, and thrust from his hips he made sure I knew, without a doubt, that he loved me. With that realization came my orgasm, barreling forward, crushing everything in its way, annihilating all thought and awareness leaving me to float listlessly on its wake.

His mouth moved to my neck, stopping at the spot just behind my ear. Where he knew barely there kisses would make me lose all presence of mind, prolonging the exquisite pleasure he inflicted. His weight shifted to one side, supported with his forearm, his hand on my shoulder to keep me in place, while his other hand moved to my breast. His fingers caressing the soft flesh while his thumb flicked at my nipple. I arched into him trying to get more—more of his fingers and his mouth; more of his cock moving slowly in and out of me.

"Kat," he breathed into me. "You feel so perfect."

I felt his words everywhere, on my neck, in my heart, between my thighs.

Seduction was the challenge and Brad was killing it.

I buried my face in his neck, letting his unique scent surround me. The heat from his body warming me. The sounds of his pleasure sending me over the edge once again.

"Brad… oh!" I grabbed at his ass, locking him in with my legs around his waist, pulling him tighter, trying to get as much of him as I could. My body going fluid and tense, satiated and greedy. My legs spread wider, hips pushed higher, grabbing, pulling, needing, wanting.

"Oh Kat, baby, fuck, so tight, so sweet, so good." His strokes grew shorter and faster, like they did when he was close.

His beautiful face transformed to something otherworldly when he was ready to come. Never had I seen something so magnificent, so powerful. His head flung back, body arched, hips thrust forward, cock buried deep, pushing harder, grinding down. As I felt him release inside me, I came one more time with a cry. An explosive, spine-tingling, love filled release.

Easily the best sex we'd ever had. And we came together. How poetic for engagement sex, right?

26

BRAD

Tonight is movie night at Lexie's winery and I invited Stacy. A move I'm already regretting. But fuck if I'm going to sit back and watch Kat move on without me, without also have a soft body beside me to cushion the blow.

Already feeling tense, I get ready for an afternoon run, fighting the urge to run by Kat's house. That would take me out of my way by over an hour of running time and I really need to spend the afternoon working on my floors. My dad sold me his house earlier this year, the same one I grew up in, and I am working on renovating it when I have time off. A single-story Craftsman style, with a large front porch, a small front yard, a large fenced backyard, three bedrooms, two bathrooms, with a detached garage.

I started the renovations with the master bathroom. Knocked out a small linen closet, the shower/tub combo, and the wall that separated the toilet. Then added a smaller separate shower, a raised claw-foot tub, glass sinks, heated floors, and built-in storage. I threw up a few clerestory windows for natural light and changed out the existing window to a prairie style. Sage green and dark gray tiling on the walls, off-white ceramic mosaic floor tile, and a custom stain on the wood cabinetry and trim.

It wasn't until I finished that I realized I'd created Kat's dream bathroom.

Which is why my current project is refinishing the hardwood floors. Something more broad in scope, yet ever pervasive to the living space, so I could convince myself I was doing it just for me and no one else.

Annoyed with where my thoughts have turned, I finish my sixty-minute run in a little over forty-five minutes. Not slowing until I turn up my front walk and take a second to admire my flower garden. Having recently discovered a love of plants and gardening I like to see the transformation from seed to plant or seedling to mature plant. There's a strategy in planting foliage depending upon the time of year and how the sun hits the area. My front deck has become a showcase for my annuals and perennials. And, at the risk of sounding like a pussy, they make me smile whenever I see them.

I enter the house panting and sweaty, only to be greeted with silence. I keep thinking I should get a dog, but it seems unfair with my schedule and no one else here to care for it. If my dad hadn't moved into a small "no pets allowed" apartment when he sold me the house, I could leave it with him while on shift. I'll bet he would have loved that. With a sigh, I throw my keys on the table by the front door and head into the kitchen to grab a water and a beer; then drink them in that order.

I fall into bed after rubbing one out in the shower, intending to lie there for a moment. Only to wake three hours later when my pager goes off. I call in to the station, halfway hoping they are calling me in so I can't take Stacy out tonight. It's just that my team is on call as backup for a neighboring city in case they're called out. We cover their house until they get back.

Which means no wine for me tonight, disappointing since I'm a fan of Lexie's wine. Glancing at the clock, I realize I have just enough time to change my clothes before I need to leave to get Stacy.

I push down the dread that rises in my throat and head out the door.

27

KAT

I get to movie night at *Lovestone* a little early so I can spend time together with Lexie before it starts. We sneak away to her office so I can catch her up on the last day. I intend to talk about the case but go in a different direction as soon as I open my mouth.

"I let Bauer get to me so I can distract myself from Brad. Even though it's never going to happen. Not with either one of them. But especially not Brad. And I know it's just me, but I also know he knows me well enough to realize it's just me and that's why he still has hope. But it's not going to work, I can't be with someone who has seen me so weak. When he was with me, I was weak, physically and emotionally. He never got to have me when I was strong, not for more than a couple weeks anyway."

I lift my wine glass to take a drink, trying to mask the way my hand shakes with a swirl, but Lexie notices. She reaches over to squeeze my free hand with hers. I take a deep drink of my wine and let out an even deeper breath.

"He's seen me when I couldn't even make it to the bathroom before vomiting. When running out of Kleenex would set me over the edge and make me cry for hours. When I was so exhausted I couldn't even sleep. I just laid there in a near catatonic state consumed in a pity party for one. And I know that should make me want him more because I'm guaranteed that he'll always take care of me, but instead it feels the opposite."

My chest tightens. I'm feeling emotions I'm just not willing to feel right now. Maybe never again. "What is fucking wrong with me that I don't want someone in my life who will make sure I'm taken care of? I mean what kind of emotional masochist am I? Everyone looks for that in life, someone to have their back, someone to pick them up when they are down, someone to be their strength when they feel weak.

"I have no problem letting you guys do that, and I love you for it. But when it comes to Brad, I just can't let him in. It makes me feel sick inside at the thought of him taking care of me again. Especially after what happened with his mom."

I start to cry.

"I don't want to be alone. And I can't keep stringing Brad along, which is what I feel like I'm doing every time I let him do something for me. But, at the same time, I don't want him to go away."

I cover my face with my hands and rub my forehead.

"Ugh! I've just got to make a choice and stick to it. Right? I mean, don't I? Does that make sense?"

She grabs my hand and squeezes softly. "Of course, it does, sweetie. Now take a breath."

"It also makes me a brutal fucking bitch, doesn't it?"

"A little," she whispers. "But an understandable one. I mean, not everyone can go through what you went through, not once, not twice, but three times and come out unscathed. And by that, I mean, you know, mostly unscathed."

We both laugh at that. Mine an ugly half cry, half laugh. Hers, a light tinkling, like when glasses meet in a toast.

"Kat, you're the only one who knows what you need and the only one who knows why. It really doesn't fucking matter what anyone else thinks because they aren't the ones in your head and in your heart. So, no matter what you think you *should* want or what your mom thinks you should want, or even what Rem and I think you should want, you need to just want what you want!"

"That's a lot of wants."

"Yeah." She laughs. "But you know who taught me it doesn't matter what anyone else wants for you, it only matters what you yourself want?" Her eyes soften as they meet mine.

"Me," I whisper.

"You," she says.

I reach over and give her a hug. "I love you, Lexie."

"Love you back, beautiful girl," she says. "Now let's get some more wine and watch our favorite movie!"

Remi has The Date picking her up and they are meeting us there. We ended up inviting Bauer to join us for the movie since he's never seen *Goonies*, but he claimed to have too much work with the case.

As usual, the tasting room is hopping and Lexie's staff is doing an amazing job of multi-tasking between finishing up with the last of the wine tastings for the day and setting up the movie attendees.

I wander out to the tasting room to get a glass of wine before grabbing a seat for the movie. Remi and The Date happen to walk in the front door at the same time I walk in from the office. I watch them before they notice me. I like them together already. I can see why their kiss was so fantastic. They kind of exude chemistry.

The Date is wearing a vintage *Ramone's* tee shirt, loose-fitting jeans and work boots, which somehow totally flows with Remi's tight black capris, black bustier, cropped hounds tooth swing coat, and leopard print ballet flats. His hair is short, almost like a long buzz cut whereas hers falls softly over her shoulders in loose curls. They look like models from a fucking magazine.

Just kill me now.

Remi sees me and points me out to The Date. He puts his hand on her lower back to guide her toward me. It looks so natural, like he should always put his hand on the small of her back to guide her through life.

Remi gives me a hug, "Hey, beautiful girl!" she says.

"Hey yourself!"

"This is Alex. Alex, this is one of my besties, Kat."

Alex looks at me. "I've heard a lot about you, Kat. Nice to meet you."

"It's nice to meet you," I say, giving him the biggest smile I can muster, feeling like a phony. He smiles back, looking totally genuine.

Lexie comes bouncing over, hugs, kisses, and introductions all around. "We are starting in five minutes, guys," she says handing us two bottles and three glasses. "I'll meet you in there."

She leaves then turns back. "Oh yeah, Kat? I just saw Brad and Stacy's name on the RSVP list for tonight, just wanted to give you a heads up."

Aw, come on, universe! What the fuck?

That's when I feel him walk in. Long before I even see him. I push Alex and Remi in front of me, then peek around Alex's massive chest to confirm. Yep, there's Brad and Stacy.

Yay.

Cute, little blonde, little petite, little button nose Stacy in her print capris, sweater set, and flowered sandals.

Barf!

Brad looks good enough to eat in every way my dirty little mind can imagine. Faded jeans, button-down shirt all loose and untucked with the sleeves rolled up to his elbows, showing off his muscular, tanned forearms, and his black Chucks. My weakness is and always has been guys in Chucks.

Ha! Who am I kidding? My weakness is and always has been Brad. And Brad in Chucks makes it a million times worse

My heart races. I can't let him see me. And I can't handle seeing him. Not when my emotions are still so raw from talking to Lexi

I grab one bottle from Remi. "You guys can have the other bottle, I need this one for myself," I say, with a head nod toward the door.

Remi turns to look behind Alex and sees Brad and Stacy. "I feel you, sweetie, grab our normal seats."

Our normal seats are atop some empty barrels on racks that Lexie moves to the back of the room just for us. They are close enough to the wall to use it as a backrest, and only one rack high, so easy to climb on without risking your life using Lexie's ladder. You'd be surprised at how comfortable those barrels are once you're up there. I turn to head toward them and trip over absolutely nothing, barely righting myself in time to avoid a face-plant.

I turn back to Remi to see if anyone saw; she shakes her head slightly no. But I think she's just trying to make me feel better.

I grab my blanket and my wine and climb up on the middle barrel. Leaving barrels on either side for Lexie, and Alex and Remi, who sneak in right as Lexie introduces the movie at the front of the room. Alex climbs up first, then grabs the wine from Remi in one hand and helps her up to sit in front of him with the other, all cozy-like between his legs.

Despair floods through me, I will never have that again. I will never have that special person, a one and only. A guy who will hoist me up on the barrel to sit in front of him and snuggle with me all night.

Except for Brad. Who, apparently, I'm still in love with and want back according to my subconscious. Brad would hoist me on the barrel and snuggle with me all night. But to do that we would have to get back together.

And for us to get back together, I would need to be cancer free for five years. That's the benchmark.

And, of course, he would have to be available.

Just to drive that point home, Brad and Stacy choose that moment to walk in. The only spots left are the ones in the back, right in front of our barrels.

Great.

Brad looks up and sees me there and gives me an odd look, like he wants to smile but can't bring himself to do it. Stacy looks to see who he's looking at and gives me a tight-lipped resemblance of a smile. I wave at both, suddenly hot and uncomfortable despite the cool temperature in the room. Brad spreads out their blanket and tosses some large throw pillows on it. Stacy settles in and unpacks their picnic basket.

Yes, I said picnic basket.

Like a real basket with a hinged top that opens from either side. She spreads out a red and white checked tablecloth over the blanket, then artfully arranges dishes, silverware, cloth napkins, and an assortment of Tupperware containers. A real picnic basket with real dishes and silverware and cloth napkins.

Seriously?!?

Really, cancer gods? You keep me in remission so I can watch shit like this? I mean, sure I know they're together, but I've never had to watch them for an entire evening while having their date ten feet in front of me.

Shit. Fuck. Piss.

I take a large swig of my wine, right out of the bottle, not even caring who sees me. He had to have known I would be here. I mean, *Goonies* is one of my favorite movies and it's at my bestie's winery! He must hate me and wants to see me tortured. Just for that, I don't love him anymore. And it's a good thing too, despite what I was thinking earlier, otherwise I'd be in real trouble.

Lexie makes her way back to us to start the movie. Then scrambles up on her barrel and hands me a bag of popcorn. I'd almost forgotten the popcorn! She has an old-fashioned machine she breaks out for movie nights and other events. I know it seems like popcorn and wine don't go together, but it's pretty good.

"Thanks, hot stuff!" I whisper to her. She blows me a kiss in return. Then nods her head at Brad and Stacy raising her eyebrows in question. I roll my eyes and shrug my shoulders in return, hoping that's enough to convince her I'm fine. The movie starts and I focus on the jailbreak and trying not to down my entire bottle of wine in one chug.

I realize I'm going to need a second bottle when I've drunk over half of mine by the time Chunk is doing the truffle shuffle. Brad is drinking lemonade, probably Stacy's home-made recipe.

Ugh.

I can't see his pager on his belt from where I'm sitting, but I'm guessing he must be on call if he's not drinking. Stacy has prepared the epitome of the perfect picnic: fried chicken, potato salad, beans, rolls, and apple pie. I'm hoping the chicken is cold and rubbery.

As though she can read my mind, Stacy turns back to us and whispers, "Hey, if you guys are hungry, we've got plenty of food." She elbows Brad and gives him a look.

"Yeah, sure, plenty." He turns to talk to all of us, but it's only me he looks at. I can barely make out his face in the dark, but I feel his piercing gaze to my core. Right on cue all the blood in my body rushes to my face.

This can't be happening. He's here with Stacy. And I'm over him. I'm having lunch with him tomorrow to reiterate just that. Just because it hasn't happened yet means nothing.

I hold up my popcorn in response to his offer and smile. He shrugs one shoulder as if to say. 'next time then.' I try to stay focused on the movie, but I find myself tuned in to the Brad and Stacy show instead. She's sitting primly, perched upon her pillow with her legs folded and off to the side. I don't think she's touched a thing on her plate; she continues to drink Diet Coke from a can with a straw. Someone should really warn her about the dangers of aspartame.

Brad's lying on his side, holding himself up on one elbow and eating with the other hand. His shirt stretches across his biceps and back, showing the movement of the muscles each time he reaches for something or brings his fork to his mouth. I remember what it was like to run my hands over those muscles and dig my nails into that back. God, why do I keep forgetting how fucking good looking he is?

"Quit drooling," Lexie leans over to whisper in my ear.

"I'm not!"

She gives me that look that tells me she doesn't believe me, but that it's okay. I hold up my now empty bottle and look at her pointedly; she responds with some crazy acrobatic move that has her half on and half off the barrel, but a bottle magically materializes when she sits back up. She takes a big chug before she hands it to me. I give her a thumbs up. I so very much appreciate that not only is she not angry with me for disrespecting her wine by chugging from the bottle, but she's joining me in doing so. I love that girl!

We're both about to chug when Brad's pager goes off.

"Ha!" I say it aloud before I mean to. Happy with myself for knowing exactly why Brad wasn't drinking. Annoyed as fuck with myself to now be in the direction everyone is looking to see who's talking and what the noise is.

Brad whispers an apology at the same time I try to save face by loudly announcing, "It's okay. Hunky firefighter off to put out fires and all."

He leans over to whisper something in Stacy's ear then gives her a kiss on the cheek. A chaste kiss I notice, feeling triumphant.

Brad gives me a look with a furrowed brow and cocked head. I shrug and smile an attempt at an apology, then close my eyes and tap my heels together three times and whisper, "There's no place like home," to try to return there.

When I open my eyes, I'm still sitting on my barrel, Brad has left, and everyone's attention is back on the movie. At least this way I'll only have to deal with Stacy when the movie is over and not the emotional steamroller that is Brad and Stacy on a cozy picnic date five feet in front of me. I hand the bottle back to Lexie and resume shoveling popcorn in my mouth.

My phone buzzes, I pull it out of my pocket and see that it's Bauer.

"Hang on," I slur softly. Then I get off the barrel and head out of the room so I can talk without disturbing anyone watching the movie.

"Whassup?"

"Are you drunk?" he asks.

"Pfft. No. Working on it. Wanna join us?"

"Some of us work for a living."

"I work—"

"Save it. He returned Madison Taylor, she's in the hospital. It's looking like the same MO. But he's got a third girl, Makayla Jones. Got her with the puppy at the park routine if you can fucking believe it. I gotta go. Call me when you sober up."

He hangs up on me. I try to call him back, and he sends me to voicemail. All three times. I google *Madison Taylor returned* on my phone, but nothing pops up. Then I try *Makayla Jones kidnapped,* and strike out again. I give Bauer one last chance to answer his phone when I call.

Four strikes and I'm out.

This isn't even my job.

Or my concern.

Or my problem.

I go back to my seat in the barrel room, share more wine and popcorn with Lexie, finish watching one of my favorite movies and shoot death glares at the back of Stacy's head.

Alex and Remi give me a ride home after the movie, I make Remi ride in the backseat with me so I feel better about my third wheel status. She wastes no time in grilling me about Brad. "So, what was up with you and the Sexy Ex?"

"What do you mean? Nothing was up."

"Don't forget who you're talking to, it freaked you the fuck out when he walked in. Then you couldn't take your eyes off him all night. Then you announced to the entire barrel room that he's hunky."

I sigh a big *I regret everything I've done over the past three hours* kind of sigh. "Yeah, that didn't go down exactly the way I was hoping it would."

"It's okay to still be hung up on him, you know."

"I'm not. Or at least I don't think I am. But the other day when I tried to summons my go-to two guys, one girl double-penetration fantasy with my vibrator, Brad kept popping into my head. One me. Two Brads. Now I can't stop thinking about him."

She chokes down a laugh. "You have a go-to vibrator fantasy? How did I not know that?"

"Yes. Don't judge me."

"I would never—"

Alex clears his throat loudly. "Uh, ladies, just a reminder I am in the car."

"Sorry, Alex!" I say, not even remotely embarrassed.

Remi's mouth drops open and she shoots me an accusing look.

I continue, at a lower voice, "I invited Brad to lunch so I can remind him it will never work between us, then he can move on and marry Stacy and I can move on and get cancer again and die or something."

"I gotta say Kat, I'm kind of amazed you haven't done that yet."

"What? Died or talked to Brad?"

She rolls her eyes at me.

I continue, "It's not exactly easy to crush someone's hopes you know. Again. Deliberately. And again."

"Yours or Brad's?"

This time I shoot her a dirty look. "I'm serious, this won't be fun."

She reaches out and squeezes my hand, a sad smile on her face. "I'm sorry, sweetie. I know it's got to be hard on you."

I half smile back.

Alex pulls up in my driveway, I thank them for the ride and give Remi a hug and kiss. Then, on impulse, I lean over the front seat and give Alex a kiss on the cheek. "You've heard me talk about sexy ex and vibrator fantasies; I think we're close enough for cheek kisses now."

He smiles. "Agreed."

I head inside fully prepared to open another bottle of wine and drown my sorrows about Brad in the hot tub that he bought for me.

28

KAT

I can't get my brain to turn off and nothing that is running through it makes sense. I'm not making sense of Brad and my thoughts about him.

Am I still in love with him?

Did I ever stop?

Why did seeing him with Stacy bother me so much?

If you had asked me a few weeks ago, I would have told you I was over him. It was easy not to think about him back when I thought I was imminently dying and going through treatment.

Well, that's not entirely true, I'm not sure if it was easy not to think about him. But I knew I was correct in my convictions of not tying him to me for the rest of his life. Or, rather, the rest of mine, I guess that will come first, right? At the time I said I loved him enough to let him go, I just want him to be happy. I'm not the girl that will make him happy whether or not he thinks I am. He's wrong.

I grab my iPod, plug it into my speakers and cue my 'Sudden Death' playlist. It's the one I listen to when I really need to wallow in self-pity and despair. But instead of grabbing a bottle of wine and getting in the hot tub, I lie on my couch and look out at the ocean. The best thing about my place, aside from being on the water, is the floor to ceiling windows that make up every west-facing wall. The night is pitch black, which is perfect for my mood. I lie there long enough to lose all sense of time. Long enough for my buzz to wear off.

Which just won't do.

And how I find myself standing in the kitchen, wine opener in one hand, wine bottle in the other. I mean, if you can't use a terminal illness as an excuse to drink all night and feel sorry for yourself, what can you use it for?

Mere moments into my self-indulgent pity party, I am a sloppy, snotty mess. *Love Actually* is playing on the TV with no sound and I keep replaying all the sad scenes. My bottle of wine now half empty, a considerable dent made in the industrial-sized bag of gummy bears, and a mostly used roll of paper towels. Because they hold up better to tears and snot than tissues. Everything that has ever been wrong or ever will be wrong in my life is working its way out of my system via tear ducts and nasal cavities.

I get a text from Remi asking me if I'm okay after seeing Brad and Stacy. I tell her I'm just having a blah night and can't sleep, but it's fine I'll be better tomorrow. I need to feel sorry for myself for a while. She tells me to text her if I need anything.

My tears are close to drying up when I hear a knock on the door. I'm not expecting anyone, especially not this late.

Within seconds there's knocking *and* the doorbell, and . . . a woman's voice yelling. I wrap myself in my blanket and move to unlock the door, only to have Remi push her way in.

"What are you doing here?" I ask.

"Well, sometimes the self-pity wallowing nights are meant to be spent alone, and sometimes they aren't. Besides, I brought wine and gummy bears and ordered Chinese delivery on my way here"—she pauses and looks around my living room—"I see you started without me." She leads me by the blanket over to the couch and sits me down.

"How far into it are you?" she asks. I'm not sure if she means my pity party or the movie. So I answer for both.

"Just half a bottle, so it's good you brought one. And Hugh Grant's sister just realized that Hans Gruber really bought the necklace for the office tart."

"You're mixing movies."

I wave my hand in the air. "And stupid Brad . . . is just . . . stupid and stuff."

She leans over and hugs me. "I wondered if it would be hard to see him on a date. Why he took her to your bestie's winery is beyond me. He had to know you'd be there."

The look on her face makes me start to cry all over again. "It's not just Brad it's everything. It's my life. I'm going to be alone. No one will hold my face to kiss me goodnight at the front door. And I don't want to be alone. I'm convinced the cancer is going to metastasize and come back in some random fucked up place. I know that I'm supposed to stay positive, and I try to but then there're nights like tonight and I just can't stay positive anymore.

"I can't do it. I will never make homemade lemonade and plan picnics with real plates. I will never be that girl that wears a sweater set and capris and looks country club pretty and wrinkle-free. And it's not even about Brad, not really. Or maybe it is. Fuck! I just need time to wallow and think as many negative thoughts as I can come up with. And then it will be tomorrow, and I'll be better, I promise."

She sits down next to me on the couch and pulls me into a hug, my head resting against her chest while she strokes my hair. "First, everyone hates the girl that wears a sweater set and capris. And by everyone, I mean absolutely everyone. So, you don't want to be her, anyway. Second, you take whatever you need whenever you need it, beautiful girl, and if there's something you need that I can give you, you tell me.

"Otherwise, I'm just going to guess at what you need. Like right now, I'm going to go call in sick to work tomorrow, open this bottle of wine, and then join you on the couch. We'll eat Chinese, line up additional movies, open more wine, and make a sleepover of it."

"I'm not good company right now, Remi," I tell her.

"Well, that works, because I'm not looking for good company, I'm just looking to sit on your couch, get drunk, and watch movies. With little to no interaction. Except maybe pass me another egg roll or pause the movie so I can go pee."

I smile up at her gratefully,

"I'm lucky to have you Rem," I say. "And your boobs make fantastic pillows."

She laughs. "Ditto, mama. Ditto a thousand times, on both counts. Be right back."

She's back on the couch in a matter of minutes, having commandeered a wine glass for herself. She fills her glass, refills mine, grabs a handful of gummy bears, presses play on the remote and settles herself in for the rest of the movie. By the time our third tear-jerker movie ends, it's almost morning and we've conquered our own body weight in gummy bears, Chinese food, wine, and tissues.

29

KAT

We go out on the balcony to watch the sunrise with hot coffee and cold Chinese. The people watching was always good at sunrise and sunset. And by people, I mean hot guys jogging in shorts and little else. "Did I ever tell you that Brad's company frequently runs this stretch of the beach?"

"Really?!" She tilts her sunglasses down and peruses the beach more carefully.

I laugh. "They usually run later in the morning."

"Do you know this because you see him or because you know his schedule?" she asks, grinning.

"Both," I tell her, ducking my head. "But whenever I see him, I hide behind the patio set so he doesn't see me, but he always looks up."

"Does he see you hiding?"

"Probably, I know it's lame. I don't know why I do it."

She laughs at me. "Hey, speaking of guys . . ." she points up the beach toward a group of guys, all wearing navy blue shorts and shirts, running down the beach. My heart beats faster. I'm pretty sure it's guys from Brad's station, it's the only one close enough that they'd be running at this beach. And I have no idea if he's with them.

"I gotta go to the bathroom," I mumble to Remi and run inside the house.

"Chicken!" she calls back at me.

I take my time in the restroom, then stop to grab us some orange juice and acetaminophen. I can hear she's talking to someone when I return a few minutes later.

"Okay," she yells at the group. "But tell him that Kat and Remi say hello and we miss him!"

I rush to the balcony only to see the backs of the guys jogging farther up the beach, back toward the station house.

"What the hell, Remi?!?" I smack her on the upper arm. "What did you say?"

"Oh, settle down. I only asked if they were from A-Shift, but they were from C-Shift. They said B-shift was out helping another city with a big fire somewhere else and that they paged A-Shift in to cover the other city's firehouse until they got back. I didn't know they did that, that's cool. Anyway, so I asked if they knew Brad and they said yes, so I told them to tell him that Kat and Remi said hi."

"And that we missed him," I fume.

"Well, we do," she said.

"No, we don't! We just saw him last night. That was dumb!"

"Kat, you miss him in the global sense of the word, as a fixture in your life, not because you haven't seen him in a long time."

"Well, I don't need him knowing that."

"Why not?"

"Ohmigod, Remi, really?"

"Come on, Kat," she says. "You know you want to be with him. You made that obvious last night. And he wants to be with you. Tell him to ditch Stacy and make you both happy."

"Stacy makes him happy."

"Bullshit. You're good for him. And he's good for you. And I've told you plenty of times that your head is up your ass where he's concerned. And so has Lex. So, everyone who loves you the most knows he's good for you and that being with him is the right thing, and yet you still sit here acting like a fucking martyr."

"I am not acting like a martyr. Take it back!"

"No way! And I'm being serious here, Kat. If you don't give him another chance, I will tell him you've been secretly pining for him all this time and that you've never stopped loving him and that he should keep trying to get you back with any means possible. And then I will tell him you have a shrine built to him on the inside door to your medicine cabinet."

"It's not a shrine!"

"It's a fucking shrine. You covered that door with pictures of him and of the two of you."

"So what?"

"So, you still love him. You still want a future with him. And, sweetie, I gotta tell you, there is no one who deserves to be loved like you do. You have been through hell and come out of it fighting. Don't you want someone fighting next to you?"

"I have you guys for that."

"Someone fighting next to you that you can have sex with?"

"I can have sex with you guys."

"Quit being obstinate."

"Fine! Fine! I'll think about it. Whatever. Change the subject"

"So, what's new?" she asks.

"Well, I've got a creepy stalker who planted a camera on my balcony."

"Holy shit, no way," she says, looking around. "Where? Are they watching us right now?"

"Uh, over there." I jerk my chin in the direction of the camera. "And I don't know. If there's a red light on, then probably. But if not, then no."

"And you wait until now to bring this up?" she asks. "We've been sitting out here all morning."

"I know, I'm sorry. I forgot."

"How the hell do you forget about a hidden camera?"

I shrug my shoulders. "Chemo brain."

"You're not in chemo right now. Jeez, Kat. Is that it right there?" she squints in the direction I indicated and points her coffee mug.

"Don't point! And quit looking around! We can't let the creepy stalker know we know the camera is there or we won't catch them."

"This is all sorts of fucked up Kat. No way am I sitting out here when someone might be watching us."

I follow her inside. "I'm sorry, Rem. To tell you the truth, I'm kind of used to it now."

"How can you possibly be used to a hidden camera on your balcony?" she asks.

"I don't know," I tell her.

"That's just weird. And a little sad. How did you find it?"

"I didn't, Brad found it."

"When was Brad here?"

"The other night—"

"My god, you tell me nothing!"

"It was just because they thought I had an intruder—"

"An intruder? What in the actual fuck, Kat? Are you okay? Was anything taken?"

"I'm fine, it was a misunderstanding. But I had a whole slew of them here: Brad, Ethan, Bauer, and two other cops."

"Kat! I can't believe you didn't tell me you had an intruder!"

"It wasn't really an intruder." I explain to her what happened that day with Brad seeing someone and Detective Sherman screwing up the dispatch call.

"I can't believe I spent all night here not knowing any of this. It's weird and really unsettling." She shivers. "Anything else major happen in your life you haven't shared with me?"

"Well, you know I'm supposed to have lunch with Brad today, right?"

"What the fuck, Kat! You tell me nothing! You said you were thinking of inviting him, not that you are going."

"It's the lunch where I tell him we're never, ever getting back together."

"I'm sorry, were you not the other person in the conversation about two minutes ago? The same person who wallowed over this guy all night long. There is no way this is going to be the lunch where you sever all ties and break it off completely. I guarantee it."

"We'll see," I say half wondering if she's right.

30

THE STALKER

Hers was the first camera I planted. Even before Kitty Kats. I put it right in her bedroom. Hiding in plain sight. And no one has been the wiser. Each time I watched her video feed, my anticipation grew.

I knew once I got her with me, it would all be worth it.

I sit down to review my work. The pictures are exquisite. Though there was never a doubt they would be.

Her hands behind her head, that beautiful blonde hair spread out over her arms and across the bed. Budding breasts barely peeking through sheer silk and lace, long, lanky legs bent at the knee and off to one side. Her hip cocked, making the bottom of her negligee ride up, affording the smallest glimpse of the side of her panties.

A classic boudoir pose.

Bright shiny red lips, longing to be kissed. Blue eyes that pop with a hint of eyeshadow. As mother always said, it must be just a hint all the way across the lid, because too much eye shadow will make a person look clownish. And no one wants to look clownish. A touch of blush that make her cheeks shine pink.

Photographic genius.

Thanks to mother, I am familiar with makeup and its application. At first, I hated it when mother put makeup on me. She said it was because I was a pussy and pussies wore makeup. But after a while, it became something that we did together. Like how we played the game together. I never saw mother play the game with Ronald. She never put makeup on him or called him a pussy either. I'm sure that made me her favorite son.

I always listened, like a favorite son should, and I played the game every time she asked.

Thinking about the game stirs things inside of me that I don't want to think about right now. Things that make me want to rub my cock and puke at the same time.

Dinner.

Dinner will appease me.

I set the oven to 400 degrees and pull tonight's choice from the freezer: Banquet Salisbury Steak. I don't particularly care for Salisbury Steak, but I do like the dessert that comes with it, so it's a frequent purchase.

Forty-five minutes remain before I need to wake the girl to give her something light to eat and make sure she drinks her juice. For her, I have only things that are easy to swallow.

The thought of the girl swallowing makes my breath shallow and my heart rate increase. Would she swallow my spurts?

My cock hardens forcing a groan that both delights and disgusts me. I allow myself a few seconds to indulge in the fantasy before grabbing at my ears and pulling down sharply. Any way to use pain to purge the images from my mind. Nails digging into the skin behind my ears as my fingers search for purchase.

It's not enough.

Panic sets in.

I never should have thought about mother and the game.

She's the reason I take the girls.

This beautiful girl with her big eyes and porcelain skin. Full bow shaped lips, so naturally red and juicy. How would they feel when touching mine?

I'm lost to the fantasy again.

I slip my hand inside my pants and start to rub.

I need to finish before the shame sets in and fills me with remorse and fear.

Much too soon the girl's face morphs with mothers. Her purity distorted by the whorish ways that define my mother.

Mother laughing. Taunting. Destroying.

I push the heels of my hands into my eyes, wishing I had the nerve to pull them out. Incapacitate them forever. Anything to avoid seeing the images that continue to sabotage my mind.

31

KAT

I go through my closet again, but nothing in there is calling my name. The thirteen plus outfits scattered around my room don't seem to do it for me either.

Not that I should care, this lunch isn't to impress Brad, it's to cut him off completely. We can't be together. And it doesn't matter how bad either of us may want to be.

Not that I want to be. My reasons are solid.

No matter what Remi says. Or how many pictures of Brad I still have hidden in my house.

I shut my eyes, take a deep breath, and spin three times pointing my finger as I go. My go to for deciding on an outfit when I can't otherwise decide.

I take my time dressing: slim fit boyfriend jeans, my bad-ass cowgirl rodeo belt, beige ankle boots, and a slouchy, low cut white tee tucked in just enough to look unintentional. I let my hair dry naturally so it has just a little wave to it and apply minimal makeup and lip gloss. I spritz a little of his favorite perfume on as my finishing touch, though I'm just not sure if that's to purposefully be a bitch or not. Grabbing my purse, I take a deep, cleansing breath, put on my sunglasses, and head out the door.

Since lunch is my idea, I'm not sure what he thinks will come of it. But I know what I must do and I'm not remotely prepared. Even though I know it's best for both of us.

I get to the restaurant early so I can get my bearings and prepare myself emotionally for this talk. It's a casual seafood place right on the water, and I got us a table outside on the patio. Magnificent view, pelicans circling, a soft breeze with the light ocean aroma. It would be romantic if it weren't so tragic, if I didn't still have feelings.

When I see him walking up I realize, too late, that said preparations should have been literal. As in a tequila shot. Or twelve.

My breath catches.

Somehow in the last twenty-four hours, I've forgotten just how beautiful he is. He looks good, as in take-him-home-and-keep-him-in-bed-all-afternoon good. His hair is tousled—probably from running his hands through it too many times. And even though his sunglasses hide his eyes, I know they are shining bright and blue behind them. The rest of his outfit just makes him look like sex on steroids: low riding jeans snug in all the right places, a tight white tee-shirt that shows off his pecs and arms. He may be my ex, but I'd still choose to fuck him every minute of every day over anyone else.

I asked him to meet me at a newer restaurant we'd not been to as a couple just so there wouldn't be any competing memories to mess with our heads.

Or maybe just my head.

Because now that he's here, I have to wonder if this re-breakup is for him or me.

Is it because I'm so afraid of hurting him if something happens to me? Or am I more afraid of hurting me if it doesn't last? If I'm afraid of hurting him, what's the worst that will happen? The cancer comes back and I die?

So, I die, that hurts him, but what do I care? I'm dead. And if he hurts me, well shit happens, right? Nothing can ever be good all the time. If having cancer has taught me nothing else, it's taught me that. All goodness ends. And most times that end is heinous. I mean, whenever you get too used to goodness, it turns bad. Everybody knows that.

Well, everybody but Brad.

Because nothing bad ever happens to Brad, at least not until me.

I'm Brad's bad.

32

BRAD

I almost didn't agree to meet Kat for lunch. I mean, I'm not sure what her game is but I know she's seeing that guy. If she thinks we're going to meet so she can tell me about it in person, she's dead fucking wrong.

They've already seated Kat at a table outside when I arrive. As always, she takes my breath away. She stands to hug me and I have to force myself to let her go when she moves to sit back down.

"Hey," I say as I sit across from her.

"Hey," she says. Her voice cracks as though she's crying or about to cry. I reach across the table and cover her hand with mine, running my fingers lightly across the back. Her skin is so soft.

"How are you?" I ask.

"I'm doing well," she says. "You know, the usual, trying to catch the bad guys, finding creepy stalker cameras on my balcony, drinking too much wine at movie night."

She takes her hand away from mine and moves it back to her lap.

I hate that I miss her touch.

"Are you resting? Taking care of yourself?" I ask.

"I am, thank you for checking… and for caring."

"Always. Speaking of the camera, anything more come from that?" I ask. I'm still freaked out by the whole thing, that someone is watching her, has been for days, maybe weeks, and no one has caught him or do anything. I should be there with her, protecting her.

"Nothing yet," she says. "But we think we are close. The computer police are working on trying to trace it now using the things that make the cameras go."

"Is that tech speak? Things that make the cameras go?" I tease.

"It is."

I can tell I've embarrassed her when she looks away from me. She's not the best with technology and can be a little self-conscious about it. But she's so fucking cute when she's embarrassed that I can't help but tease.

Besides, I'm just biding my time until I work up the nerve to ask her what I really want to know. What the fuck is going on with that guy she's working with.

Bauer.

How can she be with him? I don't see it. He's a fucking douche.

I look around and catch the eye of a lady at the next table. She looks me up and down appreciatively, giving me that look that says I could have her for the afternoon if I'd like. I look away quickly.

I've got enough going on between Kat and trying to break up with Stacy. No need to complicate things further.

"How's Stacy?"

I'm not expecting that question from Kat. And I doubt she really cares. But I answer anyway. "Fine."

"And, the two of you are doing well?"

"What's with the small talk, Kat? You don't give a fuck about Stacy or how we're doing."

She says nothing.

"She's not you," I say. "But I guess we're okay, considering."

"Considering?"

She's going to piss me off if she keeps going with the inane questions. "Oh, come on. This is really how we're going to play this?"

She looks at me, her face blank.

"Considering she's not you, Kat. Is that what you want to hear? That I can't handle moving on from me and you?"

"Um."

"She's a sweet girl. I care about her," I say. "Not enough to pursue anything further. Speaking of . . . how's the guy?" If she's going to ask me about Stacy, then I'm going to ask her about the dick-wad she's seeing.

"The guy?" she asks, trying to look confused. But I see right through her facade.

"Bauer."

"Uh, fine, I guess," she says. "Working hard and all that stuff."

She's going to make me dig for information.

Typical.

"And the two of you?" I ask.

"The two of us?"

"Are you repeating everything I ask you?" I ask her.

"No," she says. "I don't understand why you are asking me about this?"

How can she not understand? She's seeing someone else, someone she used to see in college. And according to Mavis, she's happy. In love, even. If I were a better person I would just be happy for her and let it be.

But I'm not a better person.

I'm a selfish person.

And I want her for me.

And that she's with someone else pisses me off more than I care to examine.

"This is how we are playing it, right? You ask about Stacy, I ask about Bauer."

"Okay," she says, drawing the word out.

I don't know why she's pretending to be confused. She started this.

"So, the two of you are well?" I ask her. "You're happy?"

"Sure," she says. Then she shrugs her shoulders like it doesn't matter. "I mean, he's smart, creative. Knows what the fuck he's doing, which is nice."

What's that supposed to mean?

Knows what he's doing with what?

I narrow my eyes even though she can't see them through my sunglasses.

"Are you happy with him?" I ask.

"Yeah," she says. "I'm happy. Some of the guys in the past have been real idiots, you know that."

What the fuck does that mean? If she means me, I may have to fucking kill her right now. With my bare hands.

I raise my sunglasses so she can see my eyes and the look of red-hot anger I'm sending her way. Her face softens as she looks at me. Fuck I miss her. A pang hits me square in the chest, so hard I lose my breath.

Fuck it. Go big or go home.

"Kat, I don't want it to be like this. Fuck. You know that I'm still in love with you. I'm just hoping you'll eventually realize you're still in love with me too. I mean, let's be real, he's never going to be as good for you as I am," I say.

"Why would—" she starts to say something, but I'm not going to let her interrupt me.

"Let me finish," I say. "No one will be as good for you as I am. You don't belong with him. The same way I don't belong with Stacy."

"But, I'm not—"

"In fact," I continue. "My plan was to break it off with Stacy, after movie night, but I got paged in. It was stupid of me to invite her anyway. I mean, shit, the only reason I even went to the movie was to see you. I knew you would be there, and I miss you. Every day, Kat, every fucking day I think about you and I miss you. I'm breaking it off for good tonight with Stacy. Then, I am going back to a full pursuit of you with nothing on my conscience. Fuck that guy. We belong together."

I sit back, satisfied with what I've said so far. I follow Kat's glance to the next table, one of the ladies blows me a kiss. I turn away, disgusted. Kat is trying hard not to laugh. I should find it funny, but the whole thing makes me even angrier.

"Tomorrow you'd better be ready for me," I say. "Because I am not giving up this time, Kat. There will be no walking away. No broken engagements. No trips to jail."

"That's exactly why I wanted us to have lunch," she says.

Good, we're on the same page. Relieved, I relax into my chair, waiting for her to continue.

"You need to let me go," she says.

Okay, that's not what I was expecting her to say next.

Not at all.

33

KAT

I realize I'd better get this over quick-like. I hurry through what I have to say before he can misinterpret or interrupt.

"You need to let me go. Even if you aren't with Stacy, we won't work. I can't be with you. Even if your mom hadn't died from the same fucking disease I have, I can't be with anyone who has seen me how you have."

"What are you talking about?" he asks.

"The bulk of our relationship was me with cancer. And we both know I never would have survived that first go-around without you. But then it came back. And we don't know if that will ever stop. It may never go away."

I take a breath.

"I can't ask you to be a part of that. I can't ask you to commit yourself to a life of caretaking and hoping for miracles. To living in constant anticipation of when it will resurface and how. Living in fear, always seeing me as a victim, a helpless, weakened victim with one foot in the grave, living life to the halfway point instead of to the fullest. That is no way to live, and it is especially no way for *you* to live."

I gulp the rest of my wine, signaling the server for another, fully prepared to keep drinking until it's time to pour myself into a LYFT.

"You are perfect and incredible, everything a woman wants in a partner. You have so much to offer - you are vibrant and funny, loyal and loving, giving and generous, and just totally fucking all around wonderful. You deserve for a woman to give all of that back to you. You deserve someone who gives as much as she takes.

"And that's all I can do for you is take. And soon you'll resent me for it, and then we'll either have an ugly and bitter breakup, or you'll stay with me because I have cancer and you'll hate me for it. And then I'll hate you for hating me and staying, and then we'll both be bitter only without the breakup. And it will destroy you.

"And then it will destroy me. And I can't have that. I can't be the one that destroys you. Not again. You're beautiful and you don't deserve that. And I don't deserve you."

That's when I feel the tears stream down my face. I look away from him toward the water, hoping the ocean breeze will blow them dry before he sees them.

"Are you through?" he asks.

When I glance back at him, I can see he's angry. Furious really. Like he's vibrating with it. I've never seen him like this, face set like stone, eyes hard, tone cold.

"Um, yeah?" I answer him like it's a question. I hate it when women speak with an up-tone. I hate it even more when I speak like that. I clear my throat and try again.

"Yes," I say with more finality.

34

BRAD

I take a deep breath to rein my anger in.

It doesn't help.

"First." I lean over the table toward her to make sure she hears every word I say.

Clearly and accurately.

"YOU don't fucking tell ME what I do and don't deserve. You don't tell me what I need in a relationship.

"Second, I'm a grown fucking man, capable of making my own decisions. You don't get to decide anything like this for me.

"Third, you can barely figure your own shit out for yourself, so never presume to think you even fucking come close to knowing what is best for me. For fuck's sake, Kat!

"Is that what this is all about? Some stupid fucked up notion you aren't good enough? Or that I'll tire of you? Of the cancer? Is that even your decision to make? No! It's not! You are not qualified to make that decision. You think it's so bad I've only known you for the time you've had cancer. Well, baby, that's all you've known of me either.

"So, what the fuck? Do you need someone who treats you bad? Who forgets about your treatments? Who doesn't want to put you on a fucking pedestal and worship you? What? Only women who DON'T have cancer get those things? What about all that bullshit you're spewing during your pep talks to the cancer patients? Is that just for their benefit? More of your 'do as I say but not as I do'?"

I want to fucking hit something. I can't believe the absurdity of this conversation. How can she really feel this way? Does she really think so little of herself? So little of me?

"This is absolute and complete bullshit, Kat!"

"Keep your voice down," she says.

"I will not fucking keep my voice down. If people don't like it, FUCK THEM." I look at the ladies at the next table, sure that's who she is referring to, they look away quickly. I keep talking.

"YOU do not know everything. You may think you do, but you don't. Just because you prance around helping the police with shit does not mean that you have a handle on anything else. Especially not relationships and even more so not a relationship with me.

That we are even sitting here with you thinking you are cutting me out of your life is pathetic, Kat. So fucking pathetic. Don't you think if I didn't want you then a month into our relationship, when you were first diagnosed, would have been the best time to end it? So, what, you think I will put myself through that, put *you* through that, put our families and friends through all that just to leave you later? Are you that fucking insecure? That closed off? Well?"

I know she doesn't have an answer to that. I can tell by the look on her face. But I need something from her right now. I need her to admit she's wrong. That I'm right. That we will be together.

"I don't know what you want me to say," she whispers.

She starts crying.

I'm such an asshole.

I don't want to make her cry. I want to make her listen. I want to make her understand. I want to make her change her mind. But I never want to make her cry.

"Fuck, Kat." I lean across the table, grabbing her face in my hands and trying to wipe her tears with my thumbs. She's so fucking beautiful. Even when she's upset. How could I do this to her? What kind of monster am I?

"God, baby, don't cry," I tell her. "I'm sorry, I didn't mean to yell at you or make you cry. You make me so frustrated sometimes."

"That's what I'm talking about," she says. "I'm frustrating and you'll tire of it and then you'll leave."

"Kat, I asked you to fucking marry me."

"When there was no evidence of disease!" She cries even harder.

"Jesus Christ. Was I supposed to ask when you were in treatment? My bad. I'll do it differently next time," I say.

"Brad, it will never go away. Never! It will always be with me, hanging over my head like a black cloud just waiting to rain toxic poison all over my life. I can never live a life without the fear of wondering if the cancer will come back. If it does, I won't live a full life. It will kill me. It's just a matter of when."

"Everybody fucking dies, Kat."

"I know, but not like this." She moves to blow her nose, and it makes a loud honking noise, which makes her laugh. Before I know it, she's bent over in her chair laughing and crying, sounding almost hysterical. Sure she's having some sort of mini breakdown, I move to her side of the table and pull her into my arms.

God, she feels good.

"It's okay, baby. It's going to be okay. Shhh. I'm here," I tell her. "It's okay. I'm sorry." I push her hair out of her face where it's sticking to her tears. "You're so beautiful, Kat."

And then, even though I know it's wrong, and even though I know she probably won't reciprocate, I lean in, and I kiss her.

But she opens for me and it feels amazing. I grab her head and deepen the kiss. Because I've missed this so fucking much. And right now, I feel like everything is right in the world. In this one moment, my life is perfect.

"Brad?"

Kat pulls away from me. I look at her, but she's looking behind me. I stand and turn around.

Fuck.

"Aw, Stacy… shit…"

Stacy looks like she's ready to cry, her eyes watering as they shift back and forth between Kat and me.

And now I've made two women cry today.

"I... I was just going to see if you wanted to get dessert after your lunch," Stacy stutters. "I wanted to make sure you were okay. But I can see now you are fine... really... more than okay. I'm... I'm gonna go."

She runs toward the entrance of the restaurant.

"God dammit! I'll be back."

I turn to go after Stacy. Wanting more to stay with Kat. Knowing that's an even bigger asshole move. Also knowing as soon as I go, Kat will leave.

"Kat, don't move!" I tell her.

Fuck!

35

———————

KAT

I'm stunned.

What the fuck just happened?

I stand up, throw a bunch of money on the table, and head for the nearest bar, pulling my phone out to text Lexie and Remi as I go.

I find a bar down the street and order a bourbon on the rocks because this is a hella serious situation that will require major reinforcements. I know from experience that this, on top of the wine earlier, will not settle well but I don't care.

I kissed Brad. I *kissed* Brad. I kissed *Brad*.

Shit. Fuck. Piss.

What does it mean? Why did I do it? Wait, really, he did it and I just took part. Right? That's not nearly as bad as starting it.

I mean I don't think I kissed him first. Did I?

Why did he have to look SO good today? Why do my hormones have to be so out of control?

I made him cheat on Stacy. Oh god, I'm a cheater. I am a horrible person. And she saw us. She saw us cheating on her.

I finish my drink in one gulp and order another. The heat of the bourbon slides down my body like an elixir.

He felt so good. So right. So right I can't even remember now why I ever left him. Only an idiot would do that, clearly. He's hot, he's successful, he's a fucking firefighter! He was the cover on last year's calendar. You don't leave a calendar cover firefighter unless you're an idiot.

Right?

And that's not just the hormones and the bourbon talking.

Or is it?

I'll ask the bartender. The place is empty, he'll probably like having someone to talk to. Like I'm doing him a favor by asking him for advice. I wave him over, my vision is a little blurry, and that's when I remember that I never ate my lunch and now I've had three glasses of wine and one and a half bourbons on an empty stomach.

"Can I get peanuts? And keep 'em comin'."

He brings the peanuts over. "You doing okay?" he asks as I shove an entire handful of peanuts in my mouth.

I look at him as I chew; he seems nice enough. "I have a problem." Little bits of peanut blow all over the counter in front of me. "Sorry." I cover my mouth with one hand and try to brush the peanut bits to the floor with the other.

"Is it a guy?" the Bartender asks.

"Isn't it always?"

He nods his head in agreement.

I start talking. "I left him, but for a fantastic reason, but he always kind of hung around and I know he still loves me and I thought I was over him, only now I think I want him back, except I asked him to lunch to break it off for good, but then he kissed me and I gotta tell you, that kiss rocked my world, until his girlfriend showed up and caught us, so now I'm a cheater and a horrible person and not only did I not break it off for good, but I kissed him, and she saw and now it's just going to be a mess, and all I can think about is how good he looked and how great he felt."

I pause and take a big breath. He nods his head in agreement. I keep talking.

"See, I had cancer, and he was wonderful all the way through it and we were going to get married and there was going to be fireworks because he knew I had fireworks on my list, and it was going to be amazing, and then the cancer came back two weeks before the wedding and I broke it off with him because it's not fair to him that he be tied to someone he has to take care of all the time and who might die or throw up or lose her hair or something else equally horrible."

I pause again to take a breath, a drink, and a few more peanuts.

The Bartender slides me a glass of water. "Sounds rough." He moves down the bar to help a new patron.

"It is!" I call after him.

He seems to be taking a long time with the new customer. I amuse myself by intermittently putting peanuts directly in my mouth or tossing them in the air and trying to catch them in my mouth. I'm zero for five with catching them in my mouth so far. Usually, parlor tricks and bar games are my jam. Just not today.

By the time I hit my third bourbon and fourth bowl of peanuts, I'm starting to wonder where the hell Lexie and Remi are. I say as much to the old guy nursing a beer a few stools down. He looks at me.

"What part do they not understand about emergency 911?" I ask a little slurrily. I hold up my phone to make sure I'm still getting reception, squinting slightly at the glowing screen. "They really need better lighting in here."

He continues to look at me.

"Not a big talker, huh? Well, if they don't get here soon, I'm gonna have to talk to you." I point at him, my finger wavering.

I might be drunk. "More peanuts!"

My phone buzzes on the bar top. "Sexy Ex keeps calling you know," I say to whoever might be listening. "And I keep hitting ignore. Boop! Just like that. And there goes the call. Sent off to voicemail land. Boop!"

The old guy raises his empty beer glass.

"Cheers!" I say, raising my glass to him. The bartender sets down a full pint in front of him.

"Is it late?" I ask him as he passes by. "You haven't seen my friends have you? Lexie and Remi?"

The bartender shakes his head and refills my water glass. "And I have no new texts, right?" I hold up my phone to show him.

"No," he says. "But you do have that one there that you haven't sent yet."

"Which one?" I pull my phone back to look at it more closely. He leans over the bar and points to the screen.

"That one," he says, pointing to my earlier emergency 9-1-1 text to Lexie and Remi. I look again.

"I never sent the goddamn text!?!?"

"You never sent the goddamn text," he confirms.

"Well, shit, no wonder they didn't respond. Better hit me again barkeep, it's gonna be awhile."

I hit send on my text.

And then I make the bartender double check, just to be sure.

36

KAT

Remi gets there. She gives me a hug, then orders herself a dirty martini, extra dirty, and me a cup of coffee and a burger with fries.

"Oh, a burger with fries, that sounds good, god why didn't I think of that? You're a genius, Remi!" I blow her a kiss before launching into the retelling of my lunch with Brad, how good he looked and how the ladies at the next table clearly thought so as well. How he was so angry and how hot that was. And finally, the kiss and then Stacy.

I bury my head in my arms on the bar top. "Ohmigod Remi, what was I thinking?"

"You were thinking that once upon a time you were going to marry this man and you love him, sweetie. There is nothing wrong with that."

"What if I wasn't thinking that?" I sniffle. "What if all I was thinking was I wanted to kiss him. So I did."

"Is that what you were thinking?"

"I don't know! I'm never thinking. I mean, I called off the wedding. I have sex with total strangers. I don't even ask their names. I've even thought about having sex with Bauer. And, one time I got off to it with my vibrator. And Bauer is yours. See what a shitty person I am? This is why I have cancer, isn't it? Because I'm such an awful person."

Remi laughs. "Sweets, first off, Chance Bauer is not, nor will he ever be, mine. Second, any woman in her right mind would use a vibrator to rub one off to a Bauer fantasy because he's hot as fuck. I can't stand the man, but even I can admit that. But if you ever tell him I said that I will cut your tongue out and feed it to my imaginary cat."

Remi takes a long draw on her martini, then grabs a handful of my fries and pops a few in her mouth. "As far as kissing Brad, he had already told you he still loves you, we all already know you're still in love with him even if you don't always like to admit it. So, really, the problem is with Brad. He has no business being in a relationship with Stacy when he is still in love with you. He's in the wrong." She finishes off the fries in her hand before wiping them on the napkin in her lap. I grab my own napkin and stick it on my lap, wondering if I will ever be as refined as Remi.

Lexie bounces in. "I can't stay long," she says. "I've got a hella busy night at the winery. We are racking all the Cabs and I've got to get back, it will take most of the night. Oh, thank god, food!"

She eats the bulk of my burger in a couple of bites while I fill her in on what happened at lunch. Intermittently murmuring the proper empathetic and outraged epithets. Until, far too soon for my liking, she gets up to leave. She gives me a long hug and a kiss on the cheek.

"What? No earth-shattering words of wisdom as to how I should fix my life?" I ask her.

She looks up, lips scrunched, before saying, " . . . *it was a million tiny things that, when you added them up, they meant they were supposed to be together. . .* that's how it is with you and Brad."

Remi and I both look at her.

"That was beautiful, Lex," I gush. Remi nods in agreement.

"Come on, guys!" she says, "Sam Baldwin? You know, Tom Hanks in *Sleepless in Seattle!*"

"Ohhhh," Remi and I say simultaneously.

Lexie rolls her eyes at us, then says, "Quit fighting it, Kat. Just be happy and have that happiness with Brad." And with that, she blows us a kiss and is out the door like the little whirlwind she is.

I turn to Remi. "That's a great movie. I'm surprised we didn't think of it the other night."

"Are we not going to mention the other things she said?" Remi asks.

"Nope," I tell her. I look around the bar we are in. "I think I'm done with this place. I need chips and salsa. And maybe a margarita."

Remi laughs. "We can do chips and salsa, but I'm not sure you need a margarita. Let's go."

37

BRAD

I run after Stacy, finally catching up to her in the parking lot. "Stacy, please stop, just talk to me."

She stops but doesn't turn to face me. "There's nothing to say, Brad. On some level I knew this day would come, I thought you were man enough to tell me first and not cheat."

"It just happened, I didn't mean to. I'm sorry if I hurt you. I have always had feelings for Kat, and I was honest with you about that." I grab her upper arm and spin her to face me.

"I know," she says, tears streaming down her face. "You're right. I guess I thought with time that would change. It didn't seem like she wanted you back. I just wish you would have said something."

"I meant to last night, but then I was paged, and I already had these plans with Kat…"

"Save it, Brad. I don't need to listen to your excuses right now. You're right, you never promised me anything, but you still fucked me, and that's got to count for something."

And there it is.

I knew that was coming, and it made me sick to my stomach. Because she's right. I loved to pretend that if I told her I wasn't emotionally invested it didn't matter what I did. But I was wrong.

"You're right, Stacy, fuck." I take a step back from her and run my hand over my face roughly. "It was wrong of me to do and I'm sorry."

"You're an asshole."

"I am." I don't want to argue with her, I know she's right with everything she's saying. I behaved like a total asshole. "Are you okay? Do you need a ride home?"

"Getting rid of me already?" she asks, bitterly.

"No. . . I just. . . I want. . . I didn't mean for it to go down like this. And I want to make sure you are okay."

"No, I'm not okay," she says. "But I'm sure I will be."

"I hope we can still be friends," I say, instantly regretting it.

"Don't count on it," she says.

I can't hide the relief on my face fast enough.

"Oh my god, you're actually relieved. Just when I think maybe you're a decent guy, you totally prove that you're still just an asshole."

I have nothing to say to that. I move to give her a hug goodbye.

"Don't touch me," she says before turning and walking away.

I don't wait long before returning to the table Kat and I were at. I should have known she wouldn't stay at the restaurant and wait for me. Everything has been cleared and new table settings are out.

"Fuck, where did you go, Kat?" I mumble. The server comes out and asks me if I forgot something. "I'm pretty sure my pride is gone, maybe my dignity and self-respect as well. Seen those anywhere?"

She looks confused for a second and then laughs, still unsure.

"Thanks anyway."

I walk down to the beach. I can go one of two directions, toward the firehouse or towards Kat's house. Neither seem appealing so I sink to my ass and sit where I'm at in the sand

and wait for the sunset. If I'm going to wallow in self-pity over how I've completely fucked up my love life, I may as well do it with a view. I continue to call Kat's cell, but she has either turned it off or is hitting 'send to voicemail' every time she sees my name show up on the screen.

I don't know how this entire situation got so fucked up. How can she think I would leave her because of the cancer? She's in remission, and she's already planning for it to come back. I'm not naïve, I know the chances of it happening a third time are greater than not. I know it could metastasize, and that if it does, it will probably continue to metastasize until it kills her. That's not a good reason for us not to be together while we wait for that to happen. She cheats us both out of something good.

After that kiss I know she's wrong and I'm pretty sure she knows it too. It's a choice; all she has to do is make the choice to be together, and we can be. It's so easy, why can't she see that.

I rest my forehead on my knees and stare at the sand until my eyes burn. Not looking up until someone sits down beside me, hoping despite all logic somehow it's Kat. Trying to mask my disappointment with a smile when Lexie settles in the sand beside me and rests her head on my shoulder.

"I thought I recognized the back of that head," she smiles up at me.

"Hey Lexie-loon," I say. "What are you doing out here?"

"Oh, you know," she says as she waves her hand aimlessly in the air.

"Did you see Kat?" I can't help asking.

"Yes," she says. "How're you doing?"

"So you know what happened?"

"Well, I know her version of what happened, yes."

"Where is she?"

She takes a deep breath before answering. "Look, I know you want to make this right, but I think it's best you don't see her right now. She's not right in her head, and I think it would make things worse. She feels awful for what Stacy saw."

"Stacy and I broke up," I tell her.

"Before the kiss?" she asks.

"No." I hang my head.

"Why don't you call her in the morning. Give her the night to calm down and see things a little more coherently. She's with Remi and there's no one better with helping you see things clearly and pragmatically than Rem."

I hesitate before speaking again. "When given the choice, do you think she's capable of being happy?"

Lexie raises her head from my shoulder and nods it slowly in thought; she knows what I'm talking about. We've had this discussion about Kat before, that she seems to be punishing herself for getting cancer, and she can't bear to let herself be happy.

"I do. I think she wants to very much. I also think she believes she is saving you from yourself and it creates an emotional war inside her and so far, the unhappy side is winning."

I snort out a laugh. "How does that help me exactly?"

Lexie smiles at me, placing her hand on my shoulder where her head just was.

"I read an article about Chris Pine once, something he said stuck with me. He said that dating someone on the opposite end of the happy spectrum as you only serves to teach you an incredible amount of patience," she shrugs. "I'm good at reciting great advice from other people."

I always forget just how pretty Lexie is, especially with the pink hair, it gives her an edge that her natural blonde doesn't. When she's blonde, she's cute. But with the pink hair, she reminds me of a blue-eyed Sydney Bristow from *Alias, Season One*. Total badass, combined with a bubbly personality, and a heart of gold.

"You know, one of these days," I say to her. "There will be a guy you can't let go of, and that can't let go of you, and he will be the luckiest guy in the world." I reach up and smooth her hair behind her ear.

She smiles big. "Thanks B! This is why I love you!"

"Back at ya, Lex." My smile more on the sad side.

"You gonna be okay?" she asks.

"I'm good. I'll hit the gym on the way home and work some shit out, then maybe hit up Ethan and see if he wants to grab a beer. Don't worry about me."

She stands and looks down at me. "Ok, well if you need anything just know I straddle the line between you two, and I always will, no matter what. I'd stay, but I've got to get back to the winery."

"Thanks for the talk. Have a good night, Lexie."

"You too!" She waves over her head as she trots away.

And I'm alone once more.

38

BRAD

I stare at the water until the sand cools to the point it feels wet on my ass, letting despair seep through my every pore. Deciding to forego the gym, I just hit Ethan up for the beer.

He meets me at *The Recovery Room* a short time later. The server brings us a pitcher of beer along with two chilled pint glasses and a basket of pretzels as I begin to tell him about my afternoon.

By the time I get to the part about the kiss, my emotions have run the gamut from and we're ready for a second pitcher of beer and a new basket of pretzels.

"At least you finally broke up with Stacy."

"I know. Man, I don't think I can wait any longer for Kat."

"What do you mean? Are you finally moving on, for real? Letting her go?"

"No, I need her back. I want my life with her. Now."

"You can't rush this shit. Not when you want it to last forever," he says.

"Tell me the truth, you read that in a fortune cookie, didn't you?"

"Nah man. I saw that shit on Instagram. Pansy ass wording reminded me of you."

"Fuck you," I say, laughing. "And fuck that, I don't care if it makes me a pansy ass, I want her, for as long as her forever is going to be. I'm tired of dicking around. When she kissed me back today, it was like nothing had ever changed."

"Uh-huh, because she wants some o' dat?" he says, waggling his finger at me, motioning from my head to my toes.

"You think she doesn't?" I ask, suddenly feeling unsure.

"Look," he says, getting serious again. "She knows you guys belong together; she's just scared. She's wasting valuable time, don't let her do that, man. Put on your big boy panties. Get pissed. Get fired up. Channel your inner John McClane and get your fucking girl. Don't let her do this to you any longer. This isn't the Brad Matthews I know. This is a pansy ass. And pansy asses don't get the girl. Brad Matthews gets the girl. So, go get the girl!"

"Just like that?"

"Fuck yeah, just like that."

"Go get the girl," I repeat. Nodding my head as his advice slowly sinks in.

"Yes, fucker. Go. Get. The. Girl."

I keep nodding. The idea seeming more plausible with each downward motion.

"What about the guy?"

"What guy?" he asks.

"The one from college? That Mavis says Kat's in love with."

"She kissed you today, brother. Fuck that guy."

"Yeah, fuck that guy."

"You ready for this?"

"I'm ready for this." I'm feeling charged up, ready to pound my chest. I stand and begin to bounce in place, stretching my head from one side to the other, loosening my arms, like a prize fighter going into the ring.

"That's what I'm talking about." Ethan raises his pint glass to me. "Can I get a yippee-ki-yay, motherfucker?"

"Yippee-ki-yay, motherfucker!" I say, a little too loudly for the environment, then push my beer toward Ethan. "I'll let you know what happens."

"Good luck, brother!" He yells after me. But I'm already out the door and texting Remi to find out where she and Kat are.

39

KAT

We arrive at *The Crazy Burro* and I'm happy to see Maureen is working. She seats us in our regular spot. "Hello loves, two margaritas? Or will you also need a third?"

"Just two," I blurt before Remi can say otherwise and insist I don't need one. Margaritas make me happy. And so do chips and salsa. And right now, I want to be happy.

"No margaritas," Remi says. "Just water and coffee, please." Remi looks at me, eyebrows raised.

I narrow my eyes at her. "Hair of the Dog. Don't judge."

"I don't judge. And its only hair of the dog when you're hung over, not when you're still drunk."

"I'm fine." I wave my hand in the air at her, not totally convinced she's wrong. But also not willing to admit it aloud.

I realize I'm still hungry after we get our chips and salsa and I mow through half of them in a matter of seconds. Probably because Lexie ate my burger and fries. Since Remi hadn't eaten yet either, we order dinner.

We don't talk about Brad again, which I am grateful for. It's been an emotionally exhausting day, and I just want to relax a bit. Which is hard to do when Remi keeps checking her phone and texting someone.

"Who do you keep texting?" I ask her.

"No one," she says, looking a little guilty.

"You better not be talking about me with Alex." I'm amazed she would do that while I'm sitting here. Not only that, but with someone she's not even sleeping with.

"You know that does not penetrate the friendship bond, right?" I ask. "You only get to tell people you are consistently fucking all the crazy shit that happens with your girlfriends. And only if they are the only one you are consistently fucking. You can't do that with guys you are just dating." I point my finger at her accusingly.

"I'm not telling anyone anything. Chill out and drink some more coffee."

I do as she says, albeit reluctantly. But start to feel better between the food, water, and coffee. I'm about to tell her so when she looks up and gasps. Whatever she sees behind me surprises her a little. I turn to see who it is when suddenly I'm grabbed by the arm, pulled out of my chair, and dragged toward the rear exit of the restaurant.

By Brad.

I look back at Remi.

"I've got your purse," she says. "Just remember I love you!"

Next thing I know we are outside, and he's got me pushed against a wall in the back alley. "And, remember this," he says before he captures my lips with his. He's kissing me. I'm kissing him. My world is tilting on its axis, yet I've never felt more centered. More grounded.

Until I remember Stacy.

"Wait," I mumble against his lips. "What about Stacy?"

He raises his head and looks at me, taking my head between his two hands, gently stroking my cheekbones with his thumbs. "You are the one I love. The one I want to be with, Kat. The only one. Stacy and I are over, we broke up this afternoon. I should have done it sooner, I was just being stupid, and I'm so sorry for that."

I nod dumbly, barely registering anything outside of he broke up with her. "I want to ask if you're okay, but I want to kiss you more." I grab his shirt front to pull him toward me, but he holds back.

"Remi said you aren't involved with Bauer. That's true, right? You don't have feelings for him?" he asks me.

"Bauer? Pfft. No. Remi likes him. Even if she didn't I can't be involved with anyone, you know that."

"Anyone other than me," he says.

I stand there a minute, trying to gauge my mood. I'm in his arms. I feel safe and protected. And right.

It's the right place for me to be cancer or no cancer.

I look up at him, giving just the hint of a nod.

He kisses me softly. "I know you're afraid, I am too. But we can do this. We are stronger together. I won't ever be stupid again. You are it for me. And I know that you feel the same way. We belong together. And if I have to take you to bed and keep you there until you agree that's exactly what I'll do."

I lose myself in his eyes, with his thumbs stroking my cheeks and his hard body pressed against mine. I've hardly digested what's happened before he's kissing me again, and I'm kissing him back.

"Wait." I pull away from him again, barely getting my senses back. "What if we can't. . . "

"Can't what?" he asks. "Can't love each other? Can't be together? Can't take care of one another? That's bullshit, Kat! You're mine. I plan to take care of you until the day one of us dies. Yes, it will probably be you before me. Yes, I will take care of you when you are sick. Yes, it reminds me of my mom, and that sucks. But it doesn't change how I feel about you. Or how I will put your needs before mine, always. And put you on a pedestal where I can worship you properly, like the goddess that you are. And treat you with reverence you deserve. Because you are that incredible and you deserved to be worshipped and revered. I don't care what happens, I'm not leaving you again, and I sure as hell am not letting you leave me."

He grabs my hand and pulls me farther into the back alley where no one can see us. Where I can see everything in his eyes. His feelings laid out bare and raw. His love for me so obvious and intense. It takes my breath away.

Yet still I stay silent.

Unsure of how to respond to the flurry of emotions his words have unleashed inside me.

"I don't get you. Why can't you let me love you? Why can't you let me treat you the way you deserved to be treated? Fuck, Kat, don't you realize just how special you are?"

"No. . . " I whisper.

"So, what? I'm supposed to treat you poorly? Is that what you want? Huh? Should I just fuck some sense into you? Right here, against the wall."

He keeps going before I can answer. "You want me to treat you like shit? Like you aren't special? Like you aren't my entire fucking world?" His hand fists in my hair and he pulls my head back sharply, forcing me to look him in the eye.

"Too fucking bad, Kat. *You are my entire world.* You are every-thing." His breath is heavy against my face.

I want to say something in response, but I can't get the words to form on my tongue.

"Are you hearing me?" he asks. "Do you get it?" He pushes my back against the wall, his body pressing into mine, his cock hard against my stomach. "Christ, Kat. I'm going to fuck you senseless right now. If you still don't get it, then we'll get to fucking some sense into you later."

I take his hand from the back of my head and place it over my rapidly beating heart.

I am hearing him.

And I want him to know just how much.

I pull his head toward me. "You jump, I jump, right?" I say against his lips, giving myself over to this man I cherish more than anything else. Letting myself have what I want now, and what I've wanted all along. Losing myself in his kiss, a kiss that quickly goes from soft and loving to hot and all-encom-passing.

His tongue pushes into my mouth, unrelenting and fierce, punishing in its pursuit. My head spins and my scalp scrapes against the wall. The sharp pain with the intense pleasure making me moan.

My hands twist in his hair as I keep his mouth connected with mine. Afraid to even stop to breathe for fear this won't be real. He pulls my leg up around his waist and grinds his hips against mine. The friction amazing.

I'm going to come from dry humping. The thought makes me want to giggle and groan at the same time. I use his shoulders as leverage and raise my other leg to wrap it around his waist, locking my ankles behind his back.

"Fuuuck! Kat, missed you so much, baby." His voice is muffled against my skin as he kisses and nibbles his way toward my breasts. The heat from his mouth penetrating my shirt, my nipples harden, begging for attention.

I keep working myself against his cock, the pressure building, and when he pulls the tip of my nipple into his mouth I explode. Not caring who hears my cries as I clutch at his shoulders to keep from melting down the wall. Brad gives me a moment's reprieve before he bites down, hard enough to smart. I pull my head up sharply to look at him, his steely eyes look back into mine,

"Uh uh, my little firecracker, this is no time to rest, I'm not through with you yet," he whispers, using his hips to keep my listless body pinned against the wall as his hands push my shirt up my chest, then pulls my bra cups down past my tits to finally attack them bare.

My head falls to the side and I'm lost in the pleasure all over again.

"Fuck, Kat. I could spend an eternity with my mouth on your tits and still not get enough." His mouth sucking, tongue laving, teeth biting, lips pulling. My head dizzy and my body wrought with desire. The sounds of pleasure and heavy breathing making me hotter. The rough of his stubble scraping against my nipples as he moves from one breast to another. I'm going to come again.

I moan into his hair, loving the smell of him: cedar, and soap and man.

He groans into my cleavage. "Fucking love the sounds you make, woman."

"Need you, now." We move as one to get my jeans off one leg and Brad's unzipped and around his thighs.

"No turning back now, we do this, that's it. You're mine." His cock positioned at my entrance. My legs wrapped around his waist. One tilt of my hips downward and he's inside me. Part of me is so crazy with want I'd agree to anything. Especially if it means I'm his again.

I meet his eyes.

And tilt.

Twin sighs of relief and pleasure as he fills me. A car starting sounds in the distance, headlights flicker across the wall beside us. I don't care if we're seen. Nothing matters except this. This is the right thing for me.

And him.

I clutch at his shoulders and bury my face in his neck as he pushes through every barrier I've ever erected.

In. Out.

Breaking down walls.

In. Out.

Demolishing insecurities.

Picking up speed. Growing intensity. The stucco from the wall digging into my back. Our every movement amplified, bolstering my heart, scrambling my brain. Part of me wanting to regain control. The other part not caring if I ever have it again.

"I need more. I want to feel you." I pull at the opening in his shirt, wanting to claw it off him, craving skin against skin. I wait for the buttons to fly as the material comes apart.

Nothing.

"What the fuck?" I stop.

He looks up from my breasts.

"What is this like some kind of industrial strength reinforced fucking firefighter shirt?"

His body jerks and his eyes twinkle.

"Why can't I—" I pull again.

Nothing.

"Are you laughing at me?" I ask, unsure if I want to join in or gut-punch him.

He throws his head back and lets it go, laughing until he's breathless and red in the face.

"You should see your face," he says trying to regain control of his mirth. "It's like confusion and anger and then more confusion."

"I'm glad you find this so funny," I grumble.

"Oh, come on, everyone would find this funny!" He's still laughing.

I can't help but join him. He's right. Most people would find it funny. Lest I forget, one of the things I love most about Brad—one of the things I *need* most from Brad—is the way he can make me laugh at anything.

I begin to unbutton his shirt the old fashion way, one button at a time. His cock, still inside me, jumps at the contact. The situation may be laughable, but I still want to feel his bare chest against mine. I get it open, buttons intact, and push up the white tee underneath it. His chest makes me breathless for an entirely different reason as I run my hands up his abs to his pecs.

"God, you're perfect." I lean in and lap at his nipple with my tongue, much like he did with me. He sucks in a breath as I bite at him gently, before pulling my head up for a kiss so intense I'm left dizzy. Barely able to stand as he pulls me off his dick and lowers my feet to the ground.

Giving me no time to regroup, he spins me round so my front is facing the building.

"Hands on the wall."

I bend forward, hands braced on the wall, my forehead resting against my fingers. He pulls my hips out and shoves his cock inside me with one brutal thrust. I cry out at the intrusion at the same time loving every inch as he goes. One hand pulls my hair aside giving him access to my neck. The other reaching around my front to find my clit.

"Brad." I moan.

I'm going to come again. Fast and hard.

"Kat, you fucking wreck me!" His breath is hot against the side of my neck. His lips nibbling lightly at my collar bone, sending delicious shivers down my spine. "So tight, so sweet." His voice so low, he sounds hoarse.

"Brad, I can't, oh god, I need—"

"I got you, baby," he says. His fingers work my clit relentlessly until he annihilates my world and everything I've ever known. Wave after wave of pleasure courses through my body. My defenses gone, all that remains is an empty hull waiting to be filled with his love.

"Oh, I'm going to come." Brad's arms tighten around he as he thrusts - one, two, three times before releasing into me with an animalistic roar.

How could I think I could ever live without this?

We stay that way for a while, chests heaving, minds spinning, hearts overflowing as we slowly return to earth from the orbit that spun us out of control.

He pulls his cock out slowly and I miss him at once as our combined juices trickle down my thighs. Brad pulls his pants up and situates his dick, pulls off his shirt and t-shirt before using the latter to clean me. Softly wiping at the insides of my legs, erasing any trace he was there.

Like with his dick, I miss it when it's gone.

He spins me to face him, pulls my pants up, and adjusts my bra and shirt. He looks me up and down slowly, then takes my face in his hands and kisses me. Soft and slow. So full of love my heart wants to burst from the feelings he evokes.

"Baby, did I hurt you?" His eyes dance back and forth over my face and he caresses my cheeks. My hands cover his so every part of me can be touching part of him, not wanting to separate. Dreading the moment he'll step back and this spell will be broken.

"Not at all. That was incredible."

He smiles back. "It was, wasn't it?"

My lips return to his. "So incredible."

He takes my hands into his and lowers them to my hips. Our bodies pressing together like missing puzzle pieces—the other half of a whole. "We should go before I lose control and fuck you against this wall again." He turns toward the parking lot, pulling me with him.

"Wait," I say. "I need to get my purse; Remi has all my stuff."

"It's all been taken care of," he says. "She will put it in your house and lock up after."

I realize what she was doing. "Oh my god, you're who she was texting!"

He has the courtesy to look embarrassed. "Guilty. But it was me who approached her, so don't be angry with her."

"I won't. I'm not," I say. "Especially not when I'm riding high on the bliss that is post multiple orgasms."

"I'm glad I could fuck some sense into you," he says smiling. "But no more talking about the past. I plan to take you home and worship every inch of this luscious body."

"Oh yeah?" I ask.

"Oh yeah," he says.

Then he leans down to whisper in my ear, "First, I'll make you come with my fingers and use my tongue to lick you clean. Second, you're coming again from my mouth."

I shiver against him as he describes what he will do, his breath hot against my cheek.

"Third, you're riding me baby, so hard that you come all over my cock," he continues.

"Uh huh," I pant.

"Then I'll fuck you from behind, while you hang on to the headboard, until you come again."

"Ok," I whisper.

"Then, and only then, will I let you rest up for round two." He helps me into his truck closing the passenger door after me. He rounds the front of the truck to get in on the driver's side, pumping his fist in the air and saying something that sounds a lot like, "Yippee-ki-yay, motherfucker."

I laugh. Certain I hadn't heard him right since it sounded like he was quoting John McClane. "What did you say?"

"Nothing. Just thinking about something from earlier today," he says.

"Were you watching *Die Hard* again?" I ask.

"No, it was a conversation that Ethan and I had," he says settling in and starting the engine.

I scoot across the bench seat until I'm sitting next to him, and lay my head on his shoulder, looking up and batting my eyelashes. "I'm not sure if I should be happy that you think about Ethan and the conversations the two of you have when you just finished fucking me."

He grabs my hand and places it over his hardening dick. "Does that feel like I'm thinking about Ethan?"

"I don't know," I say. "Maybe the two of you have grown closer in the last year. Maybe I need to show you what you'd be missing." I run my hand down his length, feeling his dick jump at my touch.

"Don't get me started again, at least not here." He grins.

"Or what?" I ask. He turns and kisses me hard before pulling out onto the street.

"How did I ever think I could let you go?" I softly ask a few minutes later. Not sure if he heard me, and not expecting a response.

"It wasn't my idea," he says.

"No," I say. "I guess it wasn't. I can't believe I've been so stupid."

He laughs then kisses the top of my head. "If you're a good girl, I'll fuck that stupid right out of you when we get home."

I smile. "Yippee-ki-yay, motherfucker!"

40

KAT

I wake early, unaccustomed to having someone else in my bed with me, despite Brad having been there all night. I check to see if he's still asleep. His eyes are shut, his chest rises and falls slowly with each breath. My phone buzzes from the nightstand, I roll over to see who it is.

Bauer.

"Missed me already, huh?" I speak quietly moving to the side of the bed, so I don't wake Brad.

"Did I wake you?" he asks.

"Not really. No."

"I need—"

Brad sits up behind me and puts his hands on my upper arms. "Everything okay?" he whispers into my free ear.

"Cookie, is that a man I hear? Are you cheating on me already?"

I turn and nod to Brad that everything is okay, into the phone I say, "It's just Brad."

To which Brad raises his eyebrows at me questioningly and Bauer says, "Just Brad, huh?"

Brad grabs the phone from me. "She'll call you back," he growls before tossing it aside on the bed. "Just Brad, huh?" The look on his face is fierce.

"Funny, that's what Bauer said," I whisper.

I scoot back toward the headboard as Brad advances. He stops in front of me, running his hands up my legs, pausing at my knees to spread them wide before continuing forward. His gaze steely and mouth firm. "Let's get one thing straight, my little firecracker, I am not, nor will I ever be, *just Brad*."

"I didn't mean it like that."

"No?" he asks as he slides his hands up my thighs, getting closer and closer to my core. He rubs his cheek on my inner thigh as he places my legs over his shoulders. "How *did* you mean it?"

He runs his tongue down one thigh and up the other. My head is reeling. I grab his hair and try to force his mouth to where I want it.

"Not until you answer my question," he says, grabbing my hands with one of his and pinning them against my chest, forcing me back against the headboard.

"What, uh, what was the question?"

"How did you mean it?" he asks with a quick flick of his tongue to my clit, making me squirm.

"Oh! Brad, please!"

He blows gently on my clit; the cool air makes me quiver. "How did you mean it, Kat?" He pulls my clit into his mouth alternating sucking it into his warmth, then blowing to cool it down.

I struggle to remember what he's asking me.

Oh yeah. *Just Brad.*

"Um. There's no *just,*" I thrust my hips toward his face, "there's only you."

"That's right, baby, there is only me. And no one else." He pulls back, running the scruff of his cheek up and down my inner thigh, his breath heavy on my clit.

"I'm so close," I whimper, not knowing how it's possible when he's barely touched me.

"Okay, baby." He thrusts his tongue inside of me. Kissing me as though it's my mouth, driving me crazy with every stroke until I am over the edge.

"Oh, Brad. Only you! Always you!" My orgasm rips through me with something close to violence. Shredding any coherent thought leaving my body pulsing in its wake. I slump to the side, my core unable to keep me upright, my limbs no better than wet noodles.

Brad moves to sit beside me, pulling me to his lap and onto his cock in one fluid motion with his front to my back. "Spread your legs for me baby." He pulls at my thighs, the motion pushing me forward and further down his length.

"Oh yeah." My voice is low and guttural as Brad pauses so I can adjust to his size. He starts to move his hips before I'm ready. Hitting places I didn't know existed as he pistons his hips, bouncing me on his cock. My breasts flap painfully but I don't care.

"Touch yourself," he pants into my ear. I reach down and rub my clit, pushing it down against his cock. I use my middle finger on myself and apply pressure to the sides of his cock with my fore and ring fingers.

"God you feel good," he moans. "Ride me, baby."

My head lolls back against his shoulder, he bites at my exposed neck making me moan loud. I thrust my hips back toward him, changing the angle slightly.

"Oh, fuck yes," he whispers. "I gotta make you come again baby, I'm so close." He reaches one hand down to meet mine at my clit, his fingers moving fast as he works me over. I feel another orgasm build; his other hand reaches around and pinches my nipple and I start to break apart. Brad thrusts harder. Faster. I soar into my third orgasm. My head thrown back, crying out as he thrusts up one final time growling through his own release.

He gathers me in his arms and pivots us on the bed so we're spooning.

"Good thing you did that, I can't move," I tell him.

He chuckles and kisses the top of my head, murmuring endearments. I feel completely fulfilled. Not just sexually, but in every way possible. Marveling again at how I ever could have thought I could be without him. He's that extra push I need when I feel like I can't go any further.

Sigh.

"I can't let you go," I murmur.

"What's that, baby?" he asks.

I turn to face him. "I can't let you go. It's horrible and selfish and wrong, but I can't do it."

"I don't want you to let me go. Why is it so wrong? We love each other, we should be together. We are meant to be together. You are it for me, Kat. There is no one else."

"I *will* die. And you *will* be alone. And the thought of you being alone kills me." My voice breaks. I'm going to cry I can feel it.

"So, what I'm hearing is, either way, you're dying. We stay together, you die and I'm alone. Which kills you, except you're already dead. We don't stay together, I'm alone, which kills you. Either way, you die, so we may as well be together in the meantime."

"That is some seriously fucked up logic," I say.

"But you can't argue it, can you?"

Before I can answer, my phone rings, I get up to answer it and see it's Bauer again. He starts talking before I can even say hello.

"Cookie, if you are finished playing doctor with Romeo, we've got real shit going on here at the station and I could use your help."

"I wasn't playing—" I start, but he continues before I can get a word in.

"We're dealing with a serial, here. Sherman's bringing in a profiler, he'll be here in about an hour. Don't be late." He hangs up before I can agree or ask questions.

I look at Brad. "I'm going to grab a quick shower and head to the precinct, I guess," I say.

I get in the shower, welcoming the warm spray over my sex-sore body. I am half hoping Brad will join me. But if he does, I'm afraid I won't be going anywhere in the next thirty minutes. He steps into the shower moments later, but with two mugs of hot coffee, and my seventeen morning pills.

"You're my hero!" I tell him and take a big drink, then down my pills. He added the perfect amount of cream and sugar. I sigh, feeling content. He just smiles and sits back on the shower bench, drinking his coffee and watching me.

"I think you're making me nervous just watching me that way," I tell him.

"You *think* I'm making you nervous? Aren't you sure?"

"Right. I'm pretty sure anyway. I can't concentrate when you're staring at me."

"I like staring at you. Get used to it, I'm gonna be staring at you every chance I get for years to come," he says. "Besides, what do you need to concentrate on?"

"I have to wash my hair and my body and stuff."

"I'll wash your hair and body and stuff," he says, waggling his eyebrows suggestively.

"No funny business. I think you broke my vagina; I'm going to be bowlegged for weeks."

He sets his coffee down and moves toward me, a wicked smile on his face. "No funny business, I promise."

Forty minutes later, having engaged in just enough funny business with Brad to put another smile on my face and an extra spring in my step, I'm dressed and out the door. My outfit matched to my sunny mood: blue/orange/red floral maxi skirt, a white tank top, and a jean jacket. I left my hair down to let it dry wavy, and paired my outfit with chunky jewelry, jeweled Egyptian style flat sandals, and my super cute straw Kate Spade purse I bought last week. Retail therapy at seventy percent off.

It's going to be a good day. I can feel it.

41

THE STALKER

I grab a razor blade and start slicing the skin between the fingers on my left hand. Anything to make the memories disappear.

Mother is calling me to the couch and asking me to sit on her lap. She wants to play the game. She's lonely and needs company. I am too big for her lap so my legs stuck out awkwardly. One leg stretched to her side along the couch, the other bent at the knee with my foot on the floor beside hers.

It's not enough. I cut at the skin on the tips of my fingers and underneath my fingernails.

She pulls my head to her chest, stroking my hair lightly, rocking us both back and forth. The hand holding me to her moves from my back around to my thigh. I watch as her fingers crawl up my leg towards my crotch. Her breath is getting shallow and faster.

. . .

I get the oil from the cupboard, the one that makes it hurt the most. Sometimes it's enough, just remembering how it's going to feel, to stop the memories from forming.

Mother tells me to put my hands around her back, leave them there. I do as she asks. I always do as she asks. What she does to me next feels good. I hate when it feels good. But I hate more that it's her who causes it.

Tonight I need to make everything hurt if I want to forget.

I pull oil into the dropper and place my hand palm up on the table.

"I don't want to," I whisper knowing no one is listening.

It's going to hurt.

A lot.

My hand shakes as I place drops on the cuts between each finger and then under each nail, crying out from the excruciating pain.

I grab my left wrist and squeeze as hard as I can, hoping to alleviate something.

Anything.

The pain a constant buzz running through my body. I wrap my left hand in a wet towel. The heat from my hand flares— emanating, burning through the towel from within. Tears stream down my face. It's nothing less than what I need. What I deserve.

It's only fitting that I hurt because I'm not a good person. I've known for a long time that I would grow up to be bad, and that I will always be bad. That's all on me. I'm the monster now.

Mother asks the man to join us. The one who usually just takes pictures. The game is going to change again. I start to cry. Mother tells me not to be a pussy. I don't want to be a pussy. The man laughs and says he'll show me what it feels like to be a pussy. He comes towards us, undoing his pants and slowly pushing them down his thighs.

42

KAT

I get to the precinct in just under ten minutes, leaving me ten minutes to spare from when Bauer wanted me there.

I blow past the intake desk, singing a good morning to the agent on duty, and head up the stairs to the little conference room. He is on the phone when I walk in the room but still gives me a dirty look and points repeatedly at his watch. Who still wears a watch these days, anyway? Doesn't everyone look at their phone to see what time it is? Plus, I'm early.

He ends his call just as Sherman pokes his head in the room. "Got anything?" he asks, looking at Bauer.

Bauer shakes his head.

"All right, the profiler will be here soon. I'd already sent him the file, just in case. The rest of the guys are in con room two."

Bauer then lets me know they discovered a hidden camera inside a teddy bear at Makayla Jones' house last night.

"Oh god, was he recording the little girl?" I ask. "I can't believe it. How did he do it? How did it work?"

"It doesn't look like the camera records, just streams. So, he would have to grab a screenshot if he wanted a still of anything. But, when he broke into the house to leave the pictures, he planted a remote activated nanny cam with an internet feed, so he was able to watch Makayla whenever he wanted to." He continues with some added tech speak about USB power sources, radio frequencies, and VPNs that I tune out.

"So basically, the picture thing was just a front for planting the cameras, because we always assume they took something when there's a break-in and not left something—"

I interrupt to ask him the only thing I'm really wondering about now. "So, was there a camera at Sofia's house and Madison's house too?"

"We sent units to check. I haven't heard back yet, but I'm going to assume the answer is yes. We still hesitate to disable them until we can track the signal. But Sherman has sent guys to personally warn the remaining two families, Kendall Martin's and Addie Shaw's, about what they should and should not allow their daughters to do in the privacy of their bedrooms until they catch him. We are having someone rearrange the stuffed animals in each girls' room to reduce his visibility, but not enough to make him suspicious."

"So, is the camera at Makayla's similar to the camera at my house?"

"They are similar, though yours is more robust. The cameras hidden in the teddy bears are about the size of a quarter and the camera at your balcony is about the size of a lemon. They aren't super high-tech, you can get them online for forty dollars, but they are definitely easy to hide."

Sherman knocks on the door frame as he walks by to get our attention.

"He's heading in, let's go."

Bauer and I head to conference room two. It's a room usually used for lectures and presentations. Instead of tables and chairs, it's got those little chairs with attached desktops for everyone to sit at. The desktop tips up and you can fold it down to the side when not in use.

"I love these chairs! I haven't seen these since high school," I say.

I grab a seat and tip my desktop up and over my lap, then up and over to the side. Then back again. Sometimes it's the little things that are entertaining.

The rest of the task force is not as amused as I am. In fact, some guys can barely fit their beefy frames in the desks. Looking like caricatures of themselves folded up and contorted.

Sherman enters the room. "The profiler is here. He'll be in soon. You will listen and give him respect. He knows his shit. Don't waste his time. He's here as a personal favor."

"I thought that's what we had her for," one guy says, pointing at me.

"You a profiler?" Sherman asks looking at me.

"Me? No, not a profiler."

"That answer your question?" Sherman asks looking back at the officer. Then shuts the door without waiting for a response.

Everyone looks at me, I'm sure wondering what my role in all this is then. I have to be honest at this point with so little to go on, so am I.

~

The profiler shows up a short time later. No pun intended. Gasps of surprise ring though the room.

"That's right, I'm a little person," he says. "Make the little things count, appreciate the little things in life, you're almost tall enough to be taken seriously, you'd make a good armrest, you must be a positive person since you're always looking up, you gotta hand it to short people sometimes cause they can't reach it otherwise. Blah, de-blah, fucking blah. Okay? Get all your laughs out now, all your little jokes. Got it all out? Great, now fuck off, sit up straight, and listen. Take notes if you're too stupid to remember what I say. I'm an offender profiler, not your babysitter. I don't have time to repeat myself and I barely have time for questions."

Everyone in the room sits up straighter, I grab my pen and paper, ready to take notes; even if that makes me stupid in his eyes.

He writes a few things on a whiteboard:

Male. Organized. Blue-collar worker. Single. No kids. Lives alone. Works with his hands.

. . .

Then starts talking. "Okay, first and most important, these two girls will not be his only victims. If he hasn't already, he will take more girls. Similar age and social standing, but not necessarily similar in looks and appearance. He likes little girls, but they aren't in any danger from him. At least not physical danger. He wants what he thinks they represent, which is innocence."

I try to take notes as he gives us information, especially since everything he is saying is filling in every blank we've had with this whole investigation. But he speaks so fast, it makes it difficult.

"He was more than likely sexually assaulted as a child, repeatedly. So he probably won't do the same to these girls though he has the predilections to. And let me be clear, just because he has not sexually assaulted yet, does not mean he won't."

The thought of that makes me sick to my stomach.

"Right now, we are dealing with a pedophile, people, and make no mistake, there is a difference between a child molester and a pedophile," he says. "A pedophile gets his rocks off by thinking about children in a sexual way. A molester gets his rocks off by abusing children in a sexual way. Many pedophiles never move on to molest. Let's hope this guy stays that way. My guess is he's taking pictures of these girls to use later, for his own pleasure. He's not a distributor of kiddie porn. Questions?"

Wisely, no one speaks up.

"Now, here's what's needed from you idiots. He's got a specific number of victims for a reason. Figure it out. There could be an order to the victims. Figure it out. You already know who the victims will be. Keep them safe. Questions? No? Good. I hate questions."

He leaves without waiting for a response or saying goodbye. Everyone in the room seems a little stunned. Bauer speaks first.

"Okay, let's get guys on the other two girls immediately. Anyone not still on shift, go home and get some rest. I need you fresh." He claps his hands and everyone sort of scatters.

"What about you?" I ask him.

He looks exhausted with dark circles under his eyes, a scruffy face and messy hair. Just not in a good way, and definitely not like the Bradley Cooper from *The A-Team* movie lookalike I've grown accustomed to.

"I've been here all night, and I'll be here all day. Nothing is changing that." He moves to stand, his body getting stuck in the desk. It rises with him, caught around his hips.

"Fucking desks! I've always hated them," he says, pushing it down his legs and trying to step out without falling.

I laugh. "Did you have the same problem back in school too?"

Which is when it occurs to me.

"Bauer, what if that's how he knows them?" I think aloud. "The girls. What if he works at their school?"

"That's not a bad theory, Cookie." He rubs at the scruff on his jaw for a moment, lost in thought. "Okay. Let's find a single guy with no kids who works with his hands at the school."

43

KAT

"I think we need to stakeout the school," I tell Bauer.

"Hang on, Cookie. We need to figure out who the guy is first. Then we need probable cause. Then we can try to find him." He takes a sip of coffee. Then grimaces at the taste.

"I'll get you fresh coffee, you figure out who this guy is so we can have a stakeout," I tell Bauer.

There's no fresh coffee in the break room. So, I make a fresh pot, feeling extremely helpful now that I'm solving cases *and* making coffee. I text Brad as I wait for the coffee to brew.

ME: Guess who had a feeling and broke the case wide open?

BRAD: Bates?

ME: Ha. No. And it's Bauer. You know that.

ME: But not Bauer who broke the case wide open. That was ME!

BRAD: I never had a doubt, beautiful. So, who is it?

ME: Who's who?

BRAD: Who's the bad guy? What's his name?

ME: Oh, I don't know. We still have to figure that out.

BRAD: So, really you put a tiny crack in the case? And not really broke it wide open.

ME: Whatever. Shut up. I have to go, I'm terribly busy.

BRAD: I love you, baby.

ME: Uh huh.

BRAD: Be safe.

I get back to the room with Bauer's coffee and a cup for me.

"Cancel the coffee order, Cookie. We gotta go. I've got a name."

"You've got a name? Like who the guy is? Already? How?"

"Anonymous tip."

"Anonymous tip? Don't we get like hundreds of tips, what makes you think this one is legit?"

"We won't know for certain until we catch him. But there was something different about the tip, something different about his voice and the way they left the tip. Most tippers want to self-aggrandize and make more out of their tip than it is. This guy left his tip quickly: the guy's first name, Gil, and that he would take another girl today, then he hung up. But when we ran the name through the database guess what came up?"

"What?"

"One Gil Iverson. Groundskeeper. Sail Point Middle School."

"Ohmigod, I was right!?"

"Did you doubt that you were right?"

"Always."

"Well, good thing for you, Sherman never doubts you're right."

Sherman pokes his head into the doorway. "Let's go, we've got an address and a warrant."

It always amazes the criminal defense attorney in me at how quickly the bureaucracy in the police department can move when it really wants to.

44

———

KAT

We pull up in front of Gil Iverson's house in a matter of minutes.

"I feel so bad-ass," I tell Bauer. "Going on a raid!"

"You're staying in the car, Cookie, especially in that outfit."

I look down at my tank and skirt, not seeing what he means.

"What's wrong with my outfit?" I ask.

He scoffs in return and gets out of the car to follow Sherman to the front door.

I know this is a cute outfit. Plus, I have a good eye for fashion. I mean, not in how Remi has an eye for fashion, but enough so I don't look like an idiot. I take a sitting selfie of the outfit anyway and text it to Remi asking her if there is something wrong with my outfit.

Yes, I can be that shallow. Don't judge. Remember, I'm dying and shit.

The house is in a slightly older section of town where a lot of the transient and migrant workers live and most of the homes are rentals, not owner occupied, and therefore in varying degrees of disrepair.

Gil Iverson's home is no exception.

The grass is yellow and sparse. He has dead flowers in window boxes by what I'm assuming are kitchen and living or dining room windows. There's a one-car garage off to the side, which still has the wooden door you raise by hand. A car sits in the driveway covered with a tarp weighted down with cinder blocks on the ground at all four corners and one on the roof.

I get out of the car to go check the make of the one under the tarp. I'm betting it's a white car that looks like a police car, without the red and blue lights. Sure enough, I win that bet. This is almost too easy.

My phone dings with a text, causing me to shriek and take in my surroundings more carefully. The neighborhood is quiet. No one is out, nothing seems amiss, as near as I can tell I'm the only one awake for blocks. Except for the guys inside.

The text is from Remi, reassuring me that my outfit is on point.

Take that, Chance Bauer!

I hurry back to the car and send Bauer a quick text to let him know what I've found. And that I am still waiting in the car, mostly. He and Sherman, and the two backup officers come back to the front of the house moments later, empty-handed.

"The house is clean," he says. "But there is a room that was clearly set up as a photography room and another that was for the girls to sleep in. We've called in the crime lab guys to dust for prints and anything else they can find. The two badges will wait here in case he returns, and we will go stakeout the school."

The excitement builds inside me again. Not only are we catching the bad guy, but we'll nail my creepy stalker at the same time. I can get rid of that stupid camera and finally be able to enjoy naked hot tub again.

Mmmm, naked hot tub.

Mmmm, naked Brad in the hot tub.

My body heats, I flush all over.

"You okay, there, Cookie?" Bauer asks. "You look a little red."

"Yup!" I stare straight ahead not willing to look him in the eye in case he can read the thoughts on my face. "I'm doing good."

We've already established I don't have a good poker face and the last thing I need is Bauer knowing what's in my mind.

45

THE STALKER

My Kitty Kat is not getting it. It makes me worry that she's not the one. I've left her so many clues and she's not noticing any of them. There's no way she's this dense. The rest of the cops? Sure. Pretty Boy? Absolutely. Chubby Cohort? Without a doubt. But my Kitty Kat, she's the one.

She's got to get this.

I watch her every move, willing her to see me. Pay attention to me. To what I've left for her to find.

It's right there.

I'm not saying it's enough to irrefutably allow her to catch me. What would be the fun in that? But it's close. She can connect the dots she's just not trying hard enough.

She's spent days with Pretty Boy at the police station. The looks on their faces at the ends of the days telling me they've figured nothing out. I can't make this any easier. Kitty Kat is just going to have to up her ante.

If she doesn't, I'll have to handle it myself, and that outcome won't be pretty.

46

KAT

The school parking lot is still empty when we pull in. School doesn't start until seven fifty a.m. and its barely seven a.m. now.

"Now what?" I ask Bauer.

"Now, we wait," he says.

I pull out my phone to check my messages. Not surprisingly, no one has tried to reach me since the last time I checked it about two hours ago. I resume an earlier game of Candy Crush, turning the volume on my phone down so that Bauer doesn't know what I'm doing. He's immersed in his own phone anyway.

"I can hear Candy Crush," he says. "Don't you have anything better to do?"

"Nope," I say with a smile, "I'm still trying to beat level sixty-five, I'm on a mission."

"Sixty-five?" he scoffs. "Amateur."

"I just started playing."

"When, yesterday?"

"No."

"Well, when you're finished playing, the guy drives an older blue Toyota Corolla. Keep an eye out for him just in case," he says.

"Got it." Before I can put my phone away, it beeps with a text from Brad. A smile overtakes my face.

BRAD: Good morning my beautiful firecracker - my shift just started, so I may not have time to contact you again today. Just want to make sure you know how much I cherish you. Every single part of you. There is nothing in this world that is more important than you are. I'll be thinking about you - today and every day. Stay safe. I love you.

I swallow the squeal that wants to break free from my chest.

Giddy.

I feel giddy.

A sure sign that something bad will happen soon. I swallow that thought down too. Burying anything that dare try to cloud over the sunshine I'm feeling. I'm too fucking happy to let my happiness bring me down today.

ME: I love you back. I'll be thinking about last night, today and every day.

Not my finest response. But then he's always been better with the mushy stuff than I am.

BRAD: Now I'm thinking about last night, and I'm hard.

ME: Oh! Sexting at work, I like it! You 'hard' is my favorite!

BRAD: Don't start something you can't finish.

ME: Step into the bathroom - I'll 'finish' it. ;-)

BRAD: On my way!

"Hey!" Bauer says, "pay attention, there's a blue Corolla!" He slaps me on the shoulder with the back of his hand.

ME: Gotta go, babe - sorry!

BRAD: Nobody likes a tease!

I put away my phone and return my full attention to Bauer and the blue Corolla. The hair on the back of my neck stands up - I feel excited and terrified at the same time. The car circles the lot slowly, then parks and sits there for a moment. I can't tell who is in the car. The driver appears to be stalling. After a moment, a woman gets out and walks toward the school. She's alone.

"Shit," Bauer says.

"You can say that again," I say.

"Shit," he says again.

"Smart ass," I reply. "Do we even know for sure he will come here today?"

"Yes and no, it's mostly a hunch. But I have faith in my hunches."

We sit in silence for a few more minutes. I'm tempted to pull out Candy Crush again. I swear I have the attention span of a four-year-old lately. Just sitting here is driving me a little crazy. I hate having absolutely nothing to do but wait.

"Waiting has got to be the most mundane and wasteful activity ever," I tell Bauer.

"Actually," he says without looking at me. "It's a very disciplined activity that requires intense concentration and focus. Often it produces amazing results, especially compared to the time spent. The ratio of time spent versus results gained is in our favor."

"I don't even know what that means," I tell him.

The parking lot fills up, I pull out my phone to see what time it is.

7:40am.

He could get here at any time now.

47

KAT

We sit for almost an hour, watching the lot continue to fill, kids streaming into the school, parents rushing off after they drop them off, teachers speed walking to classrooms. And then, just as fast as it started, the activity slows and dissipates completely. It frustrates Bauer and puts him on edge.

"How much longer are we going to sit here?" I ask.

He ignores me.

I check my messages - nothing new and exciting that would pull me away from here.

I sigh loudly.

Bauer still says nothing. I take a breath to sigh again when he suddenly sits up straighter in his seat.

"And here we go," he says. I follow his gaze to the driveway of the lot, sure as shit, a blue Corolla is pulling into the lot. I squirm in my seat.

The car circles the lot around the outer edge then parks at the far end away from us. A man gets out. He looks like a guy you'd barely notice if you passed him on the street.

Short brown hair partially hidden by a navy baseball cap, jeans, brown t-shirt, tennis shoes, and dark sunglasses. He appears clean shaven with a slight build, medium height, and a barely noticeable limp on his right side.

He does a visual sweep of the parking lot, then bends down into the car for something. He straightens, looks around once more, then hurries across the lot to head into the school.

"It's him. I know it is. What do we do?" I ask.

"We don't want to spook him, so we wait to make sure it's our guy, and to see if he makes a move." He pulls out his walkie and tells the other officers we've spotted our guy and to stay alert but stand back and wait for further instruction.

Another two minutes pass with nothing happening. "Aargh! This is killing me!" I tell him.

"You and me both, Cookie," he says.

We see him appear from one of the hallways to the school. Only he's not alone. A young girl is walking next to him.

She's about half his height with curly red hair, wearing a yellow t-shirt with a unicorn picture on it, jeans, gray hoodie, and sandals. She does a little hop skip with every other step, trying to keep up with him. But also looking excited. I wonder if it's Kendall Martin.

He's not holding her hand, or seeming to force her, but he is walking close to her, bending down to her height when he speaks. His head continually moving back and forth as he visually sweeps the lot, trying to see everything around him at once.

"Do not approach. Stand back. Repeat, do not approach," Bauer says into the walkie.

"How do we know that's not just a dad and his daughter?" I ask.

"I don't think so. He looks nervous, and he's not holding her hand crossing the lot," Bauer says.

They reach the car and the man motions for the girl to stand back and turn around, which she does. He opens the door and leans in as though to get something. When he emerges from the car, he puts his hand over her mouth from behind, and she falls into his arms within seconds. He lifts her up and places her in the car's backseat, then rushes around to the passenger side.

"What's he doing?" I ask Bauer. He's got the binoculars, I can't see the action nearly as well from my vantage point. He ignores my question and tells the officers through the walkie to stand down once again.

Can't they listen and follow directions after the first time he tells them?

I can see that he's doing something on the passenger side of the car, I just can't tell what. He finishes whatever he was doing, then hurries back around to the driver's side, gets in, and backs out of the parking space quickly. His tires squeal as he rushes to escape the parking lot.

Bauer speaks into the walkie, "Move in. Repeat. Move in and apprehend. Do not shoot. Child in the car. Repeat. Do not shoot. Child in the car. Someone get over to that fucking parking space and see what he was doing."

Police cars materialize from all sides of the lot, quickly blocking the escapes and cornering the blue Corolla. Someone radios Bauer they've recovered an unconscious girl from near the vacated parking space, propped up against another car.

She looks like Makayla Jones.

Another officer radios they've stopped the car. But the guy refuses to get out. And that he's got another girl unconscious in the backseat.

She looks like Kendall Martin.

"What's going on? Why don't they pull him from the car?" I ask.

"We don't know if he has any weapons. We've got to make sure the girl is safe. And if he hurts himself, we can't question him."

Bauer's phone rings, he answers it. Whatever he's told does not make him happy.

"Let's go," he says.

"Where?" I ask.

"The perp will only get out of the car if you're there."

"Uh, there, where?"

He doesn't answer. Instead driving the car across the lot to the Corolla.

Officers stand in a perimeter around the car, guns at the ready. Everyone looks tense. But no one more so than the driver.

"Whoa. Ok." I exit Bauer's car slowly and begin my approach to the Corolla even slower. I'm apprehensive even though there are armed police officers everywhere.

Bauer puts his arm out to stop me about a yard from the blue car. The man in the car is looking straight ahead. He's taken off the baseball cap, but the sunglasses remain.

I hear sirens and see the rescue truck from Brad's station pull into the lot. A shiver runs through me at the thought of seeing him in action. His rig pauses at the perimeter and Brad gets out with his medical kit in tow. The guys point out where Makalya Jones was found and Ethan speeds to that side of the lot.

People from inside the school have heard the sirens and are gathering around the perimeter of the action. The buzz of the crowd growing louder with each passing second. With everyone forming their own theory as to what's happening and why.

"Get this area cordoned off now!" Bauer yells at whoever is listening. A second, larger firetruck pulls into the lot, blocking the view for the bulk of the bystanders.

"I want kitty cat to get in the car." I hear from inside the blue Corolla.

Does he mean me?

"I want her to get in the car." He's louder now. All activity around us seems to stop.

"You," he says pointing at me. I look around hoping there is someone else close by.

No luck.

I really don't want to get in the car.

"No." Brad is standing behind me, his voice resonates deep and sure.

This is why I love this man.

"Get in the fucking car!" The guy screams. He raises the gun in his right hand and lays it on the dash.

What was once a rising buzz of the crowd is now a deafening silence.

All it takes is one person to start shooting and we'll all be in the crossfire.

"What about if I'm next to the car?" I ask in the general direction of the blue Corolla.

"Kat, no!" Brad says. "It's not safe."

Ignoring Brad, I inch closer to the driver's side.

The guy looks over at me. Behind those sunglasses, he could be anyone. That's how ordinary his facial features are. Even if I committed his image to memory now, I doubt I could pick him from a line-up tomorrow.

"If I get in the car, will you let the little girl out?" I ask him.

He nods once. "You get in the car, then he gets her out," he says motioning to Brad.

"Kat," Brad says, his tone menacing. Even though I know it's not me he's mad at per se, it's still scary.

"It's fine," I tell Brad, hoping that will pacify him. I walk around to the passenger side of the car and open the car door. Kendall Martin is lying in the backseat, her body limp and nothing like the little bundle of energy that had been walking beside the man earlier.

"Don't do this, Kat. Please," Brad says under his breath, but still loud enough for me to hear. "I just got you back. I can't lose you again. Not yet."

"Get in the car, kitty-kat," the man says, his voice rising to a shrill.

I'm half in the car, still trying to decide if this is a good idea when Brad looks at me pleadingly, shaking his head. He moves toward me, arm outstretched.

"Stop!" the man yells, pulling the gun from the dashboard and pointing it in Brad's direction.

Brad stops.

"Get in!" He shrieks, turning to me, still pointing the gun at Brad.

I'm in the passenger seat with the door closed in a matter of seconds.

The man is breathing erratically. But, this close, and without the baseball cap, I can see without a doubt it's Gil Iverson.

"Gil?"

He turns his head toward me. The gun follows. "You know me?" he asks.

I nod, hesitant. "I know you're Gil Iverson."

"It wasn't supposed to end like this," he says.

"How was it supposed to end?"

"Once I was saved."

"How were you going to be saved?" I ask.

"Not how, but who. It was you, kitty-kat. You were supposed to save me."

He pauses.

"But you failed."

48

BRAD

I see Kat get in the car.

"Goddammit!"

I stop myself from hitting something.

Someone.

Bauer moves to stand beside me. He puts his hand on my shoulder.

"If you don't get her out of there, I will," I tell him.

"The guy has settled down since she got in."

"He still has a gun pointed at her," I say.

"And we've got three times as many pointed at him."

"That helps how?"

He sighs.

"This is your fucking fault. If anything happens to her—" I say.

"I won't let anything happen to her," he says.

"*I won't* let anything happen to her," I say.

"Look, I know this is hard to deal with. But just let us do our job. Don't play the fucking hero, all right?"

He walks back to where Detective Sherman is standing and they all just stand there, watching the car, waiting for something to happen.

Fuck this.

I move toward the car. Ethan grabs my arm to stop me.

"Give it a minute, bro. Kat's dealt with criminals for a long time. She knows how they think, she won't do anything stupid," he says.

"Then why'd she get in the fucking car, E?" I run my hand over my face, frustrated and scared. "I just fucking got her back."

Ethan pats my shoulder twice, in a move I'm sure is meant to be reassuring, but just makes me more tense.

I clench my fists, then relax my hands a few times. Roll my head around and loosen up my shoulders.

Getting ready for action.

49

KAT

Gil still has the gun pointed at me. His eyes flit back and forth trying to see everything around us at once. Brad paces back and forth in our periphery, shaking his arms and rolling his head on his shoulders. Clearly agitated. His actions doing nothing to help calm Gil.

"How was I going to save you?" I ask.

Gil stares at me, for a long time. So long, that I'm afraid I've turned him off with my question.

"You spoke to me. When they interviewed you on the news. You spoke to me through the TV screen and your words went straight to my soul."

"What did I say?" I ask, not remembering what he is referring to.

"That I deserve a second chance. And that one false step doesn't have to detonate the landmine that is my life. You said I could be turned around, rehabilitated, and redeemed," he pauses. "But you were wrong."

"How was I—"

"GIL IVERSON." Sherman's voice booms through the police bull horn, making us both jump. Gil turns back and forth trying to see where the voice is coming from, the gun twisting back and forth with him. I try to lean away from it each time it points at me.

"Uh, can you give us a minute?" I yell toward the car window.

Kendall stirs in the back seat. "Mommy?" she asks, her voice groggy.

"It's okay, Kendall," I tell her.

"Don't tell her that!" Gil says. "It's not okay. Nothing is okay!"

"I don't know you," Kendall says to me.

She turns toward Gil, "I don't know you either." She looks around. "Why are the policemen here?"

Then she screams. Loud and long.

Gil covers his ears, rocking his head back and forth. "Make her stop! Make her stop!"

The gun goes off, shooting through the roof of the car. The noise is disorienting.

Kendall screams louder.

My head spins. I shake it trying to get the ringing in my ears to stop. Time slows and everything turns to a fog. Gil is talking but I can't make out what he's saying. Kendall cries from behind me. I don't know how to make sense of this. How to get out.

And then it doesn't matter. Because I'm out of the car and in Brad's arms. Bauer straddles Gil on the ground, fastening handcuffs over his wrists and Ethan is carrying Kendall to the medical rig.

"Baby, are you hurt?" Brad asks, running his hands over my body searching for injuries.

"I'm fine," I tell him.

He leads me off to the side of the chaos and pulls me tight against him.

"My god, baby, how could you get in that car? Do you have a fucking death wish? What were you thinking?" he says to the top of my head, his voice muffled by my hair, his body shaking.

"I was thinking there was a little girl in the car. I couldn't leave her in there."

"That's what the fucking police are for, Kat. Not you. You won't be working with Sherman and Bauer again. Period." He sighs loudly, his body relaxing a small degree. "God, baby. Promise me you won't put yourself in a situation like that again?"

I open my mouth to disagree with his trying to dictate what I do but decide now is not the right time. So, instead I lie.

"I promise."

He looks at me sharply, knowing I'm lying. But is it really a lie if both know it is?

One of the techs calls Brad over to help check Kendall and Makayla. He wraps me in a blanket and makes me sit in the back of the rig first.

"Don't move," he says, pulling me into a hug and kissing me firmly on the lips before stepping back to go help the other guys. An action I'm sure is frowned up while on duty at active call sites.

Brad gives Kendall a slight sedative to calm her down and hooks her up to oxygen. I get a little shiver watching him in action, his movements calm and confident.

The ambulances arrive and Brad and Ethan help get the little girls onto gurneys and inside. Both girls will be admitted to the hospital and checked out, in addition, Makayla will also be checked for injury and rape. I shudder at the thought of the poor girl having to endure a rape kit examination.

Gil sits in the back of a squad car and Bauer is standing near it, talking to a man, who I assume is the principal of the school. Both are speaking in hushed tones and nodding their heads gravely.

Stacy approaches them from behind.

Why is she here?

I forgot both girls are in her class, she's their teacher.

Can this day get any better?

Her eyes widen when she sees me. I keep my face blank.

I hear her tell Bauer and the principal that she has contacted the parents of each girl and they'll be meeting them at the hospital. Then, loudly, she says, "I can't believe this happened. And to my students. How do we feel safe again? How do I help them feel safe again?" She starts to cry. The principal pats her on the back, awkwardly, and motions to Brad.

Brad approaches slowly.

The principal must think they are still dating. He points Stacy toward Brad and nudges her in his direction; she turns into Brad clinging to his shirt and crying. He rubs her back and looks at me from over her head, an apologetic look on his face.

I don't need to be watching this.

I drop the blanket from my shoulders and jump off the back of the rig. I swear my movements catch Stacy's eye, and I watch in fascination as she fakes a fainting spell crumbling to the ground.

At least I'm pretty sure it's fake.

Brad catches her in his arms and carries her toward the same rig I've just jumped out of as people scurry around us.

"Kat," he says as we pass one another. But I continue past him toward Bauer trying to get lost in the crowd.

"What's next, boss?" I ask when I reach him.

"You doing okay?" He looks concerned.

"Aw, you don't need to worry about little ol' me."

"You were in a car alone with a psychopath who had a gun to your head. Of course I'm worried about you."

"I'm good."

"We're headed back to the precinct; I'll get one of the guys to take you home."

"Why can't I go to the precinct?" I ask.

"One, I don't think we need you there. Two, you should rest. Three, your little prince charming over there will blow a gasket if I let you do anything else on this case."

I realize I'm completely exhausted. An all-night sex-a-thon with Brad, combined with waking up so early, and the adrenaline rush I've just experienced is causing a crash in a big way.

"I think I will go home if that's okay."

Sherman approaches us. "We've Mirandized him and he's willing to talk."

"That's great!" Bauer and I both say at the same time.

Sherman runs his hand down his face. "He's only willing to talk to you," he says, meeting my gaze.

And they say there's no rest for the wicked.

I turn to Bauer. "You heard the man. Let's see if we can get this guy to talk."

50

KAT

We arrived at the precinct in record time. I had to press ignore on two calls from Brad during the drive. So, it shouldn't have surprised me when he showed up at the precinct a short while later.

"Did you even let one of the guys check you out?" he asks, once he finds me.

"I'm fine, Brad. You could have checked me out if you weren't so busy rescuing fainting damsels in distress." I feel petty and jealous saying it. But it doesn't stop me.

"Dammit, Kat—"

"Ready?" Bauer asks. I hadn't even heard him approach.

I nod.

"What's going on?" Brad asks.

"The perp agreed to talk," Bauer says.

"What's that have to do with Kat?"

"He'll only talk to her."

"No. No way," Brad says.

"It's fine," I say. "Bauer and Sherman will be in there with me the whole time."

"Actually . . .," Bauer says. "He wants to talk to you alone."

"Alone?" I ask, my voice squeaking. I mean, I may act like a total bad-ass sometimes, but I'm really a marshmallow inside. The last thing I want to do is be in a room alone with this guy.

"Absolutely fucking not," Brad says.

"He's chained in. And we'll be right outside the door," Bauer says ignoring Brad. "Surveillance will be on the other side of the mirror recording everything. Even if something could happen, which it can't, we'd be to you in a matter of seconds."

"Nothing will happen cause she's not going in there with him," Brad growls.

"Not your call, man." Bauer just looks at him and the two begin a mini stare-down.

"Okay, okay," I say as I step between them. "I'm going to talk to him," I say facing Bauer. "And he's chained up," I say as I turn to face Brad. The two just keep staring at one another.

I look from one to the other and get zero in return.

I wave my hand between them.

Nothing.

It's like I'm not even here.

"Fine, I'll be in the room with the bad guy if anyone needs me," I say to no one in particular. As much as I may like the alpha-attentiveness of two guys fighting over me, it can really take its toll on a girl. I need a nap.

I reach for the door handle with a yawn, suddenly unable to move. Brad has grabbed hold of my arm, immobilizing me.

"Let go, Brad," I say.

"You aren't going in there," he says.

"Uh, I think that's up to—" Bauer starts.

"Mind your own business," both Brad and I say to Bauer at the same time.

Bauer holds up his hands in a surrender pose and backs away down the hall.

"Let me go."

"No."

"You're being ridiculous, it's totally safe. He's chained to the freakin' floor for god's sake."

"If you won't be safe for your sake, then at least be safe for our sake. We just found each other again," Brad says.

"I'm not *not* being safe," I huff turning toward the door.

"Don't do this, Kat, or—"

"Or what?" I meet his gaze, daring him to try to force me to do anything I don't want to. He can't. And he knows it.

Brad stays silent. His teeth clenched and eyes hard.

"That's what I thought," I say.

∼

"You came," Gil breathes.

"Didn't you want me to?"

"Yes, but I didn't think it would happen," he says.

"Why not?"

He doesn't respond.

"Why did you do it? Why did you take those girls? Did you rape them?" I ask him, getting right to the point.

"No! I never touched them, not like that! I only took them because I couldn't help myself. I never wanted to hurt them, I needed something more to curb the cravings. Something that was just my own. I'm not that kind of person. I like to watch, to look, that's all."

I look at him with what I'm sure is total disgust on my face.

"I shouldn't have come here," he says. "This was a mistake."

"Come here?" I ask. "You didn't come here; we captured you."

"Only because I let you, I needed you to. You caught me because Ronald practically told you where to look."

"Who's Ronald?"

"Ronald called in the tip. But you know, I don't think I'm mad at him for that, I'm kind of relieved to be honest. I'm tired of hiding." He sighs and deflates back into his chair.

"Ronald knows about this?"

"He's known all along. But he looks out for me. Even if I was capable of hurting the girls, he would have stopped me before I'd gone too far, I'm sure of it."

"Are you saying he watched you with the girls?"

"He watches everything."

"And you let him? He doesn't stop you?"

"He can't stop me, I'm stronger than he is," Gil says.

"He's not stronger than I am. I just let him think he is." It's still Gil talking, but his voice has changed. I study him for a moment, his entire demeanor is different.

He has a split personality.

"Are you . . ." I start. "Am I speaking to Ronald now?"

"You are. I am Ronald," Gil/Ronald says. "Gil's protector. I help him when a situation gets too tough for him to handle in an emotionally effective way. I am happy to answer any questions you may have about the abductions, the cameras, and the pictures. However, you should know that I am not the one who abducted the girls, nor did I take the pictures. Further, I am not attracted to underage females. I prefer a mature woman who is a little rough around the edges, someone who doesn't mind getting dirty. Someone like you."

I'm surprised he thinks I'm mature. Until I realize he doesn't mean emotionally and that he also said I was rough around the edges.

What a dick.

"Are you saying I'm—" I stop myself from saying anything more. I don't want to egg him on. I take a deep breath and try another tactic.

"If you are not our perpetrator, what makes you think you can help us?" I ask him.

"I know everything Gil does. He doesn't always know that I know, but I do. I'm omniscient in our body. There is no way to envision the atrocities Gil suffered as a child. To understand, one would have to have lived it because the human brain can't process that kind of information, or endure it, without protecting itself. By shutting down. Splitting apart," Ronald says.

"You say Gil suffered these things, yet you share the same body and the same mind, how is it that you did not suffer the same?" I ask him.

"I stepped in to protect Gil. Gil is weak, everything affects him, everything that touches him has a lasting impact. I have no feelings. And with no feelings comes the inability to be effected. There have been few times where Gil is strong enough to do something without my knowledge."

"Like when he kidnapped the first girl?" I ask.

"Yes. But it wasn't long before I knew and confronted him," Ronald says.

"How long?" I ask.

"Maybe a week, not much longer. He doesn't have the ability to lock me out for longer than that."

"Lock you out?" I ask.

"Yes, prevent me from taking over. As I've said before, I am the stronger of us two," Ronald says.

"Are there any more of you?" I ask.

"No," Ronald says.

"How can you be sure?"

"I'm sure." Ronald sits back in his chair, attempting a position of relaxed confidence.

"Why did Gil plant the cameras in the girls' rooms?" I ask.

"To watch them," Ronald replies.

"Why didn't you stop him from doing that?"

"I wanted to see how far he would take it," Ronald says.

"Why did he put a camera on my deck?"

"I did that, not Gill. I thought it would be funny."

"Funny how?"

"Not, funny haha. More like funny ironic. All the sudden there you'd be in his camera feeds. Someone more age-appropriate intermingled with all the chicklets. And it gave me something to watch when he went away."

"Why me?"

Gil waves his hand dismissively. "He thinks you and he have some connection. Plus, you intrigue us in a way like no adult woman has since mother. But in unusual ways and for distinct reasons. Gil, because he thought you could save him. Me, because I want to fuck you." He pauses and tilts his head to the left; his eyes shift up to the right as though he's trying to recall something.

"We'd been following you in person for a while, but it wasn't enough. We wanted to watch you, to feel close to you. Like Gil does with the girls," he says.

"Like Gil did with the girls," I correct him. "He won't be watching anyone for a long time. Why didn't you stop him?"

"It's my job to protect him, not monitor him. This was the first time he made it so personal. In the past he has just used pictures he has found to satisfy himself. And when the urges got too strong, he used a castration medication. But I must admit that is not my favorite, for selfish reasons.

"This was the first time he picked specific girls and watched them on camera, track them, and then take them. The strength and control and planning that took was a heady experience to watch." Ronald has a look of awe on his face.

"This was Gil unlike I've ever seen him. In some ways I was proud of how he handled this, and in how he's handled himself with this," he says.

"So, sometimes Gil is in control of what's happening, like when he self-medicates to control his urges," I say, trying to confirm what he's telling us. Trying to wrap my head around the whole idea.

"Yes, Dissociative Identity Disorder is not as plain as black and white. It lies in the gray areas of explanation. Every person and every situation can be different. Even though I am the stronger one, there are still times when Gil is stronger than me—"

He stops talking, then laughs.

"Even now, he tries to argue his strength," he says, his smile wide. "The times that he is stronger are not often or constant, but they are there. It is important to remember that my purpose is to protect Gil from situations that he can't handle on his own. Even though I want him to be strong."

"So, he didn't physically molest any of the girls?" I ask.

"No, he did not," Ronald says.

I'm relieved he didn't hurt the girls in a physical way. Though I still don't understand his motivation. I ask the main question still on my mind.

"What was the point? And would you/he just keep going until you were caught? Or?"

"I can answer that."

His demeanor has changed again. And even if his voice hadn't, I'd still know I was now talking to Gil.

I sit back in my seat and try to get comfortable. I have a feeling this will take a while.

We take a late break from the interrogation to have lunch. I am tired beyond comprehension. All I want to do is go home and cry for a while, then go to bed. I want to cry for the girls and how scared they must have been. Even if he drugged them, I am sure that a small part of them was aware of their surroundings, and it had to have been terrifying.

I want to cry for their families because they had no idea where their daughters were or if they would ever see them again. And when they saw them again, what would they find their daughters had endured. I'm sure, as a parent, always wondering what he did to them and why they couldn't protect them.

And, unbelievably, I want to cry for a young boy named Gil. Who suffered through such horrifying things as a child, things that no one should ever have to endure. I want to cry for how he can be such a dichotomy as an adult. How he knows, intellectually, that his tendencies are wrong, but how he can't stop them emotionally. And how he fights those tendencies every chance he gets. I want to cry for Gil because he is a true product of his environment. I don't think he ever stood a chance to be anything but bad.

Sherman comes into the precinct break room where I happen to be nursing a cup of coffee. He sits down heavily in a chair next to mine.

"He calls me Chubby Cohort," he says.

I laugh. "Out of everything he's told us, that is what you are coming away with?"

He sighs. "What can I say?" He holds his hand over his heart. "Words wound. And his hit me right here."

I laugh at him again. Delighted with this new Sherman who is a jokester, and grateful for the sudden lightness in the mood.

"Do you think he will talk to you if I leave?" I ask.

"I think you've gotten most of what we will get from him today. We know what he did and when. We know a little of why, but why doesn't really matter. And we will know soon, with certainty, if he is distributing kiddie porn. Tech forensics have been working on his computer all day. If it helps, they didn't find any still photos or captured video feeds of you."

"That helps, thanks," I tell him. "I'm going to head out then, if that's okay with you."

"Absolutely. You've been a huge help, once again, I'm not sure we would have solved this without you," he tells me.

I smile at the compliment. "Thank you, but we both know that's not true. You would

have solved it eventually; it just may have taken a little longer." I stand to walk out the door. "Tell Bauer I said bye."

"I will," Sherman says while Bauer walks in and says, "Tell Bauer you said bye? Cookie, I'm hurt you wouldn't seek me out to give me a kiss goodbye. No hug or anything?"

I backhand him on the shoulder. "At least the level of your ego never wavers," I say.

He waggles his eyebrows at me. "With good reason. Or so the ladies tell me."

I laugh at him and wave at them both over my head as I leave the room.

51

KAT

I check my phone once I get in the car.

Nothing from Brad.

I thought he would be there waiting for me when I finished with Gil.

Until I remember that we're fighting, and he may never be there to wait for me again. In his defense, he warned me, and I didn't listen. Just went about doing my thing, like normal.

I text the girls once I get in the car. Even though I'm exhausted, I know if I go home, I'll just rehash the entire day repeatedly.

ME: Anyone up for Crazy Burro? But like now, not later? I've had a day and I think I'm fighting with Brad. I need my girls & a margarita.

LEXIE: I could use a break. :-)

REMI: How can you already be fighting with Brad? You just got back together.

LEXIE: You and Brad are back together?!?!

ME: We were. But now I'm not so sure.

LEXIE: I'll leave in 5.

REMI: Walking out the door.

I get to *The Crazy Burro* in a matter of minutes. Our favorite server isn't there, but we still get our regular table.

I order three margaritas and chips with salsa, check my email, check-in on Facebook, and sit back to wait for the girls. The margaritas arrive before they do. I take a long pull on mine, not caring if I get brain freeze, just wanting the calming effects of the tequila.

Lexie gets there first; I stand to give her a hug. "Hey, cute outfit!" she tells me.

Once again, I want to say 'suck it' to Bauer over his earlier derision of my clothing choice.

She grabs her margarita, and we cheer one another. She's wearing cut-offs, a black *Lovestone* tank top, and pink Chucks. Her hair is down today, and she looks adorable.

"You look good," I tell her.

"Pfft." She waves her hand dismissively. "That's sweet. Now, tell me everything."

"I'll tell you all about what happened once Remi gets here. Oh god, and I had to talk to the perp today," I tell her.

"Wait, are we talking about the case or Brad?" she asks.

"Ohmigod, right? I feel like I haven't talked to you in days!" I say.

"I know! Tell me all about how you got back together."

"Well, apparently he and Remi were texting after we left the bar, and she brought me here and then he showed up and grabbed me all caveman style and pulled me to the back alley and fucked me against the wall."

"What?!?!" Lexie practically screeches.

"I know. Be quiet! Anyway, it was amazing. So, fucking amazing. And then he took me home, and we had sex all night and I'm so sore, and god, Lexie, I've missed him so much and I didn't realize it."

"I know you have, sweetie. I'm sorry. I'm so glad he's back now though. You two belong together."

"That's just it, now I don't think we will be together," I say.

Remi sits down just then. She's wearing a sheer white peasant blouse, pulled low off the shoulders, with a black lacy bra underneath, paired with a full, knee-length black skirt and some sassy, red, peep-toe wedge sandals. I don't know how she gets away with wearing some of the things she does at her office.

"How'd you fuck up everything with sexy not-ex I so painstakingly put back together last night? Wasn't it any good?" she asks.

"Last night was amazing!" And I tell her what I've just told Lexie. Apologizing to Lexie for having to hear it twice. But when I get past the parts I've already told Lexie and to the part about Brad and I not being together, Remi says, "That is so not the guy who was texting me last night. I find it hard to believe that guy would ever leave you."

My eyes fill with tears. "Why do I always fuck this up?" I ask.

"You haven't fucked anything up. It's just a little fight. Fights happen all the time," Lexie says.

"What if it isn't just a little fight? What if I've finally gotten what I want, and I've just thrown it away? It wasn't even that important to talk to the perp. I just dug my heels in when he said no. I'm so stupid," I say.

"Oh shit, I got salsa on my blouse, I'll be right back," Remi says.

"I don't see anything," I say. But she's already heading for the ladies' room. In her defense, she is way more particular about clothes than either Lexie or I.

Remi returns to the table a short while later and we order our food. I tell them about the case and how it all played out and how my intuitive feelings helped. And I tell them about Gil, and I swear that by the time I've finished, they feel sorry for him too.

"It's weird to feel sorry for someone whose actions are so repellant, right?" I ask.

"Yes," says Remi. "But we are more feeling sorry for the boy he was and the life he could have had then we are the adult pedophile of today."

"You think so?" Lexie asks.

"Definitely," Remi says.

"Well, that would make me feel better. To know I'm not sympathizing with someone I'd like to see rot in hell," I say. "Even though I really kind of am sympathizing with him."

"I still say it's normal," Remi says. "But more importantly, cheers to a job well done, my kick-ass crime fighting friend!" She raises her glass toward the middle of the table.

I blush at the compliment, but of course still cheers to it.

My phone dings with a text from Brad. My breath catches in my throat. I open it and it looks like a picture. Of a green blob.

"What is this?" I show the picture to the girls.

"Beats me," Lexie says.

"It looks like a tree," Remi says. I look closer and she's right.

I get another text from Brad.

BRAD: Watching Ethan rescue a parrot and a cat from a tree.

ME: A bird and a cat? You're texting me this, why?

BRAD: Lady accidentally let the $10,000 bird out. He likes it in the tree. Cat jumped on the opportunity, pun intended, now both are stuck about 20' up. Thought you'd enjoy it.

ME: I'm sorry, did you say $10,000 bird?!?!

BRAD: Yep. And that's Ethan half in half out of the telescope platform trying to get in a position to at least rescue one or the other.

ME: So that's what the picture is. It looked more like a green blob.

ME: For some reason I thought you'd be texting me an apology.

BRAD: Apology? For what?

BRAD: Wait, are you saying YOU'RE mad at ME?

ME: Yes, I'm mad at you.

BRAD: What did I do?

ME: Seriously? You're trying to dictate my actions and tell me what to do. Like some kind of dictator micromanager.

BRAD: I think you're exaggerating just a bit. Especially with all the 'dictating' you seem to think is going on. I don't like it when you put yourself in danger unnecessarily, and that will never change. What you did was selfish and inconsiderate and you didn't give my wants or needs any thought when you made that decision.

ME: Well, you knew what you were getting into before you jumped back in.

BRAD: What's that supposed to mean?

ME: I am who I am and THAT will never change. I'm going to do what I think is right when I need to, even if you don't like it.

BRAD: And how I feel means nothing?

ME: Well, when you say it like that it sounds really bad.

BRAD: Kat - you're saying you don't care about your own safety. And worse, you don't care that I care about your safety.

BRAD: I get your need to be reckless at times. Hell, I even support some of it. But, goddammit, don't put me in a position where I have to watch you purposefully risk your life. Not when we already know your time may be limited as it is. Your safety comes before all else. Just please give me this one thing. Please.

And just like that it hits me. This is my guy. Not only do I need him, but I deserve him. He's it for me and there is no one else. Really, there never has been. I couldn't be luckier than to have him as mine.

ME: Holy shit. I'm such an asshole. I'm so sorry.

BRAD: There's no reason to apologize.

ME: Yes there is. I'm so lucky to have you.

BRAD: Well, I can't argue with that.

ME: Wow, full of yourself much?

BRAD: I'll show you something full.

ME: Was that supposed to be a sex innuendo/joke?

BRAD: Only if you found it funny and me irresistibly appealing.

ME: I think it fell a little flat. But I will say this - thank you for sticking with me, even though I'm a pain in the ass, basket case sometimes.

BRAD: Sometimes?

ME: haha

ME: Notice there are no exclamations points. They are sarcastic ha's in case you didn't notice.

BRAD: Noted.

ME: I love you. Be safe. Thank you for caring about me.

BRAD: Always. Have fun, tell the girls hi from me. I love you.

We eat our food, order another round, tease Remi about sexting with Alex last night, and give Lexie a hard time about agreeing to do a wine event with her ex, Trevor.

Overall, it's just like nothing has changed in my life.

Yet everything has changed.

I have my girls; I have Brad back, I still have no evidence of disease, the last week has been crazy insane, but starting tomorrow I have my life back. And I'll have time to relax and just enjoy being me for a while.

Remi and Lexie are talking about the next movie Lexie should show at *Lovestone's* Movie Night. And I let myself zone out for just a minute so I can examine how I feel. And I realize I feel good. I'm comfortable financially which gives me breathing room to figure out what I want to do next. Because shouldn't life be about pursuing what you want?

In some bizarre way, Gil Iverson taught me that. He pursued what he wanted, to his own detriment. Because what he wanted was illegal, but he still got what he wanted, what he needed. His pursuit was methodical and relentless. Not only did he want the girls. Or at least photographic representations of the girls. But he also wanted to be set free. And in his mind, jail was the only freedom. How that makes sense to him, I'll never know. But he gave his life to it.

I want to know what I want. And I want to pursue it.

"That's a lot of wants," Lexie says smiling.

I didn't realize I'd said that last part out loud.

"Lucky for you, you have plenty of time to figure out what you want," Remi says.

"Oh, maybe you should write a screenplay!" Lexie says.

"Or a book, you should write a book!" Remi says.

And we are off and running at the mouth again. Man, I love these girls!

Hours later, I have Uber'd home, showered off the stench of interrogation at the precinct, and am now crawling into bed. Brad is on shift until six a.m. It will be weird to get used to him being here and then not being here again. With his schedule, he's usually twenty-four hours on, forty-eight hours off. But even that changes sometimes. So I will get him some nights, but not others.

Sigh.

I shouldn't already be used to him being back after just one night, but I am. I'm such a wuss. I text him a drunken good night and am asleep before I even read his response.

52

KAT

I wake up late and slightly foggy from three margaritas the night before. Brad is curled up behind me, my back to his front. One arm under my head, the other around my waist and close to cupping a breast. I move to lie on my back, trying to go slowly. His hand moves to just below my belly button as he rolls the other way to his back.

I peek over at him to see if he's asleep, his eyes are shut, his chest rises and falls slowly with each breath. I realize I'd better get out of bed before I wake him up with his cock in my mouth. He must have gotten off shift and climbed straight into bed. I ease myself out from under his arm and slip quietly from the bed, so I don't wake him. This would be a good time for soak now while I still have no disruptions.

Now that my creepy stalker is behind bars, I'm going back to naked hot tubbing as often as possible. Starting now.

I lower myself into the water and turn on the jets. As always, the feeling is one of almost immediate relaxation. I still have some unusually sore muscles in random places, thanks to Brad, and the warm water feels good swirling around them.

I get situated in my favorite lounger seat and adjust the jets to hit my lower back and feet. Both have been giving me some issues lately, just a little pain and discomfort. Probably because I have been more active, and on my feet more this last week than I have in many of the months prior. Force of habit causes me to bring my phone with me and set it on the side shelf near the hot tub. I'm not expecting a call, but this last week with Bauer and The San Soloman Stalker has made me realize that anything can happen at any time.

I'm still clearing my head and stretching my muscles when I hear Brad quietly come outside and leave me a cup of coffee and my pills on the shelf by my phone. I smile in his general direction even though my eyes are still shut. Allowing him back into to my life and to take care of me again has been the best decision I've ever made. I reach blindly for the coffee and bring it closer to my face, inhaling the deep aroma. I've always loved the smell of coffee, there is nothing else like it. I take a couple sips, wash down my pills, then set the coffee back on the shelf and get ready for my meditation.

Just as I've cleared my head and transitioned myself into a Zen like state, my phone rings.

"This had better good; you are interrupting my soak," I say into the phone, not even looking to see who is calling.

"May I speak to Katarina Walker, please?"

"This is she," I reply, sitting up and opening my eyes. It's never good when someone is calling and using your full name to ask for you.

"Katarina, this is Dr. Michaels, I am calling on behalf of your oncologist, Dr. Wilder, who as you know is on vacation this week. I've looked at your recent scans and wanted to let you know I have concerns about what I've seen, and I'd like for you to come back in as soon as possible. Today is preferable, really."

My head swims, I feel nauseous and dizzy.

"What." My voice croaks and I clear my throat. "What did you see that has you concerned?"

I hear him answering me with words like *multifocal, osseous, metastatic disease scattered throughout the lower cervical, thoracic, and lumbar spine* and *suspected leptomeningeal metastatic disease* and my phone slips from my hands and into the water.

Brad comes out to the deck, already dressed for the day.

"Did your phone ring? Is everything okay? Who would call this early?"

The look on my face must have said it all, because a minute later he is in the hot tub with me, fully clothed, and gathering me into his arms.

"Baby! Babe, look at me. Kat, what happened? Are you okay? Baby, did you drop your phone in the water?"

For a long moment, all I can do is just lean into him and try to glean a sense of safety and security from being in his arms.

I'm in a fog.

My brain isn't working correctly, I can't have cancer again. I just helped the police solve The Stalker case. I wouldn't have been able to do that if it was active again. I mean, Brad and I just got back together. Remi has a new boyfriend. There is no way that this is a convenient time for this.

I look up at him, confused. "Did you come in the hot tub in your clothes?"

"That's not important baby. Tell me what happened." He sits down and pulls me with him onto his lap and is running his hands along my arms and back.

"I think I dropped my phone," I tell him.

"It's okay babe, I've got it." He picks it up from the side shelf to show me. It's dripping wet. Good thing I got that 'life proof' case for my phone.

I take a deep breath, look up at Brad, and say, "That was the oncologist who is covering for Dr. Wilder, the cancer metastasized. It's in my spine this time."

He cups my face in his hands. "We'll get through this, Kat. Everything will be okay."

He says it with such tenderness, I almost believe him.

EPILOGUE

KAT

SIX MONTHS LATER

So far treatment is staving off the cancer. It's not diminishing, but it's not growing either. Since it's been six months, I consider myself lucky.

Tonight is the annual Law Enforcement Ball, which includes a, sometimes contentious, blend of firefighters, police officers, and detectives.

But it's hard, when we go out, to acclimate myself with my appearance again. My hair is thinning, my face is bloated, and my complexion is splotchy. I'm wearing a backless, slinky black dress, better suited as lingerie, and a dangerously high pair of stilettos. But I can't decide between my hair and a cute little fascinator hat, or a wig.

I'm sitting at my little makeup table in the bathroom, going back and forth with each on my head.

Brad comes up behind me, he puts his hands on my shoulders as he leans in to nuzzle my neck. He peeks up at me in the mirror.

"You look amazing, baby," he says.

"No I don't. I look terrible," I say sourly.

"You look amazing to me."

"I don't want to look amazing to you. I want to look amazing to everyone."

He raises one eyebrow at me.

I have got to learn that eyebrow trick.

"You know what I mean," I tell him.

"Go with the Angelica Houston looking wig," he says. "It makes you look dangerous and your eyes totally pop." He says the last part with a lilt in his voice and I can't help but laugh.

"I love you," I tell him.

"Not more than I love you," he says, his voice normal.

"God, we've gotten sappy," I say.

"It's so gross, right?" he says, his voice back to the lilt. He's in his dress uniform, and he looks amazing. I eat him up with my eyes.

"Keep looking at me like that and we won't be going anywhere," he says as he swoops down to kiss my neck again. He gets me in that spot and I groan, instantly eager and wet.

"Do we have time for a quickie?" I ask.

"Only if you put on the wig," he says.

We get to the Ball just in time to take advantage of the end of cocktail hour. I can't drink when I'm in treatment, so Brad gets me a club soda with lime from the bar, and a local craft brew for himself. We settle ourselves into a corner of the ballroom and watch the people. I'm not as up for socializing lately as I've been in the past. I see two familiar looking heads, but they disappear as quickly. I shake my head.

"What's the matter?" Brad asks.

"Nothing, I thought I saw Remi with Bauer. It was weird. I think my eyes are playing tricks on me."

"It sounds like it."

Then I see a flash of pink hair and am convinced its Lexie.

"I swear I just saw Lexie too. I think I'm going off the deep end, babe," I say. Brad turns me around to face him.

"Imagining your friends is one thing, but if it turns into dancing unicorns or scary clowns, let me know."

I laugh.

He smiles and spins me back around to face the ballroom.

"Surprise!" Both Lexie and Remi yell.

I jump so high ice flies out of my glass.

"Holy shit! What are you guys doing here?" I ask as I move in to hug them both. They look amazing. Remi is in a three-quarter sleeve, gathered red wiggle dress with a crossover neckline that shows her curves off in an almost indecent way. With her dark hair in victory rolls, eyes heavily lined, bright red lips, and peep-toe pumps, she looks like a carry-over from a pinup calendar you'd find in a mechanic's shop in the 50s.

And Lexie couldn't be more her opposite if she tried. Looking like a little punk rock pixie in a black strapless baby doll mini-dress with an extra-large glittered belt, tulle skirt, patterned black tights, and heeled ankle boots. Her bright pink hair pulled into twin spikey knots on either side of her head.

"Sexy not-ex thought you could use a little moral support on your big night out," Lexie says.

"I'm so glad to see you guys. How'd you get in?"

"Sexy not-ex got us dates," Remi says.

I turn to Brad. "Thank you," I say and kiss him on the cheek.

Ethan shows up behind Lexie and hands her a glass of champagne. He knocks beer bottles with Brad as a hello.

"So, you're the date?" I ask Ethan.

"I'm a date," he says.

"And I'm the other," Bauer says as he approaches. Handing Remi a martini, dirty from the looks of it. He holds up his glass of bourbon in acknowledgment.

"I can't believe you did this," I say to Brad. He shrugs in return as if to say it's no big deal.

"And I really can't believe you did this," I say to Remi, motioning to Bauer.

"I'm offended, Cookie," Bauer says. "The Ice Queen and I have become friends."

"I wouldn't say *friends*," Remi says.

"How about tolerating one another for an evening for the sake of a friend," Lexie suggests.

"I'll drink to that," Remi says.

"Hear, hear," Ethan says raising his bottle. Bauer drinks to it, shaking his head.

A throat clears into the microphone on the stage, and the fire chief calls for everyone to find a seat as the first course will be served soon. We make our way to our table, and Brad pulls out my chair for me and gets me situated. Then whispers into my ear that he'll be right back.

Bauer, seated to my right, gives me a little wink. I squint my eyes back at him.

The Chief, still on the stage, asks for everyone's attention.

"We have a special presentation tonight I know you won't want to miss. If everyone could please quiet down for just a moment," he says.

The room quiets.

I look around for Brad, not wanting him to miss the special presentation, but I don't see him anywhere.

"Hello." A new voice beckons from the stage.

Brad's voice.

"For those who don't know me, my name is Brad Matthews. I'm a lieutenant with the SSFD." A round of cheers and whistles echo through the room from his station mates and friends.

"I'm up here tonight to ask for your help," he says looking at me.

I lean over Brad's empty chair, to Remi, on my left. "If he asks for cancer research donations, I'll kill him!"

Her eyes twinkle back at me, but she says nothing.

"You see," Brad continues, "there's a woman here with me tonight who means more to me than I can possibly put into words." He pulls the microphone from the stand and walks across the stage with it.

"Years ago, on this very night, I met her, and she rocked my world. I'm happy to say I've never been the same," he says. A few catcalls and whistles bounce around the room. I feel myself blushing. He jumps down from the stage and walks toward me.

Lexie lets out a little screech, practically bouncing in her seat.

"Now, I don't have a lot of practice with this, I've only done it once before," he says. "And my timing wasn't the best. So, this is where you all come in." He reaches our table and stands there looking at me. If I didn't know better, I'd swear his eyes are shining with tears.

"I need your help," he says as he gets down to one knee.

Holy.

Shit.

Fuck.

Piss.

"In convincing this woman to become my wife." He pulls a ring from his pocket.

The same ring.

And he holds it out to me.

"Should she say yes?" he asks the crowd, looking only at me.

"YES!" I hear Lexie scream as she pounds on the table with her fists. All the drinks and plates bouncing in place. She's not alone though, the word *yes* resounds through the room.

I can't speak.

All I can do is look at him. This beautiful man who still wants to spend his life with me. After everything I've put him through and knowing everything I'll probably put him through again.

He wants me.

The feeling is intoxicating.

I nod my head as tears spill over from my eyes to my cheeks.

"She said yes." Ethan grabs the microphone from Brad and tells the crowd my answer. Amid the cheers, clapping, whistles and camera flashes, Brad takes my left hand in his and moves to put the ring on my finger.

Only, it won't go past my knuckle. My fingers are too swollen from treatment.

He pushes a little harder, but it won't budge.

"Oh, for fuck's sake," I say. I stick my finger in my mouth and try to get it wet enough to slip the ring past my knuckle. It moves a little, but not enough. In fact, now it won't move in either direction and my finger is turning red and beginning to throb as it fills with blood.

"Ah! What do I do?" I ask the table shaking my hand.

"We could cut it off," Ethan says.

"No!" Brad and I both say at the same time.

"I meant the ring," Ethan says. "Jeez."

"Still no!" I cry.

"Stick it in ice water," Remi says handing me a glass.

I put my finger in the ice water and it starts to feel better, and smaller. Once I can slide the ring back off again, I realize it's not going back on. And my eyes fill with tears for a whole different reason.

"Baby?" Brad asks.

"I can't wear my ring," I say, sobbing.

"We'll get it sized," he says.

"I don't want it to be bigger," I say.

I can feel snot dripping out of my nose. Remi hands me a napkin. I blow my nose and wipe my cheeks, realizing I've ruined my makeup.

"Remi," I plead, holding up my black streaked napkin.

She and Lexie get up and drag me into the bathroom to repair my makeup. I can hear the Chief is back up at the podium, making comments about the beautiful demonstration of love.

"Ha!" I say, "It might have been beautiful if my fat fucking fingers weren't so fucking fat."

"Sweetie," Lexie says. "It happens all the time. Like when I get my period, it's no big deal."

"Let's get you fixed up," Remi says.

They repair my makeup, and we head back to the table. I can see the boys bent over doing something. They straighten when we return. Brad has a shy smile on his face.

"I think I have a fix," he says.

I look at him. He reaches up and puts something around my head. I look down and see that he's tied some kind of black string together to make a necklace. The ring hanging as a pendant from the middle.

"How…" I start.

Ethan holds up Brads dress shoes, now void of laces. I look under the table and see that Brad is in his socks.

The things this guy will do for me.

I grab his face and kiss him like I've nevr kissed him before. Trying to put all my love and gratitude into that one kiss so he can know just how much I need and love him.

He pulls back after a moment, his hands now framing my face, and says, "I know, baby. Me too."

That's my guy for you.

He totally gets me.

And I can't wait to spend the rest of my life with him.

No matter how long that may be.

KAT'S SUDDEN DEATH PLAYLIST

We've Got Tonight – Bob Seger

She's Got a Way – Billy Joel

Here Come's a Regular – The Replacements

Never Let Me Go – Aretha Franklin

Lonely Sinking Feeling – Cowboy Junkies.

Last Request – Paolo Nutini

Tonight's With You – Black Rebel Motorcycle Club

Yours – Blues Traveler

Romeo and Juliet – Dire Straits

You'll Accompany Me – Bob Seger

Everlong – Foo Fighters

Maybe I'm Amazed – Paul McCartney

Wild Horses – The Rolling Stones

I Hope That I Don't Fall In Love With You – Tom Waits

I'm Not In Love – 10CC

Missing You – John Waite

Everything I Own – Bread

Jealous Guy – Bryan Ferry & Roxy Music

Stay – Lisa Loeb

Look What You've Done to Me – Boz Scaggs

When I Need You – Leo Sayer

You Are So Beautiful – Joe Cocker

Will You Still Love Me – Amy Winehouse

Without You – Harry Nilsson

Volcano – Damien Rice

The Man Who Can't Be Moved – The Scripts

Photograph – Ed Sheeran

Still They Ride – Journey

I Go Crazy – Paul Davis

Against All Odds – Phil Collins

Someone Like You – Van Morrison

Wait – Sarah McLachlan

Video Games – Lana Del Rey

Hold Me Through The Night – Beth Hart

Goodbye My Lover - James Blunt

3:00 AM - Edwin McCain

Don't Want To Miss A Thing - Aerosmith

If I Knew - Bruno Mars

All Night Long - Peter Murphy

Bell Bottom Blues - Derek and the Dominos

Hurt - Johnny Cash

You're The One That I Want - The Lennings

THANK YOU FOR READING!

If you enjoyed this book, please consider leaving a review. Hell, even if you didn't enjoy it please consider leaving one. That way I'll know what to change for next time.

If you want to know more about my books and new releases, join my newsletter!

~

Positive mental health is important at every stage of life for our psychological, emotional, and social well-being. If you or someone you know suffers from mental illness, please get help. Resources like MentalHealth.gov provide valuable information on how to help yourself and others.

~

Much thanks to such organizations as:

The American Cancer Society

METAVIVOR

Breast Cancer Research Foundation

For their tireless efforts in fighting a horrible disease. And providing support to my loved ones during their times of need. We appreciate you.

ABOUT THE AUTHOR

Denise has been reading since before she could talk. And to this day, escaping into a book is her go-to activity before anything else.

She likes to write about sassy women and semi-flawed alpha-esque men (hard on the outside and just a little soft on the inside.) Denise's female characters always have strong friendships, potty mouths, and like to drink—a lot.

Denise is loyal to a fault, a bit too sarcastic, blindingly optimistic, and pretty freakin' happy with life overall. If she couldn't be a writer, she'd be a singer in a classic rock band. Right after she learned to carry a tune. She has more purses than days in the month, an obsession with colored ink pens, and a slightly unhealthy bracelet habit.

Home is in the Pacific Northwest where she lives with six special needs Siberian Huskies and a husband (BW) who has the patience and tolerance of a saint. And, lest she forget, Denise also lives with too many to count characters inside her head, who will eventually have their stories told.

For more about Denise visit her website at: www. DeniseWells.com

Or follow her on any of the social media sites below.

ALSO BY DENISE WELLS

<u>STANDALONES</u>

The One I Can't Have, a steamy age-gap novella in **AB Worlds Age-Gap series**

The Three Way, a steamy novella in the **AB Worlds Valentine's Day Series**

Forever Wicked, a steamy novella in the **AB Worlds Halloween Party Series**

Summer Shivers, a romantic thriller in the **Summers in Seaside Collection**

Overdrive, a steamy enemies to lovers romance **in KB WORLDS - DRIVEN COLLECTION**

Pour Decisions, a romantic comedy novella in the **Girl Power Collection**

How to Ruin Your Ex's Wedding, a steamy romantic comedy

I Heart Mason Cartwright, a steamy romantic comedy

Love Off The Rocks, a romantic comedy short

Rebel without a Claus, a steamy, gay romantic short

Breaking Dylan, a coming of age story

<u>AGENTS AND ASSASSINS TRILOGY</u>

Fearless - Book One, a steamy romantic thriller

Careless - Book Two, a steamy romantic thriller

Ruthless - Book Three, a steamy romantic thriller

<u>SAN SOLOMAN</u>

Keeping Kat, a steamy second-chance firefighter romance

Romancing Remi, a steamy enemies to lovers romance

Loving Lexie, a steamy cowboy enemies to lovers romance

Seducing Sadie, a steamy firefighter romance

Trusting Tenley, an emotional second-chance at love romance

<u>ANTHOLOGIES</u>

High EX-Pectations, a romantic comedy short in the **Imperfect Date Anthology**

CAUGHT UNDER THE MISTLETOE - A Holiday Affair to Remember, a romantic comedy holiday short

STORYBOOK PUB CHRISTMAS WISHES - Mistle Oh-No, a romantic comedy holiday short

STORYBOOK PUB - Breezy Like Sunday Morning, a romantic comedy short

<u>LIMITED RELEASES</u>

GIRLS JUST WANNA HAVE FUNDAMENTAL RIGHTS - Charity Anthology

SEEDS OF LOVE A Charity Romance Anthology to benefit Ukraine - Charity Anthology

HOT AS F$#K SUMMER ROMANCE ANTHOLOGY - SULTRY SUMMER NIGHTS

LOCKED AND LOVED: An Isolated Romance Collection

SUMMER WITH YOU: Summer Shorts Collection

JUST A LICK Collection

LOVE LETTERS Collection

STOCKING STUFFERS Anthology

SNEAK PEEK - ROMANCING REMI

REMI

A drop of sweat falls from his forehead on to my face.

I reach up to wipe it away, trying not to be disgusted.

This isn't working for me.

I need to stop him before it goes too far.

He's going through the motions, all the right motions even. His angle is good, he's moving in and out at a nice pace, and he's throwing in a little bump and grind for good measure and clit pleasure.

Haha – that rhymes.

Focus, Remi.

Maybe if I touch myself.

I reach down but can't seem to wedge my hand between our bodies. He's at such an angle where his pelvis doesn't seem to be leaving mine. Yet still pumping away, I'm sure of it. I reach my hand around to feel. Yep, his ass is moving up and down.

His nicely rounded ass, I should say. I squeeze the hard, taut muscle. He groans in response.

Huh.

How is it that I can notice how great his ass is and still be getting nothing from this?

You know why, Remi. It's because you're a cold shell of a human—

I ignore that little voice in my head. The one that reminds me that I'm incapable of any real feeling or emotion. Just one more thing I can thank my parents for. The lack of any real feelings or love in the Vargas household growing up.

Don't think about that now.

I refocus my attention on the attractive man pumping away on top of me. He's trying hard. It makes me feel bad for wanting to stop him. But he's sweating. And I've got other stuff I could be doing right now.

I look at him, his eyes are closed, and his face has this dreamy quality about it. Like he's in a great headspace. Or, shit, like he's enjoying the sex.

What must that be like?

Get out of your head, Remi.

Stay in the moment.

Except, I haven't been in the moment this entire time. If I've not gotten into it yet, it's not like it's going to get any better.

It should be good though. I mean, we had two face-to-face dates that I enjoyed. And the six months of long-distance sexting and texting was good. Hot, even.

But this...

Is in person, not via text from hundreds of miles away where you can stay detached.

I never should have invited him to a champagne brunch this morning. I don't have the extra time in my schedule to waste a whole morning like this. I could be at work running lab trials like a good little scientist should. Or out with my besties, Kat and Lexie. And now I'll probably get a headache from the cheap champagne at brunch.

Fuck.

"Can you stop?" I ask him, my jaw clenched, as he grunts and thrusts above me. He doesn't seem to hear me, so I give his chest a shove.

"Yeah, baby, give it to me," he says.

"Hey, Alex," I say, tapping him on the shoulder instead. "Stop, this isn't working for me."

He stops and looks at me with his head slightly cocked, a confused look on his face.

"Off," I say gruffly, as I start to sit up, still pushing against him.

He rolls off me, pulling out as he goes, and turns to lay on his back beside me.

"What's the matter?" he asks, his chest rising and falling rapidly and his tone annoyed. He looks at the ceiling, forearm resting on his forehead, as he tries to catch his breath.

"This isn't working for me."

"What does that mean? What's not working for you?" He leans up, cocking his head, and squinting his eyes as he asks his questions.

"The sex isn't working for me. I'm just not feeling it," I say.

"Not feeling it? How can you not feel it? Am I doing something wrong?" He looks down at his dick.

"No. It's just me."

"Are you just not in the mood? Do you want to wait a bit? Maybe change positions? I can go faster. Or slower." His brown eyes wide with hope.

God, I'm an asshole.

"It won't make a difference, Alex."

"Well, how do you know unless we try?" A small smile lights his face. He really is cute. Handsome even. At one point I thought he was hot, but then we settled into a rhythm, got to know one another better. His humanity started to show and, well, I hate that part. When someone starts to let their walls down and you see things like weakness. I hate weakness.

"It's not going to happen. I don't know how to be any clearer. The sex *is not* working for me. I'm not going to get off. I don't see a reason to continue."

"How do you know you're not going to get off?"

Wow. He's so much more persistent than I thought. I need to shut this down. He needs to leave. I want to shower, change my sheets, and get on with my day.

"I just know, okay?"

"Okay," he says drawing out the word. "Maybe I could—" He reaches for me.

"I don't think so," I say, trying to be gentler.

"Okay, that's a little harsh—"

"I'm sorry." I guess he didn't get that I was being gentle. I get out of the bed and walk naked to the bathroom. "I don't mean to be harsh. I just… I think it's best if you leave now. If you'll excuse me, I'm going to take a shower and, uh, stuff."

I close the bathroom door behind me and turn on the shower. Then make the mistake of glancing in the mirror. My normally, carefully coiffed black hair looks like a back-comb teasing experiment gone bad. My makeup is still intact though, thank god. That's what hundreds of dollars at *Sephora* will get you. I pat at my face, trying to push down whatever moisture may have been there. I don't sweat, but I do gently perspire at times.

"Remi."

I hear him outside the bathroom door, still trying to talk to me.

"Alex, just go. Please. I'm sorry it didn't work out."

"If that's really what you want," he says, sounding petulant.

"It is." I keep my voice firm.

"Okay. I'll call you later," he sighs.

"You don't have to call me later."

"You don't even want me to call you?" he asks, sounding surprised.

I turn the shower off and open the bathroom door—at least put his boxers on. It's a start.

"I don't want you to call me. Not to be rude, I think it's best if we don't see each other anymore."

"Wow. Okay. I thought at least we'd be friends."

"We did have a good time." I gesture to the bed. "Before we had—"

"Okay, okay, I get it," he says. "You don't need to keep reminding me."

"Well, I hope you have a good rest of your day."

"Seriously, Remi? You stop me in the middle of sex to tell me it's bad, get out of bed, ask me to leave your house, and then tell me to have a good day? What is wrong with you?" His voice rising to a shrill at that last question.

So much.

I can't help it; his question makes me laugh.

After a brief pause, he laughs with me. His lightly muscled abdominal muscles contracting.

He really is good-looking.

I consider changing my mind about him, then shake my head, ridding it of such a thought. I grab a robe from the back of the bathroom door and put it on, then reach my hand out to him, "Friends?"

He takes my hand and shakes it. "Friends." He grabs his pants and puts them on, then looks at his watch. "I guess if I leave now, I can still make my game."

"Game?"

"Yeah, the law enforcement basketball league."

"You're in law enforcement? I thought you did IT consulting work." I try to rapidly think back to when he's talked about his job in past conversations. How had this not come up before?

"I do. But I specialize in IT for police departments."

"Oh. I had no idea."

"Does that make a difference?" he smirks and runs his hand through his sex-tousled hair.

Kinda.

I fight the urge to run my fingers through it after him. I've always found law enforcement sexy.

What is wrong with me?

"No." I laugh slightly. "I just have friends in the police department and the fire department."

"Why did you think I was traveling to two different regional police departments over the last six months?"

"Well, I wasn't really thinking about who you were working with. Or where you were working. Just that you were traveling for work."

"My base is out of San Soloman, but they lend me out to other divisions as a consultant. So, this last gig was two different locales, one in NoCal and one in the Central Coast. But both were PC refreshes," he says as he finishes dressing.

"Oh." I have no idea what a PC refresh is, but I don't want to ask him for fear that he'll try to explain it to me, and then he'll never leave.

"Anyway, the annual ball for San Soloman law enforcement is coming up. I was going to ask you to go with me."

"That's sweet, but I can't."

"Can't or won't?" His face hardens. I've made him mad. I try to soften the blow of rejection. "Can't. I'm actually already going."

"Weren't we still kind of dating, or at least talking, up until a few minutes ago? Or… is that why you stopped me earlier? Because there's someone else? Why did we even get together today then?"

"No. Believe me, that is not the reason. I wanted to get together with you today, I didn't realize it was going to go like it did." I don't blame him for being frustrated. If I were him, I would be too.

"Then how are you going to the ball?" he asks.

"I'm going as a favor to a friend."

He looks skeptical but doesn't question me further.

"Okay, well, maybe I'll see you there, then. If I go. I mean, I'm not going without a date." He kisses me on the cheek and turns to leave.

"I'll walk you out," I say.

"Don't bother," he says. "Take your shower. And enjoy your day."

"Thanks," I say. But I follow him to the door anyway so I can lock it.

"Hey," I say. He turns to look at me and I continue. "Not that it's a big deal, but if you had a basketball game you wanted to play in, then why agree to see me today?"

"Remi, we'd had two dates and then spent the next six months texting. Of course, I wanted to see you before anything else. I like you. It was important to me to see where this was going to go. I guess now I know."

"I'm sorry to disappoint you." And in that moment, I do feel bad for how this has played out. Even though a small part of me knew it couldn't have gone any other way.

He gives me a small, sad smile, then opens my front door and heads out.

Get your copy of Romancing Remi here

ACKNOWLEDGMENTS

(FROM THE ORIGINAL PUBLISHING OF THIS BOOK AS LOVE UNDECIDED - KEEPING KAT IS A NEW VERSION OF THAT BOOK)

Kat's story has been through more re-writes and revisions than I can count. Though in my defense math was never my strongest subject. Get it? Counting. . . Math. . .

What hasn't changed with Kat is my inspiration for writing her. This book is written for, and in memory of, **Courtney McMillon Bonelli**. I miss you every day, beautiful girl. Every single fucking day.

That said, I've got some people to thank for helping to shape this story into what it is today:

Rachel Radner - talented author, amazing CP, wonderful friend, emotional crutch, and voice of reason: I couldn't do this without you. Not any of it. Thank you doesn't feel like enough. Thank you. Thank you. Thank you. Thank you.

Ellie McLove - editor extraordinaire - Gray Ink: Thank you for taking a chance on me! I am indebted to you!

Linda Russell - Foreword PR: Thank you for holding my hand and helping me navigate through my first real, grown-up release. You are awesome!

Shari Ryan - MadHat Books: You saved my ass. Thank you for allowing me to take advantage of your creativity and talent.

A special thank you to **Cal Fire Captain Michael V. Neal** for helping me understand what's involved in the life of the brave firefighters in Riverside and San Diego Counties. You shared freely and gave me more info than I knew I needed. I applaud you and am grateful for your service. Note - any mistakes are mine and not his.

Scott Hoxie - your insight on rugby players and all their dirty deeds was not only helpful, but fascinating. Your time is very much appreciated. Again, any mistakes are mine and not his.

Sandi Nichols - your knowledge on guns is both scary and impressive. Thank you for helping me find a girly gun for Kat. I'm going to get shit for saying girly gun, aren't I?

To the best office bitches in the world: **Larutha**, **Bobeena**, **Bobeeta**, **Boberri**, and **Kristen** (we never did get a catchy nick-name for you, did we, Kristen?) - thank you for listening when I blathered on and on about all things "me" related where this book is concerned. And for giving me your opinions whether I wanted them or not. Ha! Just kidding, I always wanted them.

T. Greenwood - You were very kind in alerting me to the (huge) flaws in the early versions of this book. You were right. I wish I'd listened to you sooner.

It took me a while to get a feel for Kat's Sudden Death Playlist and what kind of music she vibes to. I had help. Thank you to all my FB peeps who suggested their faves - it was super helpful.

And, a special thank you to **Lorna Batting Luckinbill**, **Sandra Crayton**, **Timothy Flowers**, **Danyale Hambly Jones**, **Michelle Miles**, **Melissa Monasmith**, and **Sidney Taylor** for suggesting songs that really resonated with Kat. She appreciates it.

I can't function in life without my **Remi IRL**. Girl - you get me going when I stall, make me happy when I'm sad, and talk me down off every ledge I crawl on to. I love you. Soul sisters forever!

And, my **beloved BW** - I may fight you with every critique on my work, but damn if you aren't usually right. How one man can be so lovable and so frustrating at the same time boggles my mind. Your love and support mean more to me than I can ever say. I love you. Thank you so very much.